Contents

Soldier Spy

Book 4 in the Napoleonic Horseman Series
By
Griff Hosker

Published by Sword Books Ltd 2014
Copyright © Griff Hosker First Edition

A CIP catalogue record for this title is available from the British Library.

The first Kiss this Ten Years! __ or __ the meeting of Britannia & Citizen François

The Peace of Amiens

Maps and cartoons courtesy of Wikipedia (William Robert Shepherd) *This image (or other media file) is in the **public domain** because its copyright has expired. This applies to Australia, the European Union and those countries with a copyright term of **life of the author plus 70 years**.*

Chapter 1

December 1804

Sergeant Sharp and I were summoned, once again, to Whitehall. It seemed like only yesterday when we had been rescued from the French beach by Black Prince and Commander Teer. Although we had done that which we were ordered and rescued hostages held by the French it had been at a cost. I had expected a quiet time; a time to get to know my troopers and the new officers in the regiment. It was not meant to be.

Colonel Fenton had not been happy when the missive from Colonel Selkirk arrived. He was not angry with me but rather with those armchair generals and politicians who used us like pawns in a giant chess game. However, he knew better than to question their orders. He arranged for Lieutenant Jackson to take charge of the troop for a short time and we had taken the mail coach to London.

I had taken the precaution of having Sergeant Sharp pack us a small valise. Where Colonel Selkirk was concerned it paid to be prepared. We were also travelling in civilian clothes, our pistols were in the valise but we still carried our swords. These visits to London normally resulted in a foreign trip of some type.

Alan seemed remarkably sanguine about the whole affair. He was actually smiling as we thundered along the muddy London road with rain lashing the outside of the coach. We had been fortunate to obtain inside seats. The other three passengers were braving the outside. There were some advantages to a military warrant. The inside was not only warmer it was less hazardous than clinging to the tiny rail outside.

"Where do you reckon to this time, sir? Back to Frog Land again?"

I shook my head, "I doubt it. There is little else we could learn there. We know that Bonaparte intends to invade next year. He is gathering his army already. The regiments we saw are just the beginning. There weren't enough there to invade. He will be drafting in more. Besides, now that we know the Royal Navy will plant their ships along the Channel, it will be a stalemate. We can do nothing about Napoleon and his army but his navy has no chance of defeating Nelson."

"Did I hear that you met Admiral Nelson, sir?"

"Aye, I did. It was in Italy a couple of years ago. It was round about the time I first began to work for Colonel Selkirk. Nelson is a very clever man and he has a wonderful wit and cunning. He gives me hope for England. There might be many buffoons running things at Horse Guards but so long as we have the likes of Nelson then England will be safe."

"Are there no Generals as good?"

I realised I had spoken out of turn. Sharp was a sergeant. I was an officer and I should have watched my tongue. I tried to extricate myself from the mess. "Well, I haven't seen that many but the ones I have met have not impressed me. Who knows, we may meet one this time."

The coach stopped at St. Martins Le Grand; it was the terminus for the mail coaches. The coach went no further. We headed south towards the river. It would be the quickest way to get to Whitehall. We made our way towards St. Paul's and Cheapside. It was not the cleanest part of London despite the presence of the superb cathedral. I wished to be through the sea of humanity as soon as possible. Our smart clothes and our size enabled us to force our way through the throng towards the river. The river was the artery of the city. It was easier and quicker to navigate its waters rather than the crowded streets. It was also much safer.

The boatmen flitted around like insects on a pond. When we reached the river six of them hurtled across the water to get our trade. As in all things the toughest of the watermen won the race. He grinned up at us showing that he had lost teeth before now. He had a short clay pipe jammed into his mouth and he spoke without removing it. It was a remarkable feat.

I saw him taking in our good clothes and our case. We were being appraised to enable him to make the maximum profit from our business. "Now then, young gentlemen, the name's Jem Green, and I am the best waterman on the river. Where can I take you today?"

"Westminster Pier."

"Hop aboard and we'll have you there before you know you are on the River Thames."

As we descended into his boat I saw that he had two boys in the boat with him. Both were barefoot and looked to be frozen. Jem snapped at them. "Look lively and store that valise." He smiled at us, "Teaching my boys to become good watermen. They will have a good trade when they are older and will thank me for my sharp words." He glanced up at the pennant on the masthead, "You gentlemen are in luck, and the wind is with us as well as the tide. Hoist the sail boys!"

We were halfway towards the busy pier when I saw his avaricious eyes take in the quality of our clothes. I had ensured that both of us had the best and most durable of clothes and footwear. My sword was a fine one and had been taken from an Austrian officer many years earlier.

"We haven't negotiated a price yet, gentlemen."

I knew that he was attempting to rook us. I smiled, "I believe there are set charges along the river or am I mistaken?"

He shrugged, "This river can be a dangerous place, young sirs. Men and their belongings have been known to fall overboard. It is better to pay a little for a guaranteed arrival." He smiled evilly, "You know what I mean?"

I turned to Sharp, "The trouble is, Sergeant Sharp, that there are too many people taken in by a young face. They assume that it implies innocence and naivety." Even as I was speaking I was slipping out the stiletto I had taken from my boot. The tip of the razor-sharp blade I pricked at his throat. "Now we will pay the right price, the price that everyone pays and not a penny more." I glanced at the two terrified boys and smiled, "Perhaps your sons have learned a valuable lesson today, Mister Green, about treating customers fairly. Mayhap when they become watermen they will become more honest than their avaricious father."

His face showed his terror. He had seen someone he assumed was a young gentleman newly arrived in town and a bird ripe for the plucking. He had learned, to his cost that one should not always judge by appearances.

As Westminster Bridge loomed up I handed the correct coins to the boy while Sharp lifted the valise. "We will carry our own bags. I would not wish you to slip and drop them over the side. Good day sir."

I watched as he clipped the two boys about the ears as though they had been responsible for him losing profit.

As we headed towards Whitehall Sergeant Sharp shook his head, "And we risk our lives for scum like that."

"No, Alan, we risk our lives for the hardworking people of this country. This is London and it attracts the worst of characters but there are good people here too." Away to our left, we heard the bells of St Margaret tolling. There would be a service in the church nestling beneath the abbey. There would be good people in there and that was good to know.

The sentry barred the entrance with his musket. It was always the same when we arrived. It would be a fight to get in. I handed him my warrant letter hoping that he was one who could read. The confused expression on his face showed me that he could not.

"Sarge?"

A grizzled veteran sighed his way from the guard room, "What is it, Jenkins?"

He waggled the letter before the sergeant. The veteran barely looked at the letter but looked at us. "It's all right son, I know them. These are two of Colonel Selkirk's ghosts." He saluted, "In you go, sir." I knew that there were others like me; men who went abroad for Colonel Selkirk and His Majesty. Those who worked in Horse Guards called them his ghosts.

Colonel Selkirk's office was always messy. His dress reflected the untidy nature of his workspace. He had sleeves rolled up and inky fingers which left the inevitable stain down his cheeks and hair. He seemed to live in his office. Certainly, he was always there when we called in.

He glanced up and waved us in, "Come in, come in. I just have to finish this."

I noticed the map on his wall, which had pins and tapes attached, was of the Austrian Empire. I recognised Vienna immediately. I had done some work for Napoleon in Austria. It was where I had learned to speak some German. My curiosity was aroused. I had not expected this.

Sergeant Sharp cleared away some documents from the two chairs and made an attempt to dust them. I smiled and shook my head. We sat down and waited.

Eventually, he put down his pen and leaned back in his chair with his inky hands around the back of his neck. He smiled, "Have you heard what your friend Bonaparte has done now?"

I frowned. He was hardly my friend although I had served him in much the same capacity that I now served Colonel Selkirk. "Whatever it is I will not be surprised."

"He has been crowned Emperor," I confess that despite my earlier assertion I had been taken by surprise. It must have shown for the colonel burst out laughing. "I thought that might surprise you."

I thought of all those young soldiers who had fought for the revolution; all of the aristocrats who had lost their heads and now we had something worse than a king, France had a tyrant. "I am surprised the French stand for it. They rid themselves of a king, why should they want an Emperor?"

"Yes, it is hard to fathom eh? Still, your knowledge of the man has helped us and I believe will help us in the future." He leaned forward. "What will he do next, eh?"

"Why ask me? I am just a captain in the Light Dragoons."

"You do yourself a disservice, Robbie. You have been privy to one of the greatest generals we have ever seen." He waggled an inky finger at me, "Don't mention that outside of this room; I would be even less popular than I am. Come on, just take a guess."

I sighed, "If Nelson keeps his fleet in the Channel then he can't invade England. He must have at least a hundred thousand men there now."

"Nearer to a quarter of a million but go on."

That number staggered me and I had to regain my train of thought. "They will become bored. There are only so many parades that can keep them occupied." I glanced up at the map and smiled, I knew where the colonel was going with this. "Austria, he will want to conquer Austria. We... that is he, came damned close in Italy before we went to Egypt."

The colonel slapped the desk, "You see I knew you would be able to work it out. As it happens I agree with you but I am afraid that others are blind to it. They are thinking of sending a force back to the Baltic. They think that we can distract him there." He shook his head. The Baltic was the wrong place to risk a confrontation with Napoleon. We had fought there ourselves and been forced to have an inglorious retreat. "You have been to Vienna I believe?"

I nodded, "Yes sir. I went with an Italian diplomat on a mission from the General."

"Good. I want you to go there again. Nose around and find out if the Austrians can stand up to Napoleon's new army."

I shook my head. "I can save a wasted journey there then sir. They won't. They are reasonable soldiers but they are badly led. The French army will slice through them like a knife through butter. They hurt them in the Low Countries and in Italy. Look at Marengo."

He frowned, "But they will be fighting in their own land."

"Italy was their own country and they made a mess of it there. They just aren't good enough. More importantly, their Generals are no match for Bonaparte." I knew that man for man, the French were much better than the Austrians. I also knew that they had the talisman of Bonaparte. He never lost!

He stood, "Hmm. Then it is worse than I thought." He studied the map as though trying to find the answer there. He suddenly spun around. "There is a way but it might involve some danger to yourself and, of course, Sergeant Sharp could not be involved."

Alan had grown in the last couple of years and he stood up angrily. "With respect, sir!" The 'sir' was almost spat at the colonel. "If the captain is in danger then I will be with him. I serve this country as much as you do."

The colonel's eyes narrowed. "That is bordering upon insubordination, Sergeant Sharp."

I put my hand out to restrain my sergeant, "But in that case, sir, I agree with him. Sergeant Sharp has proved himself more than resourceful, loyal and brave." I stood. "Perhaps it would be better if we ended our association here and now. We will go back to our regiment and you can find some other fools to risk their lives for your Machiavellian schemes."

Sergeant Sharp nodded, gratefully and he turned to open the door for us. Colonel Selkirk glared at us. I do not think he was used to his orders being questioned. "Sit down both of you before I have you put on a charge."

I knew that was a bluff but we sat down anyway. I smiled, "So what is this danger into which you wish us to place ourselves?" I chose my words deliberately. It would be the two of us or neither of us.

He coughed and then he smiled back, "You are a game 'un, I'll give you that. I want you to be a double agent. Pretend to work for the Frogs and gain their trust. I can give you some piddling pieces of useless information for you to feed to them. Find out what they are about. You know Bessières and you have proved your ability to him."

I stared back at him. "That is beyond risky; that is suicidal."

He stood again and went to his drinks cabinet. He poured two glasses of whisky and offered me one. I looked at Sharp and the colonel sighed and gave one to him and the other to me. He poured himself a third. "This damned equality will be the undoing of us, mark my words." He sat down and took a sip. "Think about it, Robbie. The last time Bessières saw you was just before he left Egypt."

"I know and then I killed an officer in a duel."

"That will be forgotten, trust me. You can present yourself as having being captured in Egypt by the British and you have escaped. Having Sharp with you might even help the masquerade."

I was not so sure. I had almost been caught the last time I had ventured into France; dare I risk it again? Then the thought of

Napoleon Bonaparte as Emperor came into my mind. I had never really got on with my father who had treated me more like a serf than a son but I knew that he would want me to do something about this upstart who was going to take France down the road to disaster. I thought of all my brave comrades who had been abandoned in Egypt and I knew that they too, would want me to take the risk. All I had to do was to risk my life and that was not much.

"Very well but your plan seems a little vague. What is it you intend for me to do?"

He swallowed his whisky. "You are correct for I have only just come up with the idea." He stared at the map. "Where would you say Bonaparte and Bessières will be?"

"I would guess either in Paris or with the army at Boulogne."

"And if we are both right then that army will soon be moving towards the east. But I think that Bonaparte will still be in Paris. He has just made himself Emperor and that means he will be lording it up there. He has to let everyone know that he is Emperor and he will be consolidating his power. Bessières, on the other hand, will be where the army is. He is the master mover of men and materiel." He peered closely at the map. "If you were going to move men quickly and easily to the east which route would you take?"

I was intrigued and I stood and went to the map. The answer was obvious; it was the blue snake which wound its way towards Austria and Hungary. "I would use the river and I would use the barges we saw in Boulogne."

The colonel slapped the map. "And by God, that is where he will be." He jabbed a finger at the Rhine. "He will be in the Netherlands."

I studied the map, as did the colonel. Sergeant Sharp said, in a small quiet voice. "But sir, won't it be obvious where he is going when he begins to move over two hundred thousand men? They won't be easy to conceal."

I knew he had a point but I had served with Bonaparte and knew better. "True, Alan, but Bonaparte is a master of moving men swiftly and deceiving his enemies of his true destination. He will move them surreptitiously. He is like a magician and he will use sleight of hand. He pretends to do one thing and does something entirely different."

"Then how will …"

"General Bessières is the great administrator. He will know where everything is going. There will be planning involving the stores that they will need and the depots they will use along the way." I turned to the colonel. "But we would need to move swiftly would we not? He will not move for a few weeks for it is winter but we have to get to the continent first. And we will need a story and information to give to him."

"You had better stay with me tonight and I will make the arrangements for your voyage."

"The regiment?"

"I will send a message to Colonel Fenton that you have been sent as a military attaché to Malta." He began scribbling and we remained seated, "Well what are you waiting for? I have done with you. You know where my house is." He scribbled a note. "Here, give this to my man. I'll be along shortly."

We took a carriage from Horse Guards to Piccadilly. We could have walked but I suspected I would need as much rest as possible before we were off on another wild jaunt.

This was the third or fourth time I had been to the colonel's townhouse and I was recognised. I would not have needed the note but it was easier this way. "I'll draw you, gentlemen, a bath each." I saw Sharp colour. He was just a sergeant and he found it hard to be treated with such deference. I suspected that Colonel Selkirk chose his servants as carefully as he did everything else.

I enjoyed being pampered. While we bathed, the colonel's man cleaned our clothes and brought refreshments to our rooms. As I wandered around the impressive house I reflected that the colonel must have money. I knew how much a colonel was paid and it would not pay for this. Sipping my wine I realised that I now had enough money to pay for such a dwelling and servants. The family import business was doing well and my half share in the ship which Captain Dinsdale sailed for me was more than profitable. When I had finished with this sort of adventure and when Napoleon Bonaparte was defeated then I might think about such things.

The colonel arrived home late and he brought many papers and material with him. He waved us into his dining room. It was already laid for dinner. He waved his arms at his servants; he looked like a demented windmill! "We have no time to sit and eat, just put the food on the side there and we'll help ourselves. And bring up a couple of decent bottles of wine too."

He laid out maps on one half of the table and documents on the other. He rubbed his hands together, "Now then. Those documents contain all the information you will need. That is intelligence which we want them to have." He grinned wolfishly, "Some of it is true, some might be true and some are downright lies. I spent all afternoon writing it. You have to learn all that… tonight!" My heart sank. "Now the two of you will have to study these maps and commit them to memory too. You can't be caught with them in your possession; at least not until you have spoken to Marshal Bessières."

I looked up, "Marshal? I thought he was a general?"

"The Emperor is rewarding those who have helped him." He laughed, "Had you stayed there Robbie who knows? You might have become a marshal yourself. Anyway, that is by the by. Let us get on with the maps."

The food and the wine were brought in and consumed as the colonel gave us as much information as he could. Sergeant Sharp was a bright lad and I saw him taking in the routes we would have to take.

"Now we can't send a ship in for you this time as we have no idea how long it will take you to get the job done. Consequently, you will have to make your own way home." Sergeant Sharp's face was a picture. "Still you are both resourceful chaps. Now read that information, Robbie, while I test your sergeant here."

The colonel fired question after question at Alan until he was sure that he knew the maps inside out and back to front. In that time I managed to absorb the names and the information I was to give to the French. I had a slight idea which facts were true for I had heard them myself but the lies and half-truths were beyond me. I would have to treat them all as though I believed them.

Eventually, he seemed satisfied. He poured the last glasses of wine and then told us how we would be getting to our destination. He handed me a money belt. "This contains gold Louis. You should be familiar with them. Upstairs are two sets of clothes for you. You have used them before. We will be leaving at first light and meeting Lieutenant Commander Teer at Greenwich." I smiled; he was a friend and, more than that, he was reliable. "I thought you would appreciate that. He will try to get you as far up the Rhine as possible. With the short days, we are having at the moment that should be perfect. I take it you have your pistols?"

"Yes sir, they are in our valise."

"Well they are French and that will help." He pointed to my sword, "And that thing is Austrian so it should aid your disguise."

I looked at the maps and the papers. "You have planned well in a short space of time sir but I am not sure that we can do anything that will change the course of events."

"You don't have to. Planting this false intelligence and discovering what Bonaparte is about might just make the difference. This Emperor is a clever chap and he is the one calling the shots and making things happen. This is our only chance to regain the initiative. If he makes his plans on false information then he might make a mistake. More importantly, you can get close to the plans and find out what he is up to. If we know where he is going to attack then we might be able to do something about it."

His face softened, "But please try to get back in one piece eh boy? I am getting to enjoy our meetings. I should hate for them to stop because you are dead."

Chapter 2

We left the Thames just after dawn. It was a foggy day. It felt dank and damp. We both had greatcoats but we were still cold. Jonathan had us wait in his cabin until we passed the Isle of Dogs. There was little likelihood of us being spotted by French agents but it paid to be careful. The 'Black Prince' had done this sort of thing before.

After we had left the estuary we joined him. He smiled boyishly. "Another adventure eh Robbie? My crew still talk about our little rescue from the beach. It brightened up their lives."

"But no prize money."

"No, one can't have everything." His face became serious. "You know I cannot return for you this time."

"I know. We shall have to make our own way out."

"You will not be able to do as you once did and use the Channel ports. They have your description there."

"How do you know?"

"We captured a couple of ships and their captains told us. There is a reward for two men of your description. It is another reason why I am happier about dropping you up the Rhine; even though it is more dangerous for us. It will be easier for you. Anyway, you are welcome to stay on deck but I am afraid that we will all be a little busy." He pointed to our valise. "I am keeping that on deck in case you have to make a sudden exit. I have four men detailed to get you ashore as quickly as we can. We may not have the luxury of time when you leave us."

As the afternoon drifted to night the cook brought us hot cocoa laced with rum and a sticky meaty stew. We were experienced campaigners now and knew that you ate when you could for you knew not when your next meal might arrive. The 'Black Prince' sailed towards the Rhine under the barest of sail. We appeared to be moving quite slowly. The Second Mate explained that the reason was to slip in unseen. "It's the sails that they see. With just bare sticks and hardly moving we are near invisible as it is possible to be.

Sergeant Sharp and I stood well away from the sailors and tried not to get in their way. I spoke to him because I was a little nervous and I wanted him to be sure of our plans. "The first thing we shall do is to get some horses. I want to get as far to the east as I can. Remember that you are still an American."

We had used this idea before. I would be the Frenchman returning from America with an American servant. Sharp had practised an American accent and he was now much better than he had been. Playing him as someone who was dumb had proved too hard for him. His French was a little better and he could ask questions when necessary. The problem was when someone answered him; he could not always keep up with the speed of their response.

"Captain says to stop talking now, sirs. We are in the Rhine."

I now noticed that the motion of the ship felt different and that it was dark and foggy. I heard the splash from the bows as the sailor threw the lead. I saw that the guns were all loaded and crewed although they were not, as yet, run out. We were in the Batavian Republic. They might resent the French presence but this was still the French Empire we were travelling through. The river seemed as wide as a sea to me although I remembered the Texel when I was a young Chasseur. There the river had been so wide that we had captured a whole fleet of Dutchmen. I felt sorry for Jonathan. He had to worry about enemy soldiers, enemy ships, a shelving bottom and being able to turn his ship around. All we had to worry about was getting off the ship.

The Second Mate came for us. He whispered, "Captain needs to speak with you."

As we walked across the quarter deck I was aware that we were slowly swinging. He was turning. Had we reached our destination? "Sorry about this Robbie." He pointed to the east of us. I could just make out some vessels on the river. "If I am not mistaken then they are the French invasion barges. I can't go any further along the river. We will have to let you off here." He paused, "Or I could take you back to London."

I smiled, "No, here will be fine. If this is the French Army then we are in the perfect spot and I wouldn't want you to get in trouble on my account."

"No, trouble, dear boy, no trouble at all." He pointed to our cases, "Mister Roberts get these two gentlemen in the boat eh. There's a good fellow."

I shook hands with Jonathan. "Thanks for everything."

"You must tell me how this one turns out when you get back."

As we climbed down the tumblehome I wondered if we would actually get back. Mister Roberts, the Second Mate, steered. He gestured with a gnarled finger, "We will head to the north shore sirs. There's a landing jetty there and I think it is empty at the moment. I and the lads will stop talking. If you need anything use hand signals." He paused, "And good luck sir. You are a mad bugger but I guess it takes mad buggers to win this war. I should know I serve with one."

There was genuine affection in his voice as he spoke of his captain. Despite his youth, I knew that his men thought the world of him and would do anything for him.

He had been correct. The jetty was empty although how he had known where it was I could not fathom. The fog was thicker than ever and seemed to hang a few feet above the river. It suited us. We gently bumped into the wooden pontoon jetty which rose and fell with the tide. Sharp leapt out and I passed him the cases. I nodded to the Second Mate as I clambered out of the dingy. I was careful not to trip over my sword. A sudden splash might bring more attention than just the mockery of sailors. By the time I had turned around the dingy was just a shadow edging back into the murk and the mist.

I could hear voices ahead of us but their owners were hidden by the fog. They were not speaking French. Sharp carried our cases and I walked ahead of him. We had to appear as though we had been seeking shelter for the night. This was always the most difficult time. Once we had been here for a day or so we would know how the land lay. We would have a better idea of where we were and we would not be the subject of intense scrutiny. I know that whoever we met would be suspicious of us, arriving after dark and with no apparent means of transport. I knew that Sharp would go along with any story I concocted. However, I could not begin my fabrication until I had met someone and gauged their questions. Poor Sharp would not understand a word that was spoken. It must have been doubly worrying for him.

I discerned a lightening of the fog which suggested buildings and the noise increased in volume. We were close to people. The stones beneath our feet became smoother and, suddenly, I almost tripped over a step. I swore in French and then stomped up the steps to the building before us.

There were a number of sailors seated at the lamp-lit tables but also a few uniforms. As we stepped into the light the murmur of conversation ceased and all eyes were upon us. "Damned robbing sailors!"

One of the uniforms, a policeman of some type stood and spoke. Although he spoke French it was heavily accented. "You have been robbed, sir?"

"As good as. I paid the captain of a cargo ship to bring me from Dunkirk to Arnhem and he drops me here. No offence but this looks like the middle of nowhere to me and not Arnhem."

They all laughed at my obvious discomfort. "I am sorry sir, you have been robbed. What was the ship called?" He took a notepad out and a pencil.

"The Marguerite or something like that. Captain Dwass was his name."

They all fell about laughing. I knew some Dutch having served here with the Chasseurs and Dwass was Dutch for soft-headed. The policeman put away his notepad. "I do not think we will find this man. He has taken you for a ride." He and his friends all thought that this joke was hilarious. "How much did you pay him?"

"A Gold Louis each for me and my servant here."

It was getting better and better for them. I had paid far too much and I had been robbed. To them, I was an empty-headed fool and therefore harmless. I had concocted the story to appear a harmless and gullible fool. They would be less suspicious of me and equally keen to rob me.

"There is a hotel here with rooms and tomorrow there are many barges which can take you along the river or you might accompany the soldiers here. They are transporting cannon up the river."

I pretended not to hear the part about the cannon. "Well as I shan't be able to get there tonight I will use the rooms." I smiled at the policeman. "Thank you for your help, officer. What is your name? I shall tell Marshal Bessières of your assistance when I next see him."

Suddenly all humour left the room as I dropped the name of the Emperor's right-hand man into the conversation. The soldiers suddenly looked sheepish.

"Klaus Winklemann sir and that is not a problem. If you will come along with me I shall introduce you to the owner of the hotel." He tapped the side of his nose. "He is a friend of mine."

I doubted that. It was more than likely that he would receive backhanders from the hotel for bringing customers whom they could cheat. I had used the accent of my father. It was haughty, high pitched and arrogant. It marked me as someone from the upper classes; these people would enjoy rooking a noble, and a foreign one at that. I played on that by sniffing disdainfully at everything and running my finger down the furniture to find imaginary dirt.

The owner smiled ingratiatingly. "I am sure I have a fine room for you and an adjoining one for your servant." He shrugged apologetically. "It will not be cheap, sir."

"Just so long it is clean and presentable. Is there any chance of some edible food?"

If he took umbrage at my criticism he did not show it. "Of course sir, I will have a table made ready for you. First, let me show you to your room."

The room was barely adequate and for the character, I was playing it just would not do. I looked incredulously around the tiny interior. "Is this, really, the best you have?" He nodded. I leaned in to him, "You know we have an Emperor now? The days of austerity are gone. You need to invest in your property, sir, for when the Emperor has conquered the rest of Europe we will all be rich and you will have a much better clientele coming through your doors." I stood and looked around again, "It will have to do I suppose but do not expect to charge me a fortune for this hovel!"

"I am sure you will be happy with the price sir."

Once we were alone, Sharp checked that the adjacent rooms were empty and no-one was within earshot. Although he would have picked up most of what we said I needed him to be clear about my story. I quickly gave him the gist of it.

"So do you reckon we will go by barge or by an army vessel?"

"I am not sure. Both have their advantages. At least this way it saves us hiring horses." Horses were good for travelling but they tended to be noticed when you reached your destination. A boat would be the focus of interest and not the passengers.

The food, when we ate was simple enough fare. The wine was acceptable. I think the owner had actually made an effort. The dining room also had many uniforms within it. This time it was the officers. They were artillerymen and engineers. That was as I had expected. Cavalrymen would not want their horses on barges; it upset them. The barges would make light work of transporting heavy objects such as cannon and siege equipment. Bessières knew his trade.

I noticed a couple of officers paying close attention to us. I kept glancing at them surreptitiously in case I knew them but I did not. I had changed a great deal since I had been a lean and young Chasseur. I had filled out considerably. After a while, I smiled at them and raised my glass. When they had finished their meal they wandered over. One of them fixed me with his gaze, "I understand that you know Marshal Bessières." I gave a slight nod of the head. "May I ask how?"

I drank some of my wine and said, arrogantly, "Not that it is any of your business but I did him some small services in Italy and Egypt."

"You are a soldier then?"

I spread my arms, "Do I look like a soldier? I am a businessman and I have just returned from America on… well, I will keep that business to myself." I picked up my knife and fork. "Now if this interrogation is over I will get back to what passes for my dinner."

The younger of the two looked angry but his older companion looked thoughtful. "I am sorry if we have caused you offence but you must know that there are English spies and saboteurs operating along the Channel coast. Last year they destroyed some valuable ordnance. We were just being careful."

"As was I. Which is the reason I travelled so far north. I have no wish to be murdered by an English spy."

"Very sensible. Now to make up for our rudeness, we understand you are trying to get to Arnhem…"

I held up my hand. "I hoped to get to Arnhem but I was heading for Marshal Bessières' headquarters. If he is the same man as he was he will be at the vanguard of this mighty army."

He smiled, "And he has not changed. We are heading for his headquarters tomorrow in one of the barges. I would be honoured if you could accompany us."

I was not sure if this was as a guest or a prisoner but I had now chosen these cards to play and I would have to play them. "That is most kind Major…?"

"Major Lafils and this is Sous Lieutenant Delacroix."

I nodded at the Major whilst assiduously avoiding the lieutenant. He looked a little like Sergeant Delacroix and me had served with him in Napoleon's Guides in Egypt. "And I am Robert Alpini."

The young man said, "That sounds Italian."

"Yes it does, doesn't it?" I gave him a bland smile. "So shall I see you here in the morning?"

The major nodded, "We will be leaving at dawn."

"As I said, major, I have done some services for Marshal Bessières; we will be ready."

"We will take our leave, sir."

They left the dining room and headed out towards the river. From the worried look on Alan's face, he had understood some of what had been said. I smiled. I would explain all later. When the owner came, rubbing his hands after we had finished he had the smile of someone who thinks he has served the finest repast on earth. "Well sir, how was that?"

"Barely adequate but fortunately I was hungry. We will be leaving with the army, before dawn. I expect a hot breakfast at five-thirty."

His face fell. "Yes, sir."

"And my bill at the same time."

Once in the room, I explained to Sharp about our journey the next day. "Isn't it risky sir? Going to the heart of their army?"

"Quite the opposite. If we had anything to hide we would avoid it like the plague. And I daresay the owner will be adding his own views too. I saw him speaking with the major just before he left. I hope I played the part of a self-important businessman well. I want no suspicions before we reach Bessières. After that, there is little point in deception for he knows me." Sharp's face reflected my own opinion. This was like walking into the lion's den and expecting not only a red carpet but to be able to walk off with the lion's dinner. I hoped Colonel Selkirk's opinion of me was justified.

There was a tiny knock on the door in the early hours of the next morning but we were already up. We did not wish to miss the barge. The fog of last night had turned into a savage frost which rimed the river with tiny flecks of ice. It would be a cold day on the River Rhine. Fortunately, the breakfast was much better than the evening meal and I happily paid the bill. The owner looked relieved that he had pleased me.

The major arrived alone. "You are ready?"

"Of course."

He led us on the reverse of our route the previous night. I could now see that there were just a handful of buildings by the dock and they obviously serviced the vessels heading up and down the mighty river. We had stayed in the only hotel and there were just two bars. A ship's chandlers and police station completed the settlement.

The barge we were to travel upon was moored next to the dock while the others were in the river already. It was wide and it was long with two masts. It would travel slower than a man could walk but it would not need to stop. There were just a dozen blue uniforms on board and I could see, from the shapes below the tarpaulins, that they were hauling cannon.

The major let me on first. "Cabin accommodation is limited but it will be warmer than on deck. Follow me."

We were in a small cabin at the stern below the rudder and the bridge. It was obviously the place where the crew would normally sleep but, having been commandeered by the army they had been ejected. The seats were functional but the major was quite correct. It was much warmer than on the deck.

As soon as we left the dock it was obvious why we had been invited on board; the major was suspicious of us. We were more prisoners than guests. I did not mind as I had expected this and I felt I would be given a much closer scrutiny at Bessières' headquarters than on a barge. He plied me with questions about my past. They were all done conversationally but they were trying to find out more about me. I had prepared well and I deflected his questions without giving too much away. I let him know that I had served in both Italy and Egypt but not in what capacity. When he asked me about Sharp I told him that I had been in America but not how I came to be there. He was interested in that country and, I have to confess, I was forced to make much up. I was just glad he had never been there.

It was dark by the time we pulled into the shore. "We are here at Marshal Bessières' headquarters. He was obviously not going to let me out of his sight. That did not worry me. He could escort me right up to the Marshal if he so chose. In fact, that might make life easier. When we stepped ashore I noticed that the young lieutenant was also with us. There were signs that this was some sort of headquarters building as there were many staff officers and their horses. The presence of the Gendarmerie was also a sign that we were in the right place. I saw no faces that I recognised, which was a relief. I needed to get to the Marshal without being asked awkward questions.

As we approached the large building festooned with the Tricolour I began to feel slightly nervous. How would I be received by the Marshal? He might have changed. Certainly, it was now a different world from the one I left all those years ago. We had an Emperor which would change things; I noticed that the uniforms I saw were more colourful and flamboyant than they had been.

The major walked right up to the sentry who stepped aside to allow us entry. He marched into the passageway and a moustachioed sergeant of the Gendarmerie opened the door for us. There was a major in the uniform of the Chasseurs à Cheval of the Guard there with a lieutenant. The major saluted and the major smiled, "Good to see you again Pierre. How can I be of assistance?"

"It is I who can be of assistance to you, Georges. I believe I have captured two spies."

I now knew why the lieutenant was with us for a pistol was placed behind my head. I felt it pressing into the back of my skull. One false move and I would lose my head.

"Do not even think of reaching for your sword or you will die before we have the chance to question you."

I had failed. I had not even made it to Marshal Bessières. I had been captured and, in all likelihood would be shot as a spy.

Chapter 3

"I protest and I insist that I speak with the marshal!"

The Major of Chasseurs stood and his face had a cold smile upon it. "Oh you will see the Marshal believe me but he is not here at present." He nodded to the sergeant. "Lock them up but leave their cases here. We will see what we can learn from them. Oh, and before you leave us, your sword please."

I unbuckled my sword and handed it to him. "Take care of it. I shall want it back before I leave."

The major laughed, "Oh you are confident I will give you that." He seemed to see the sword for the first time. "This is a fine Austrian cavalry sword. An elementary mistake I am afraid. We now know that you spy for Austria!"

I almost smiled. They knew nothing and had no evidence. We had just aroused suspicion by our arrival. As we were led away I realised that we should have tried a different approach and I had made a mistake. Next time I… Even as the thought entered my head I knew that there might not be a next time.

They threw us, unceremoniously, into a cellar in the commandeered building. There was just one weak candle lighting it and there were no chairs. All that I could see were some old packing cases. Sharp began to speak and I held my finger to my lips. I walked back up the stairs and peered through the crack in the door. There were two guards seated and facing the door. They were talking. I descended to Sharp and took him, with the candle to the point furthest away from the door so that we could talk.

I whispered, "Sorry about this Alan. It seems my carefully thought out plan failed."

"How did they know sir?"

"I don't think they do. I think they are just suspicious but that doesn't help us."

"At least there is nothing in the cases to give us away."

He was right. The pistols that were there were French and the clothes had all come from France. "Have a quick search and see if there is a way out of here."

We began to look for another door or, perhaps, a skylight. The cellar proved to be just that, a cellar to store cases the owners of the house no longer needed. It was damp and it was dirty. There were rats and mice racing around but, if they could escape through small holes, we could not. We sat on two packing cases to await our fate.

I had no idea how long we waited down there for no one came for a long time. I was pleased that we had had such a good breakfast that day. Eventually, the door opened and a light shone down. The sergeant who had escorted us stood at the door and said, "You two. Come up."

"Ah, you have realised your mistake…"

He laughed, "No, the major thought you might need to pee! He didn't want to have you stink the place up."

Disappointed, we followed him with the two guards and their bayonets firmly placed in the middle of our backs. We were taken outside. It was a cold and frosty night. There was a small hut outside. The sergeant pointed. I opened the door and saw that it was a primitive toilet. There was a hole in the ground. As the door was closed behind me I looked, in the dark, for a way of escape. There was none. I sighed and used the toilet. I opened the door and, as I stepped out, checked the area for another means of escape. While Sharp was inside I looked around to see if there was a chance of overpowering our three guards and fleeing. These were professionals and they were far enough away from me that, if I had attempted to rush them, I would have died.

By the time Sharp came out, I was quite cold. The night air was freezing. When we reached the cellar there was a tray with two stale baguettes and a jug of water. The sergeant smiled again, "From your fine clothes you won't be used to bread and water but we won't have you starving to death before we shoot you."

I was grateful for the bread, stale or not. A hungry and tired man-made mistakes and when we had eaten we lay down to sleep. There was little point in worrying. We just had to deal with the situation in which we found ourselves.

We were rudely awakened the next morning by a bucket of cold water thrown by two grinning guards. It had the desired effect. I saw the anger flaring in Alan's eyes and I shook my head. They wanted us to react. I smiled and said, "Well that saves us washing, at least."

This time there was a captain as well as the major and the sergeant in the office. Sergeant Sharp was left outside. I suspected that they intended using the divide and conquer strategy. The three of them sat on the other side of the desk and I saw that my sword and pistols were in plain view before me. They had given me a smaller seat than theirs so that I had to look up at them. It was pathetic really.

"Now then. Tell us who you are."

"I told you I am Robert Alpini. My family has land in Sicily."

"You are Italian then?"

"I was born in Breteuil. What do you think?"

"Then let us see your papers."

"I have none."

The major leaned back in his chair and spread his arms, "Then I can do nothing for you. On the grounds that you have no papers and we can find no record of your arrival in France you will be executed in the morning."

If he thought to intimidate me he was wrong. "That would be a great shame for I have information which Emperor Napoleon Bonaparte would dearly like to have." It was my turn to lean back with a self-satisfied smile upon my face.

I saw the frown pass across the major's face. This was not the reaction of a man with something to hide. The captain slammed his fist onto the desk, "He is bluffing! He knows nothing!"

"But if I do and you shoot me then what will happen to you? In my experience, Napoleon Bonaparte does not forgive easily."

Even the captain was discomfited by that. "Then tell us and your life will be saved."

"I will say this one more time; I will tell Marshal Bessières and no one else."

The captain stood, "I have had enough of this." He shouted, "Bring in the other prisoner!"

Sergeant Sharp was dragged in. "What is your name?"

We had agreed that, as he was playing an American there was little point in changing his name, merely his place of birth. His accent marked him as foreign immediately but it was hard to tell if he was English or American. I could tell the difference but I doubted that the two officers in front of me would.

"I am Alan Sharp of Winchester, Virginia, United States of America."

If they had examined, as I expected they would, our cases they would have found a forged passport from Colonel Selkirk attesting to that fact. I saw the subtle nod exchanged between the officers. The major spoke in English. It was almost as bad as Sharp's French but I think it was an attempt to win Sharp over to their side.

"Now then, Mister Sharp; our countries are allies. Your Statue of Liberty was made here in the land of liberty. Tell me, what is this vital piece of information which this man says he has?"

"I don't know sir, I am just his servant."

That was true. Only I had examined the papers and documents provided by Colonel Selkirk.

"If you are a servant then why stay with him. You could leave now and be on a boat back to America."

"He saved my life, sir, in America. I am duty-bound to serve him."

I could see that we had flummoxed them. Their ploy had failed. Then the major asked, "Where did you come from? Before you landed here?"

This would be the part where our story either saved us or doomed us. Over the meal in Colonel Selkirk's home, the three of us had debated and discussed this part of the plan more than any other.

"England, sir."

The captain slapped his hands together gleefully. "There, I told you, he is an English spy! We should shoot him now!"

The major shook his head and spoke to the captain much as one would a child. "If he is a spy then he will have information, will he not. I think his servant has just saved his life and it would be folly to kill them now." He looked at me. "Are you sure I cannot persuade you to divulge your information to me? The consequences will be that you will be returned to that rat-infested cellar. Do you really want that?"

I looked him directly in the eye. "I can assure you major that I have suffered far worse than the cellar in the service of France. I will speak with Marshal Bessières and him alone."

He nodded, "I can see that there is more to you than meets the eye." He pointed to the weapons. These are the weapons of a soldier and, in your eyes, I detect a man who, despite his youth, has been in combat. I hope, for your sake that you are telling the truth or you will be shot. Marshal Bessières is a ruthless man as I am sure you know."

"I do sir and I look forward to becoming reacquainted with him."

"Take them away!"

As we were led down to our dungeon once more I was relieved that it had been so painless. I think that I had planted the seeds of doubt in their minds. This was not the time to begin upsetting the new Emperor. We remained silent until the door was slammed shut on us and we were left to dim Stygian light and our rats.

After I had checked that the guards were not in close proximity we spoke of what had occurred. "Will they shoot us, sir?"

"They might shoot me but your American passport guarantees you more time while they check on the truth of your documents."

"But is it likely?"

I pondered that. This was the question neither Colonel Selkirk nor I could answer. It all depended upon Marshal Bessières. If he was the same man I had known all those years ago then I felt sure he would give me the benefit of the doubt. If, on the other hand, he, too, had been swept up in the Imperial fervour then he might have changed and then who knew?

Despite the major's threat of more bread and water, we were served a hot stew with bread and a bottle of poor quality wine for our next meal. After the bread and water, it tasted like gourmet cooking. We waited for two days in the dank and damp cellar. Sharp improvised some dice and we filled the hours talking, quietly, and playing dice. After two days the door opened and we expected the routine walk to the privy or a meal. Instead, the sergeant pointed at me and said, "You, come!"

I shook Sharp's hand as I left. One never knew what might happen. No words were necessary; we had talked for two days and said all that we needed to. This time I was taken to a small chamber where there was a bowl of water, a razor and a towel. The sergeant watched me like a hawk as I first washed and then applied lather to my face. When I picked up the razor I knew that it was a test. If I wanted to escape I would slash the sergeant across the throat, seize his weapon and flee. I caught his eye and smiled as I began to shave. There was relief there and, I think, a little contempt. Perhaps he had wanted me to try to escape. When I had finished I did feel much cleaner. I now knew that I would be meeting Bessières. This chance to clean up had been to avoid offending his nostrils.

The first thing I noticed as we approached the office was the increase in guards and in the quality of uniforms. This was a Marshal of France and they were taking no chances. The door opened and I took a deep breath. The major and the others had been easy to fool but this man knew me. This man had fought alongside me. He had sent me on secret missions for Bonaparte and he knew what I was capable of. This would be a stern test of my story which now seemed both flimsy and inadequate.

He looked much as I remembered him although there were now flecks of grey in his hair. He was immaculately turned out and, even though I had washed, I felt dirty. The major was there along with a captain of the Consular Guard although, as I had been told, they would soon be called the Chasseurs of the Imperial Guard. Bonaparte had high ambitions.

Bessières was writing and he glanced up, briefly, "It is he. Give him a chair and brings us a glass of wine. Sergeant, we will be quite safe now. You may leave us." He then went back to his writing and, when the door was closed, I was the subject of scrutiny from the other two officers. Eventually, he finished writing and sat back. There was no smile on his face. "So what is this information you wish to tell me?"

I was now the gambler and I made my play. "It is for your ears only, sir."

The other two looked outraged but my old commander merely nodded, "I thought as much." The door opened and a servant brought a decanter with two glasses. "Thank you, Philippe. You gentlemen may leave us."

The captain became almost incandescent with anger. "I protest sir! How do we know he is not an assassin?"

"Major, did you search him before throwing him in the dungeon?"

"Yes, sir."

"Has he any weapons?"

"Well, no sir, but he has his hands."

The argument was so feeble that Bessières burst out laughing. "I will be quite safe."

They left but I knew that they would be hovering outside the door. The Marshal poured us a glass each and held his up. "Salut! To fallen comrades."

"To fallen comrades." I did not know who he was drinking to but I had many friends from the 17th Chasseurs in mind as I drank my wine.

"Well Robbie, I never thought to see you again. To be truthful I thought you were dead."

"Thought or hoped?"

"That is unfair, I always liked you."

"Then why was I abandoned in Egypt?"

"Orders, surely, you of all people understand that."

"I suppose so and it is now in the past."

"But you have committed a crime."

28

"Hougon?"

"Of course."

"It was a duel."

"Duels are illegal but his friends claimed murder, made all the more believable by your flight."

"I was alone and the only ones who remained were his friends. I would have had to kill them all and then I would have been guilty of a crime."

He sipped his wine. "I suppose so. Tell me what happened to you?"

I took a deep breath; this was the story fabricated in Colonel Selkirk's dining room. "I hid out in Alexandria; I had some money. When the British came I fled into the desert. I don't know where I was heading but I had to get away from our enemies." My words were all carefully chosen. The colonel had told me the right words said more than their surface meaning. "I was close to death and then I was saved by a Scotsman, Sir Hew Dalrymple. He heard my story and took me under his wing. He nursed me back to health and took me back to England."

"I see and this name that you use, the Italian one?"

"That is also true. I discovered that relatives of my mother had gone to Sicily. I met one in London and I changed my name." I shrugged, "I went into partnership with them."

"And where did you get the money from?"

"I said that this English General had taken an interest in me and he loaned me the money."

That surprised him. "Really?"

I nodded. "I have paid him back!"

I could see that Bessières was intrigued now, "How?"

"I speculated with some of the family money in America and made a success with my investments."

He smiled, "Now I understand the American connection. In fact, I understand everything save for the most important one. Why are you here?"

"Patriotism. England is still at war with France and I can help you to defeat it."

He nodded and sipped his wine. Suddenly he said, "This man with you. He is English is he not?"

"He is an American. I saved his life in New York and he became my servant. He is loyal but not too clever."

He smiled, "We gathered that. And what is this vital information you have for me? This news that will ensure that the Emperor Napoleon conquers Britain?"

I recognised the sarcasm in his voice. "You and I know, Marshal Bessières, that it is with the leaders that men win wars. General Dalrymple is the kind of General that can win wars. He is the British Napoleon." I had never met the man but Colonel Selkirk had assured me that he was one of the most incompetent generals Britain had, and they had many. This was the first of the disinformation I was to seed my conversations with.

"I have heard the name but not of him."

This was like fishing. The trout was nibbling the bait. I just had to be patient. If I moved too soon it would flee. I sipped the wine, "The wine is quite pleasant."

He was distracted, "Hmn, oh yes. It is one of the Emperor's favourites." He looked up at me. "You are close to this man?"

To help the lie I pictured Sir John, the Knight of St. John who had, indeed, taken me under his wing. "He regards me as the son he never had."

"You realise the reason my people were so suspicious was because a British warship was seen in the Rhine about the time you arrived."

"I know. That is the reason my captain abandoned me. We were chased into the fog and he threw us off before we could be caught. The ship spotted us leaving Dover and followed us."

"They do not trust you, Robbie."

"I can do nothing about that but in truth, I care not. Do you trust me?"

"Of course. I know that you believe in France and will die for France."

As I spoke my next words I really meant them. "Of course. I will do anything for my country, for France!" I believed it but

Bonaparte was not France and I would give my life to be rid of him.

He smiled, "I knew that. I am pleased that you are with us once more." He spread his arms, "However, We will need to prove to these people that you are a friend. You will need to come with us on campaign."

I nodded, "That is fine but if I am away too long then Sir Hew might become suspicious."

"I understand but three months or so would be acceptable would it not? And if we asked you to perform services for us as you did before then that, too, would be acceptable?"

This was like the razor; this was a test. "Of course." I smiled, "We will be returned our weapons and our clothes?" I sniffed, "These are a little pungent."

He smiled and wagged an admonishing finger at me, "You are a rascal Robbie but I have missed you. You make life interesting." He stood and went to the door. As I had expected the officers and sergeant were hovering close to it. There was distinct disappointment on their faces as he said, "This officer and his servant are now free. Their weapons and their clothes can be returned to them. Major, arrange some accommodation for them. They will be accompanying us east."

They were, however, soldiers and they all snapped to attention. "Sir!"

The major could barely conceal the contempt in his face, "See to it, sergeant!"

As the sergeant led me away I had no doubt that the room we would be given would be little better than the cellar we had occupied. It mattered not. The marshal had accepted my story. We were not out of danger but the most dangerous test had been passed.

After Sharp had been fetched and our belongings we were taken to a tent which was close to the tents of the sergeants. They were taking no chances. There were two cots and two rather thin blankets. The sergeant grinned as he said, "I am in the next tent and I am a light sleeper."

I smiled back, "Good, for if it gets cold in the night I know that you will be ready to bring me another blanket." I received a contemptuous look from the veteran. He had been deceived by our fine clothes. He thought that I was an effete young man. I, too, was an old campaigner.

We left the river the next day and moved with Bessières and his escort along the road which led to the east. The sergeant had ensured we had the sorriest pair of horses that were available. He and two tough-looking troopers rode directly behind us. I did not mind. The Marshal rode next to me and talked as we rode. It was still an interrogation but a gentler one than that meted out by the colonel.

"How important is this General who took such an interest in you?"

"He is likely to be given command soon of another force."

Bessières flashed me a searching look. "The British are planning another invasion? Where will it be this time?"

Colonel Selkirk was a wily old bird and he knew that I would be likely to be asked such questions. I was prepared. "You know that they sent forces to Pomerania last year?" He nodded. "That and the Low Countries are easy to reach and they have their navy of course."

He seemed relieved by my answer. "We still have enough forces in the Low Countries and Pomerania is close enough to our friends in Prussia and so we have little to fear there."

I had gleaned my first piece of information. Since the expulsion of the Hanoverian forces to England Prussia was free to expand west. I suspected some collusion between Bonaparte and the Prussians.

"What kind of man is this Dalrymple? Is he a cavalryman like you or an artilleryman like the Emperor?"

"Neither. He was a colonel of the foot."

Again he was relieved, "Good. The British had good soldiers once but as their colonies showed they could be defeated by skirmishers. Your cavalry, well Robbie, you know how much better our men are. But I believe it is the artillery which will

determine the outcome of this conflict. We have the finest guns
and the finest gunners. We have more guns than the rest of the
nations put together." He nodded. "I am pleased that we have met
again for you have put my mind at rest." He slowed to look at my
face. "We will see the Emperor next week. I am sure he will be
interested to speak with you too."

So I would get to meet the Emperor. I wondered how he would
have changed. It had been some years since we had spoken. He
deserted soon after the debacle of Egypt. I knew that I had
changed. I was bigger, stronger and quicker with my weapons. I
liked to think that I had also developed my mind. A few years ago I
would have happily tried to kill the monster responsible for the
deaths of so many of my friends but now I could calculate. I could
devise the best means to defeat my enemy.

I enjoyed the ride east. I was travelling through unfamiliar
lands and I always enjoyed that. The weather was not as bad as it
might have been and we were spared both snow and rain. We were
prepared for the icy blasts of eastern wind. We gradually edged
south-east as we headed for Bavaria. It was a perfect place from
which to invade Austria and both the Bavarians and the other
German people were glad to see someone who would stand up to
the Austrian giant. Austria had always been something of a bully
and the tiny German nations looked to Bonaparte like a saviour. I
wondered if they knew just what Bonaparte was like.

We were quartered in the barracks close to the palace. At least
we were not in tents. Our guards were still as suspicious of us as
ever but that did not worry me. If we had to flee then I knew we
could affect an escape.

We had been there for a week when the Emperor arrived. He
travelled in a carriage escorted by his new Chasseurs à Cheval of
the Guard and some exotically dressed Mamelukes I remembered
from Egypt. He was ever the showman. We watched his arrival
from the door of the barracks. The sergeant's beady eyes never left
us. Once he had entered the palace Sharp and I retired to the
warmth of the fire. Sergeant Sharp had an excited look upon his
face.

"Why so excited, Alan?"

"I have never seen an Emperor before."

I shook my head and laughed. "He is just a soldier like you or I but he has given himself the title of Emperor."

Sharp looked confused, "But he rules an Empire!"

"He rules France, parts of Italy and he has these Germans who look to him for protection. Wait until you have met him and then judge."

"Will I be meeting him?"

"Probably. He will certainly want to see me and I think he will use you. Be careful around the Emperor; he is not an honest man like Bessières. He has little English and so he will speak in French. Keep your eyes and ears open."

We were left to cool our heels for a whole day before we were summoned into the Emperor's presence. I took it as a compliment that he did not bother to dress for me. He was in his overalls and, as usual, working. When we had been in Milan I had only seen him sleep for the briefest of times. Whatever else he was a hard worker. The Guards were left outside the door but Jean-Baptiste was present and I think the Emperor felt safe.

He looked up from his papers, pen poised mid-air. He waved it in front of my face. "Robbie, such a naughty boy! I ought to have you shot for what you did!"

I gave a little half bow, "I did what I had to and what honour demanded. I could not refuse the duel."

"Some said it was murder."

I looked him directly in the eye. "Why would I need to murder him?"

"You are right, Robbie, you are a killer. I am just pleased that you are a killer for France once more. Please sit." He suddenly seemed to notice Sergeant Sharp. "And who is this?"

"He is my batman." He looked confused, "Military servant. I saved his life in America and now he serves me. Sir Hew thought I ought to have a servant."

"Ah, this General Dalrymple. I have heard of him but Fouché did not think he was important."

"He is the rising star. Who would have predicted, when we served together in Italy, that a captain of artillery would become an Emperor?"

Anger flashed briefly across his face and I saw Bessières frown. Then he smiled. "You do enjoy taking risks; I am pleased you have not changed for we have a service to demand of you before you return to England and gather information." He looked at the map pinned to the wall. "If that little island thinks I have finished with it then they are wrong. I shall conquer it in good time." He looked at Sharp who had remained impassive throughout. "Can we trust this one?"

"He speaks little French sir but as I saved his life he is completely loyal to me."

"Perhaps I should keep him here as surety of your return."

I shrugged, "You know me, Emperor, if I chose to flee, I would not wait or worry about one American servant."

He gave me a shrewd look, "One thing I learned about you Robbie is that you are loyal to your friends. It is a weakness but you are right. If you do not return after this mission then I know that you are a traitor and you will be executed when I reach England." There was a cold assurance about his words and I had no doubt that he meant every one of them. He went to the map and gestured me forward. "I need you to do what you did for me as a soldier. I want you to scout the land and the armies from here in Strasbourg, along the Danube to Vienna. I need more than numbers. You are a clever soldier and a good judge of military matters. What are the defences like? What are the qualities and weakness of the commanders? It is fortunate that you came back into my service. I have soldiers who could do what you do but the fact that you speak German, English and Italian and you are a civilian means that you have more chance of passing unnoticed. Jean-Baptiste."

Bessières came forward. He handed me a leather case. When I opened it I saw that there were gold coins within and a document enabling me to pass through French lands. I saw that it was in the name of Alpini and identified me as an Italian businessman.

Soldier Spy

Bessières had been busy. He gave me a sad look. "You have just one month to return with the required information."

I looked at him with a shocked expression, "But it is over five hundred miles and it is winter."

Bonaparte laughed, "Are you becoming soft, Robbie? I can remember when you laughed at such journeys. You will do it and you will return here."

"Not on those nags we have been riding."

Bessières smiled, "No, of course not. We have four horses for you to use and they are the finest we have."

The Emperor gave a wave of his hand, "Go!"

And so we left Strasbourg in the service of the Emperor of France.

Chapter 4

I knew as we left Strasbourg, that the hardest part of the journey would be the first fifty miles or so. We would be under close scrutiny as we would still be close to the border. I decided to head north towards the fortress of Ulm. We could then approach Vienna from the north-west and be less likely to attract attention. It also meant we might be able to travel down the Danube which would mean our horses might be less damaged and we could travel further. I had calculated that we only had half a dozen days to examine the defences; the rest would be spent in travelling.

The border itself was a vague affair. There was no one place where one crossed and showed one's papers. The land was disputed and did not really belong to either of the main nations. There were small German principalities dotted all over this part of the world. In a more peaceful time, travellers could come and go as they pleased.

I knew that the French had patrols along all of the roads and I assumed that the Austrians would have the same. The best time to cross this indeterminate area would be late at night. Hopefully, we would find somewhere in Austria where we could stay and then resume our journey.

The horses were excellent beasts. I recognised the quality immediately. They moved instantly and responded to all of our commands without hesitation. That might make life much easier later on. We left the city and took a smaller side road towards the east. The weather helped us as the rain had arrived and was driving from the east. It would carry any noise towards us and prevent an enemy from hearing us approach.

We had travelled ten miles before we hit trouble. As we rounded a bend between a tree-lined section of the road we suddenly found a barrier and muskets trained upon us. There was little point in fighting and we would soon have been caught had we fled. I slowly raised my arms and nodded at Sergeant Sharp to do the same. It was hard to make out faces in the dark and even harder to detect the colour of the uniform but the muskets were unmistakable. I was just pleased that they had not fired first and asked questions later.

When I heard the command to advance, I almost cheered; it was in French. "I am a French officer and we are under the orders of Marshal Bessières."

Wisely they did not take us at our word but allowed us to close with the barrier. Six troopers appeared on either side and I saw that they were Dragoons from the 15th Regiment. The sergeant was a grizzled old veteran and he kept his men's guns trained upon us.

"Dismount and show me your papers."

A trooper held a burning torch and I took out the leather wallet. I had secreted the gold pieces on myself and Sergeant Sharp. They were too much of a temptation to be left in plain sight. I held my cloak above my head to protect the document from the worst of the rain. The sergeant read the document. I saw his lips moving as he did so. He had only recently learned the skill. He handed it back to me and nodded. Then he glanced down at my sword. "That is an Austrian sword is it not?"

I smiled, "I believe it was an Austrian officer who furnished me with the weapon." I saw the question on his face. "In the Low Countries, 1795."

"You were a horseman?"

"A Chasseur, the 17th."

He smiled, "Not a real one then." He handed me a bottle. "Here this will keep the cold out." I took a swig; it was rough brandy but welcome nonetheless. I handed it to Sergeant Sharp. "Filthy night to be out and," he lowered his voice, "Austria starts just two miles down that road."

"Then why is the barrier facing Strasbourg?"

"It isn't but our horses alerted us to your presence." He looked at them. "They are fine horses. If you wish to avoid the Austrians then I suggest you ride along the trail through the forest. They patrol it during the day but they are lazy bastards and keep to the road at night." He grinned, "We have used it to surprise them a few times.

"Thank you, sergeant."

"We cavalrymen must stick together. You had better be careful; they might be lazy bastards but they know their job. They are a nervous bunch and they shoot first and ask questions later."

I mounted, "I hope to see you again, perhaps in a month or so?"

He tapped his nose, "I will keep watch for you."

The trail was just beyond the barrier and a trooper led us there. "It twists and turns but it will get you to the other side of the border. Good luck."

The trail was clear but it had been made by walkers and not riders. We had to keep low in the saddle and we became soaked as we knocked rain from the branches of the conifers we passed. That, however, was a small price to pay for security. The track wound circuitously through the thick forests. It was difficult to hear for the dripping of the rain but we pushed on.

We had been riding for an hour or so when I smelled smoke. It was not the wood smoke of a house; instead, it was the smell of tobacco. Someone was smoking ahead. My experience told me that it would be Austrians. They had pickets out on the trail. The sergeant's surprises had been duly noted! I stopped my horse and made the danger sign for Sharp. We tied the four horses to a tree and, drawing our swords I led us forward. I used the forest rather than the trail; there was little undergrowth but we soon became even wetter. The rain dripped from the leaves and wetted us as we passed by. We were drawn on by the smell of the smoke. Suddenly something moved and I saw the light of a small fire. The movement had been a moving sentry.

We stopped and crouched until we could ascertain numbers. There appeared to be three men and they were in the middle of the trail. From their uniforms, they were Austrian Hussars. I had fought them in Italy. There was no way that we could go by them, the horses would make too much noise and we would be seen. There remained only one option, we had to eliminate them. The light was hidden as a trooper moved again. We now had their positions. I tapped Sharp on the shoulder. I sliced my finger across my throat. He nodded his understanding. I would take the one on the right and he would take the one on the left. Hopefully the third would fall easily. We separated and I held my sword before me. In situations like this it was normally the one to strike first who would emerge alive and my hands were quick.

The ground was slippery and it was hard to move as swiftly as one wished. I took it slowly. Perhaps Sergeant Sharp was moving quicker than I was but whatever the reason I was still a yard or two from the back of my target when I heard the scream of the trooper being stabbed by Sergeant Sharp. There was no point in being silent any longer and I leapt forward, the tip of my sword darting towards the man I had chosen to kill. My movement and the death of his comrade had alerted him and he spun around. My sword sliced along the back of his left hand and he shouted a curse in Austrian. I heard the clatter of metal on metal as Sharp fought with his opponent.

I was facing a sergeant and he knew his business. His sabre was out in an instant. Therein lay my advantage, it was not only curved, but it was also shorter. He would have to slash at me whilst I could stab at longer range. Even so, his first move took me by surprise; he slashed at my eyes. I had to react immediately and I jerked my head back. He quickly brought the blade around again to slash at my middle and I barely had time to deflect the blade. He was too good a swordsman to toy with and I went on the offensive. I feinted to the right. He brought his shorter sword up to counter the blow and then, spinning around, I brought my sword around to cut deep into his midriff. His buttons, trim and pelisse afforded him some protection but my edge was razor sharp and it came away red. His eyes showed that I had hurt him. Before he could bring his sword around again I darted forward and ended his misery with a clean thrust to the throat. I turned quickly. I was just in time. Sharp had slipped and the trooper was poised to deliver the coup de grace. He had a surprised look on his face as my sword emerged from his chest and he fell down dead.

"Are you alright Sharp?" I helped him up.

"Yes, sir. I just feel like an idiot, attacking early and then slipping like that."

"Never mind. Have a look around and find their horses. I'll check their bodies."

The sergeant had a purse filled with coins as well as a pass to enter Ulm. I pocketed that for future use. The troopers had some coins as well. Austrian currency was useful as it would make us less conspicuous. The sergeant's sword was better than Sharp's and, when he returned with the horses, I gave it to him.

The men had food on the fire and we quickly devoured it. Combat gave one an appetite. After we had eaten I looked at the bodies. They would be discovered the first thing in the morning and that might only be an hour or so away. The Austrians would hunt us down and we would not be able to get far enough away in a couple of hours. We had to buy some time.

"Put them on their horses. Tie them over their saddles with their hands and feet bound together."

We used the reins to tie them and then we led the three horses and their grisly cargo back to our mounts. With no reins to guide them and a rider on the back, the horses leapt down the track when we slapped their rumps. They would gallop for a few miles and then stop. With any luck, they would reach the Sergeant and his patrol. Three horses and the weapons would be a welcome bonus for men on picket duty on a wet German night. The rain had stopped and the horses would be easy to track. The Austrians would follow them and, hopefully, look that way for their killers.

We mounted and left the track until we were beyond the camp of the three dead pickets and then we rejoined it. Within a mile or so we found that we were at the main road once again. We had to move swiftly now for the relief for the three dead troopers might well be on their way from the nearest village.

The short rest had allowed the horses to recover and we made good time along the road. There was an inn ahead and I was looking forward to stopping for a hot meal and a fire to dry out our clothes. The clip-clopping in the distance of a troop of horses persuaded me to defer that decision. We kicked the horses on into the woods and hid behind the inn. I left Sharp with the horses and closed with the rear wall of the building. The troop stopped and I saw lights from the door as the innkeeper opened it.

"Well, Gustav, was it another quiet night or have you had any guests?"

I heard a laugh and then a smoky voice replied, "Just Hans and his patrol before they went on duty. You know how he likes his schnapps."

"It will be his undoing. We will return in an hour. Have something hot ready for us."

As they cavalry trotted down the road I realised what a close call it had been. We needed to put off any hope of food and make the next town as quickly as possible. When the patrol had left we cantered down the road each riding his spare horse. Dawn arrived but it was still a dull and dank day. The temperature had not risen much although the rain had, at least, not returned. There was an air of dampness which seeped into your clothes and chilled you to the bone. We were both desperate for a fire, hot food and a bed. We saw a small town ahead and I decided that we had to stay somewhere and rest if only for the horses' sake. We would be able to make much better time with fresh horses.

The town of Oberkirch was a typical Austrian town. There were inns and there were shops. What there was not was a garrison and for that I was grateful. Having decided to cut across country and avoid the Rhine I had avoided the border.

The Golden Crown looked to have a stable and accommodation. Surprisingly we were accepted without any suspicion despite the fact that I was obviously a foreigner. Sharp and I would speak in English whenever possible for this was not the language of the enemy, the French. The waiter who served us our meal was quite garrulous and we learned how lucky we had been. There had been a garrison but a month earlier it had been sent towards the border. Everyone in the town, it seemed, feared a French invasion. They were intrigued that I was an Englishman but when I said I represented an Italian exporter of wines and lemons it was accepted. I was even questioned about the trade. It was fortunate that I knew enough about it to be able to talk confidently.

After the waiter had gone I told Sharp my plan. "We will rise early and push on as far as we can. With two horses I think we can cover quite a distance. We will try to get to Ulm in two days. It will mean travelling sixty miles a day. We have to move."

Sharp smiled and shrugged, "It will keep us warm. This country is a little cold for me."

That was Sharp's way. He always looked on the positive side. And so we left for Boblinghen before dawn. It proved to be a mirror image of Oberkirch and equally focussed on business. In fact the further from the border we went the less worried were the people. Our journey was going far better than I hoped. The scares on the first night had worried me.

Late in the afternoon, as the sun was setting behind us, we saw the fortress city of Ulm loom large ahead. This definitely had a garrison. Here there would be soldiers and we would be questioned. We made it through the gates just in time. They were about to close for the night. The timing might actually have helped us for the guards there seemed keen to quit their post and become warm. Our papers were only given a cursory glance. I did not have to use the dead sergeant's pass. Once they realised that we were English we were no longer a threat. We had reached our first destination and our work as spies for Emperor Napoleon Bonaparte could begin.

I chose a large hotel in the middle of the city. We had money and there was no point in penny-pinching. The "Boar's Snout" was a lively hotel with a large stable. Our horses would not stand out there. It looked to be a hotel frequented by carriages. We would attract little attention here as there would be many such as us. The owner was a friendly fellow and he even tried to speak English to us to make us feel at home. He had the most magnificent moustache I had ever seen and I knew that my old comrade Pierre would be envious. He seemed inordinately proud of it and twirled it constantly. To give credence to our story I asked him which hotels and inns served quality wine and used lemons and olive oil.

His face became sad. "I am sorry sir. We like beer and simple food in Ulm." He leaned forward. "It is the garrison. There are over two thousand soldiers here serving three hundred guns. They make sure that we serve beer and simple food." He brightened, "Perhaps in Vienna?"

I smiled back. It served my purpose for we were heading there and I had learned much already. "That is an excellent idea. We will, however, spend tomorrow visiting your fine town so that I may gauge what your city needs that my family can provide."

We left the cosy hotel after dark. The town was a foggy miserable rabbit warren. It suited us for most people would have stayed indoors. We would be unlikely to be seen whilst we spied out the defences of the fortress city. We took our swords; it would be foolish to risk being assaulted by criminals. We wrapped up well with cloaks as well as hats. I intended to find a bar frequented by some of the soldiers of the garrison in the hope of gleaning information. Soldiers in their cups were more likely to have unguarded tongues. The walls of the city ran alongside the Rhine and that was where the seedier ale houses frequented by the soldiers would be.

We entered the first inn we came to. It was badly lit but it was crowded, filled largely with soldiers of the garrison. These were not front line soldiers. These were men who manned the ancient cannon on the wall and stopped visitors like me entering the city. They were more like militia than regulars. If the ones we saw when we entered were a measure of the city's defences then a regiment of cavalry could take it. We ordered a couple of wheat beers. Sharp had never drunk the brew before and he found it interesting. Our conversation about the beer in English seemed to allay any suspicions the other customers might have harboured.

The landlord came down to our end of the bar, "What are you two fine gentlemen doing in this part of town?" He nodded meaningfully at the others. "It is neither the safest nor the sort of place fine folk frequent."

I shrugged, "We only arrived today and we are lost. I saw your bar as a haven. We are staying at the 'Boar's Snout'."

"A fine hotel. When you have finished your beer turn right and then head towards the centre of the town. You will find it."

I nodded and we drank in silence. I listened to the conversations of those around me. They were not happy. Pay had been late in arriving and there appeared to be widespread discontent. Of course, it could be that the only malcontents from the garrison were in this inn but I doubted it. These men had no pride in their uniform and they were eking out their ale; a sure sign that they were short of money.

When we left I headed towards the walls of the fortress to see if I could catch sight of the artillery. There had been a time I would not have known the difference between the guns but I was now a veteran and I knew what could do damage to an attacker and what was more likely to hurt the ones firing. As luck would have it we came upon two unguarded guns which peered through the embrasure in the wall. While Sharp kept watch I examined them. Although it was dark I discovered much through touch. The barrels were rusted and the trunions seized. The guns would be hard to move and they would not fire true. The balls themselves were pitted and uneven. Between the rusted barrels and the poor balls, it would be impossible to aim these cannon. The windage alone would make the prediction of fall of shot a guessing game.

We headed around the rest of the wall but the other guns had men nearby making examination impossible and we hurried on as though late for an appointment. I was about to enter another seedy inn when I heard noises coming from behind it. I was intrigued. If what I suspected was true then these might be soldiers trying to rob someone. It would be a good test of my theory. I drew my sword and Sharp copied me. We slipped along the wall and peered around to the barrel yard at the back of the tiny tavern.

There were four of them and they were all gunners. They had a young man backed up against a wall. They held swords before them as though they knew what they were doing while the young man ineffectually waved his before him. Perhaps he thought it was a magic wand. I had the information I needed and I could have left but I suspect that I inherited a sense of duty from both my mother and my father. I could not leave this young man to be robbed by these thugs. I decided to intervene.

I spoke in German, "Is there a problem here?"

I saw the relief on the young man's face but the leader of the soldiers, a huge brute of a corporal snarled, "Piss off out of it before we stick you and your mate, fancy pants!"

I smiled and said to Sharp, "It seems they want us to leave." I saw the expression on the young man's face turn to one of horror. "How about you? Would you like us to leave too?"

His voice sounded high pitched. At the time I thought it was fear but I later found out that this was his natural voice, "Actually sir, I would like to leave with you."

I kept my sword in my hand as I moved a little closer and said, "There you are. You see we are welcome. Of course, you can come with us, sir. We would be…"

I got no further as the corporal roared at me and swung his sword at my head. Even though I anticipated the move had I not been on the balls of my feet he would have split my head open. As it was I was able to pirouette around so that his sword struck fresh air. I quickly sliced across the back of the knuckles on his right hand with my longer sword. He screamed as his sword fell from his damaged hand. A second gunner tried to skewer me but Sharp's newly acquired sabre slashed across his thigh and he too dropped his weapon.

Before the others could react I had my sword at the throat of one of the unwounded gunners. My voice was now cold and threatening. I spoke deliberately. "Now if I were you I would take your wounded friends and get back to the fortress and hope that my new friend here does not make a complaint to the commander of the garrison. I do not think they take kindly to soldiers robbing honest visitors."

They turned to look at the corporal who nodded. They went to retrieve their weapons. "No gentlemen, let us leave them where they lie. I would not like you to be tempted to attack us again later on." The two unwounded men helped their comrades away. I turned to the young man. "You come with me. Sharp, watch our backs." The rescued young man tried to speak but I held up my hand. "No, let us get somewhere safe and then we talk."

I had no idea where he lived but I was anxious to return to our hotel. It was central and it was safe. It was with some relief when I saw the streets brighten and found more people about the place.

I pointed to the hotel. "We are staying here. Come and join us for a drink and we can hear your story."

He smiled and nodded, "An excellent suggestion."

He had more colour in his cheeks and he appeared to be more composed. We sat at a quiet table by the fire and I ordered a bottle of white wine. I would have preferred red but I knew that it would be white or beer here. After it had been poured I held up my glass. "Cheers. I am Robert Alpini and this is my servant Alan Sharp."

"And I am Carl Philip Gottfried von Clausewitz." I saw the smile begin to appear on Sharp's face at the mouthful of a name but I gave a slight shake of my head. If he was a von then he was aristocracy and I knew just how seriously aristocrats took themselves.

"I am pleased to meet you. What were you doing in such a dangerous part of the city?"

"I am studying at the military academy in Prussia, the Kriegsakademie, and I was anxious to discover the secrets of this fine fortress."

"Surely that would have been better in daylight?"

He nodded, "I began my examination in daylight but I was so fascinated that I lost track of time and I lost my bearings. I asked those soldiers for directions and they led me to the place where you found me." He drank some of the wine and shook his head. "It has shaken my faith in soldiers."

I laughed, "They weren't soldiers. They were criminals who have avoided jail."

He gave me a shrewd look. "You have been a soldier. You handled yourself well back there."

I smiled, "Yes I was a soldier but now I sell wine."

It was his turn to laugh. "That I find hard to believe."

"But it is true. Besides, peace must come soon."

Von Clausewitz leaned forward and spoke quietly, "Do not believe that my friend. I have been sent here by General Von

Scharnhorst himself for he wishes to know about the defences of this land."

I was taken aback. "Are you not being indiscreet telling me this?"

He laughed, "Oh no. The commander here knows I have been sent by the General; they are old friends. There is nothing untoward but if someone decides to invade Austria then this is the best route." He gave an embarrassed laugh, "The General has great faith in my plans. If Austria is attacked then we will help them against this greedy Emperor."

This was news indeed. If a lowly student of military matters suspected this then perhaps the French Army was heading towards disaster. "Aren't you a little old to be still studying?"

"I served in the war against France when I was young. I realised then that the more I could learn about war the better."

"Well, we had better escort you back to your hotel."

"There is no need. It is only across the square and I will not be surprised again." He stood and gave a formal nod. "Gentlemen, I am in your debt. Honour demands that I repay the favour. If you ever need anything then do not hesitate to seek me out."

I shook his hand. "Think nothing of it. It was our pleasure. It gave us both a bit of unexpected excitement."

As we watched him cross the square I did not realise that our paths would cross again. We were not just ships passing in the night.

Chapter 5

We left Ulm and headed towards the Danube. We were not in Austria proper; this was Bavaria but it was controlled by the mighty Austrian Empire. As we headed down the main road, built by the Romans, towards Augsburg and Munich we saw clear evidence of the Imperial Army. It was only at troop and battalion strength but it was evidence that the Austrian Emperor was preparing for whatever Napoleon Bonaparte could throw at him. We used the same system we had around the Pas de Calais when we had spied on the French invasion plans. Sharp used a stick which he marked to identify foot, horse, artillery and fortresses. I had a thin sheet which I overlaid on our map and we marked the positions of the units and defences each night.

Leaving the ancient medieval town of Augsburg we trotted down the snow-flecked road towards Munich. As I rode I thought about my position. I was obeying orders but I felt like a traitor and yet I had neither affiliation nor allegiance to Austria. I suspect it was something in my blood which caused me to feel that I was being dishonourable. I just hoped that the information I took back to England would be worth the dishonour I now felt.

Munich was the most formidable place we had seen hitherto. It was old and here I saw cannon which could match those of the British although the French guns were better. The gunners, too, looked more efficient. We found accommodation and stabling close to the Ratskeller. This was the busiest part of the city and the one where we would attract the least attention.

The defences of the city were impressive as were the troops based there. I saw at least two good cavalry regiments. Strategically this was a much more important city than Ulm or Augsburg for it controlled the river approach to Vienna. However, I was sure that the Emperor's cannons might be able to destroy the ancient city walls. They looked to be medieval in nature. Artillery was in Bonaparte's blood

Sergeant Sharp was enjoying the food in Bavaria. Munich was filled with beer halls and they all served sausages with sauerkraut and pickles. It suited Alan far more than the food we had eaten in France. I noticed that Sergeant Sharp was not so much eating as devouring his food. "You look as though you are enjoying that Sharp."

"I am sir. This is proper food. It fills a man up. And as for the beer… it is the best I have had since England. No offence sir, but the food that we ate in France was not a patch on this."

I smiled, "No offence taken."

Suddenly a major of the Austrian Cuirassiers was in our face. He spoke perfect English. "You have been to France? Where are your papers?"

He was with some junior officers and I saw suspicion written all over their faces. I took out the letter identifying me as Robert Alpini and I smiled. "Yes, we visited there during the Peace of Amiens. Luckily we left before war was declared or we would have been interned along with our friends."

I could see that I had not convinced him and he clung on to the document. I was not worried; we had spares in our bags.

"And what were you doing in France?"

"What I am trying to do here; sell fine wine from Sicily, lemons and olives."

The sneer erupted across his face. "We need no such things in Austria. You are wasting your time! But what is an Englishman doing selling Italian wine?"

"My family has Italian connections. Is that a problem?" I was beginning to tire of the attitude of this Austrian officer. Perhaps I was more tired than I realised.

Sharp must have sensed that I was losing my temper and he spoke quickly. "You would be surprised, sir. Many women actually prefer wine to beer. Now as for me I can't get enough of your beer and the food is the best I have eaten. I suppose it is all a matter of taste isn't it?"

His smile was disarming and the major's face softened slightly. "You have a good servant there with excellent taste. I would suggest you leave this city as soon as possible. If people know of your French connections they may take matters into their own hands."

"Thank you for your advice and we were leaving tomorrow anyway."

"Good for if I see you again I will take you for questioning!" He rejoined his comrades and we finished our food as soon as possible.

I heard laughter as we left. I think they thought that we were beating a cowardly retreat. They could think what they liked but when Napoleon Bonaparte arrived many of those arrogant young men would lie dead in Munich's streets.

Once in our room, Sharp could not apologise enough. "I am sorry, sir. Me and my big mouth! I was too relaxed I think. I forgot what we were about."

"It is not your fault Sharp. I should have been more discreet too. We have learned our lesson and from now on we frequent quieter establishments without senior officers."

We managed to avoid being seen on our way to Vienna. The weather rapidly deteriorated as deep winter set in. The snow fell thicker and the temperature plummeted. I was grateful to see the huge capital of the Hapsburg Empire appear in the distance. We had reached the end of our outward journey.

The old Imperial city was built to impress. There were wide avenues and huge buildings. The military here were the best that Austria had. This was where their elite regiments were based as well as their generals and planners. I hoped that we would learn much from our visit. We quickly found a small inn where our exhausted horses could be stabled. I intended to stay but two nights before we headed back. We had pushed our luck but I needed our horses to be able to get us out of trouble quickly.

The owner was quite helpful and told us of the better shops which might be willing to stock our wines. Whilst riding from Munich I had decided that we needed to establish our story before we started spying. The interrogation by the major had put me on my guard. Besides, it would be just as easy to observe the city while visiting shops as wandering around looking suspicious.

Our hotel was close to the cathedral and also some of the better shops. Had I actually been after new business I would have been quite successful? As it was, by noon we had six addresses noted in Sharp's ledger which wanted more information about the products and samples. That done we headed towards the barracks and the defences of the city.

Surprisingly it was not as formidable as either Ulm or Munich. The river formed one barrier and there was a city wall. It was just too large a city to defend. An attacker could choose his point of attack and would outnumber those defending the walls. As we walked from one end to the other I realised that this would be an easier target for the Emperor than the others we had seen. In fact, with a fast-moving corps, he could probably take the city before the Austrians knew he was there.

Perhaps we tarried too long too close to the defences for I was aware that we were being followed. Had we sped up it would alert our pursuers. We were, after all, businessmen and not soldiers attuned to danger. I had to force myself to walk slowly and to peer in shop windows. I was delighted when I found a small shop selling wines. I took the opportunity to enter.

The owner was a small man and, from his headgear, a Jew. "Good morning sir, how can I be of assistance to you?"

I smiled and became a businessman. "It is more what I can do for you, sir. I represent the Alpini family of Sicily and we are hoping to begin exporting fine wines, lemons and olive oil to your fair city." I waved an expansive hand around the interior of the shop where the shelves were packed with bottles. "I can see that you already stock some fine wares and so I will offer to send you a sample of each of our products."

He smiled, "That is most generous of you. I believe I have heard of your wines. It is a pity that you did not bring samples."

I spread my arms, "We did but unfortunately they were damaged in the Tyrol."

"Ah." He searched in his desk and brought out a sheet of paper. "Here is my address. It will save your servant having to write it out."

"Thank you, sir. You are most kind." After shaking hands we left and I hoped that those who were following us would have left. I was wrong. They were waiting. There were four policemen. I smiled at them. "Can I help you, gentlemen?"

They all had fine uniforms but one looked to be a tailored uniform with more lace. He was obviously the leader and it was he who addressed us. "You can come with us for questioning."

"Why? We have done nothing wrong."

"You have been behaving suspiciously. Your swords, if you please."

We handed over our swords and my heart sank. We had been so close to being able to return to Strasbourg and now, it was likely that we would end up rotting in an Austrian prison. As we headed towards the Imperial Palace I became even more depressed. Had we just been taken to a police station for questioning I was hopeful we could have talked our way out of it but questioning by the military was a different matter. I was thankful that they had not seen us leaving our hotel. Our papers and secret map were safe from scrutiny.

We passed many guards who all took the time to observe us closely as we were marched through the corridors and down towards the cellar. We were hurled, unceremoniously, into an office with just a table and four wooden chairs. The door was slammed shut; it seemed ominously final. Sharp looked as though he was going to speak but I held my finger to my lips and shook my head. Until I knew the lie of the land we would keep silent.

Eventually, after what seemed an age, a young captain and a grizzled sergeant arrived. I had a moment of déjà vu; I had done exactly the same thing in Egypt when questioning the survivors of the attack by Nelson's ships. I became even warier and I hoped that Sergeant Sharp would be able to keep his nerve.

The officer smiled and that worried me for there was no warmth in the smile. He spoke in German. "I am Captain von Stollen and you are?"

"I am Robert Alpini of London and I wish to know why I have been arrested."

He leaned back and smiled a smile like a Nile crocodile. "Arrested? No, merely brought here to answer questions and clarify certain matters."

"Certain matters?"

"Yes, you and your servant were observed wandering around the city looking at the barracks and the defences."

I laughed and tried to make it sound an easy laugh, "We were just taking in the sights of this wonderful city of yours."

"Then why did you only visit shops and military installations? There is the opera which is famous, the cathedral, and the churches, in fact, a whole host of sights to satisfy the most curious of visitors and yet you avoided them. I find that interesting. You also avoided all of the fine eating establishments which are normally attractive to first-time visitors. Or have you been here before?"

I was beginning to become uneasy. I had been here before and in the service of Bonaparte. Had I been identified? I had changed much in those years and I was now a full-grown man. I decided to play for time.

"We had not yet got around to those. We were just on our way for refreshment having concluded our business." I proffered the letter from the Jewish shop owner. "You see I am going to send this man a sample of our wares. You can confirm this with him."

He smiled again which, once again, made me uneasy. "We already have done and he confirms your story but I think we will question you a little longer."

He stood and left followed by the sergeant whose eyes had never left me throughout the whole interview. Had he recognised me? I had no time to explain to Sharp what had been discussed. He would have to trust me. I began examining the room for an exit but, as we had descended stairs and there was no window I assumed that the only way out was the way we had entered; through the door which I had no doubt was guarded.

Time passed and no-one returned. I dreaded them finding our bags and searching them. They would find my passport for the French border and Sharp's counting stick not to mention the secret map. I had no doubt that this bright young man who had interrogated us would be able to discern its purpose. I could see the worry etched across Sharp's face. I had led him, once again, into the direst danger. I thanked God for his loyalty and his company. To suffer this alone would be intolerable.

The door began to open and I steeled myself for the interrogation becoming much tougher. The young captain stood there and then he opened the door. There, looking a little more composed than the last time I had seen him was von Clausewitz. Stollen's face looked as though he had just had to suck a lemon. "Are these the two men sir?"

He looked at me and nodded, "They are."

"And you can vouch for them?"

Von Clausewitz turned angrily to the young officer, "You dare to question my word?"

The Prussian obviously had more influence here than I had thought possible for the young captain positively quailed, "Of course not sir but we have to be certain."

"From what you have told me their story about being merchants was corroborated by the shopkeepers you questioned and you have no more evidence against them."

"Well no, sir, but…"

"Until we defeat this monster Bonaparte we need every ally we can get and it would not do to upset Great Britain at this time."

The captain's shoulders sagged in resignation. He waved at the door, "You are free to go. I am sorry for any inconvenience." He handed us, reluctantly, our swords.

"Thank you, captain. I understand your suspicion but my friend here is right. We need to stand together."

Not a word was spoken until we were well clear of the building. In fact, we had reached the cathedral before Von Clausewitz uttered a word. He had a cold look in his eye as he said, "I have repaid my debt to you and I suggest you leave Vienna as soon as possible."

He turned to leave and I restrained him, "Thank you for getting us out of there but I am not your enemy. Believe me. I give you my word that I am on the same side as you."

He brushed my arm away, "And which side is that I wonder?" He shook his head, "I do not know why but I believe you. Still, you must leave now."

"We will but tell me how did you know that we were in custody?"

"Luck. I was meeting with one of their generals, General Mack, and I saw you enter." He shrugged, "I have a little influence with the general for my family's name is known."

"Then I thank you and your family. God speed."

"And to you. I believe you will need all the luck you can muster to escape to…" he looked to the heavens, "wherever you are actually going." He held up his hand, "And I do not want to know!"

We wasted no time in returning to our hotel. It was far too late to leave. It would have raised even more questions and besides the night was incredibly cold. The temperature had plummeted and the Danube had frozen which eliminated my alternative plan to travel back by boat. We paid our bill and said we would leave just before dawn. I lied about our destination. I said that we were heading for Salzburg and Innsbruck in the Tyrol. I did not think that Captain Stollen would give up quite that easily.

After we had descended the stairs and collected the food I had ordered we peered around the street to make sure we were not being watched. We would still need to pass through the gates but I wanted to avoid being followed. I breathed a sigh of relief when I saw no one. We did not take the gate which would have led us directly to Munich; instead, we took the gate on the opposite side of the city. I wanted them to think we were heading for Buda. The information I had given the innkeeper would just make them even more confused.

The guards at the gate were not suspicious for we were heading further into the Austrian Empire; we were not fleeing and our story about trying to reach our destination in daylight made perfect sense. As soon as the road dipped out of sight of the gate we headed across country towards the fields and woods to the north of the city. It was risky riding across unknown country in the dark but we were both good riders and it was worth the risk. We rode hard until dawn. I kept making adjustments so that we gradually turned west. The snow on the ground would mark our passage but the snow-filled skies promised more to hide our tracks. If we had a day then we would be able to lose our pursuers.

When we saw the road just beyond the eaves of the trees we halted. I wanted the horses to have a little rest. We ate some of our food and then changed mounts so that we were riding fresh horses. It made all the difference and they cantered happily down the road, the snow muffling the sound of their hooves.

On our return journey west we skirted all the major towns to avoid the military. We stayed in small inns and farmhouses but we spent the daylight hours and some of the night riding ever westwards. We changed horses twice a day but, even so, they were sorry shadows of the horses they had been. I particularly wanted to avoid Munich. I almost had a permanent crick in my neck as I constantly peered over my shoulder looking for pursuit. The weather aided us for a blizzard blew up and only a lunatic would have ventured out in such weather. We were two such lunatics and we passed that dangerous hive of military activity without incident.

We passed Augsburg and Ulm in the night. We were too close to home to risk being caught. Our last accommodation was a small inn just twenty miles from Strasbourg. The room was so small that it only had one bed and the stables were less than adequate. But it was a bed and we were tired. The innkeeper and his wife made up for the shortfall by giving us one of the best meals we had eaten on our long journey. We left after dawn and I intended to reach the border just before dark to give us the best chance to slip across. I hoped that my papers would see us through without difficulty but I would take no chances.

We were close to the path we had taken in the forest when our luck ran out. The melting snow muffled the noise of the Austrian cavalry who thundered after us. Had our horses not whinnied we would not have known they were there. I turned to see Captain Stollen and a troop of Hussars hurtling towards us. I put my head down and kicked hard towards the forest. On the road, they would easily catch us. Our only chance was the forest. We were fortunate that we had recently changed horses and so, as we entered the forest, I shouted to Sharp. "Let go of the spare horses. It will slow them down."

It hurt me to let such find steeds go. They had served us well but if we kept them we would be captured and they would have the same fate. The Austrians look after their horses and I was sure that they would be cared for. Miraculously the loose horses bought us time. Both beasts slowed down and the Hussars suddenly found their path blocked. The trees encroaching on both sides prevented them from passing the two mounts and they had to stop. We had bought some precious minutes. With luck, our mounts would be fresher than theirs. The sun was dipping in the sky and that, added to the canopy of trees, made our journey darker. It suited us. We only had our swords as weapons. Our pistols were in our bags. Had we had access to them I might have risked slowing down to ambush Stollen and his men. The lack of pistols meant we would have to rely on our horses and hope that they did not come to grief.

Sharp kept glancing over his shoulder to see where the Hussars were. "I think we have a lead, sir. I can't see them on the straight parts."

"Good! We might just make it."

Perhaps I was tempting fate but, as we approached the place where we had killed the pickets there was a crack from a prematurely fired musket. This was no time for hesitation and I drew my sword, lay low over the saddle and kicked towards the smoke. The surprised Dragoon looked up in horror as my sword sliced down and split his skull. My horse knocked over a second and I heard a scream as Sergeant Sharp killed a third. More muskets fired from left and right but we were moving too fast and I heard the leaves shredded by their passage. They had increased their pickets. I wondered how many more would be ahead of us.

My horse began to slow and, as I put my hand down to pat him, it came away red. He had been struck. As much as I hated to do it I would have to ride him until he fell; it was our only chance of survival. "Sharp, my horse is wounded. Overtake me." I glanced behind and saw him shake his head. "That is an order, Sergeant!"

He spurred his horse on and he led the way. I looked under my arm and saw that the Hussars were less than forty yards behind me in the fading light of dusk. Had we been a hundred yards ahead we might have made it but they would catch us before we reached the border. It is a strange thing but when you have no hope life becomes simpler. We just had to ride until they caught us and then fight until we died. It was that easy.

I risked another look and saw that they were less than three horse lengths behind us. "Come on boy. Another few yards and..."

I got no further as the foliage on both sides of the path erupted in the smoke from fifteen muskets. The noise was so loud that I was deafened. My horse slowed and I turned in the saddle. The Austrians were beating a hasty retreat leaving bodies on the trail. The old sergeant who had shared his drink with us stepped out. "You made it then?"

He handed me a bottle of brandy and I swallowed down a mouthful, "So it would appear."

He pointed to the dead Hussars and Dragoons. "They have increased their pickets since you crossed over. You certainly stirred a hornet's nest."

I asked, "Any more brandy?"

He gave me a strange glance as he poured some more into my beaker. "You don't look like a drinker."

"I'm not but my horse is wounded. I want to clean the wound."

Luckily the bullet had only grazed my mount. He would survive. We left the sergeant and his men to harvest the bodies of the Austrians while he sent one trooper to escort us to Strasbourg.

Chapter 6

We headed directly for Bessières' headquarters. From the lack of cavalry around, I assumed that Bonaparte was elsewhere. The sergeant who had been our guard recognised us and reluctantly admitted us. Bessières, as usual, was hard at work. He looked surprised to see us.

"You are back sooner than I expected. Did you complete your task?"

In answer, I took out the map and the sheet with the markings on it. "Here are the numbers of men, horses, guns and forts."

He slapped the desk and began to laugh, "You have done it again Robbie. How do you do it?" He waved his hand, "It matters not. Now these are the numbers but…" He stood, "I forget myself, "Sergeant, bring in some coffee for us and some croissants." As the sergeant turned to go he snapped, "Fresh ones!"

Sitting down he picked up his pen, "So, you will give me the minutiae which is in your head."

We spent the next hour detailing all that we had seen. Sharp added information when I was unclear. I did not mention Von Clausewitz; just that we evaded capture.

The breakfast had arrived and I gratefully devoured it. "You have done well and proved your loyalty. We now need to get you back to England so that you can continue this work." He reached into his desk and handed me a bag of coins. "Some gold Louis; you will need expenses." He smiled, "You have already earned this and, when we have conquered England, you will have estates and houses. The Emperor will not forget his loyal friends." He went to the map on the wall. "Now, as for getting you back." He drew a line with his finger around the Atlantic coasts of France and Spain. "There are no ships which come to these ports and go to England. " His finger continued until it came to Copenhagen. "The Danes are still neutral. You will have to travel there and obtain passage on a boat to England."

I looked at the map. The journey would be about the same as the one we had already taken but there seemed to be few options available. "Very well."

"I will have a carriage made available and the papers necessary to facilitate your journey." He sipped his coffee. "Good. Now how will you send your information to us?"

The colonel and I had discussed this already. "You say there are no ships travelling from England to France but there are ships, as you say, which go to neutral ports like Copenhagen, Oslo, Stockholm and to Italy. I have connections with Italy and that, although the longer route would seem to be the best option. It may be possible for an Italian ship to deliver packages to either Corunna or Cadiz." I could see that he was following the logic of the plan we had concocted and he nodded. "I will use the ports of Naples, Corunna and Cadiz for my packages. I will address them to you. All you would need to do would be to arrange for someone in each of the ports to deliver the package here."

"That could be arranged but we will need a code." He handed me a copy of Julius Caesar by William Shakespeare. When I opened it I saw that it was in English. He smiled at my reaction. "We thought it might be better than giving you a book in French. The code is quite simple. It is a substitution code. You go through each page in turn. One page for one message. Just to make it clear you will need to write the number of the page on the letter somewhere. You underline the alphabet and then use the next letter for your message. It will be difficult at first but you will get used to it. Here," he handed me a pen and some paper. "Try it. Write '*the army will sail in May*.'"

It took me longer than I expected and I handed over the completed paper with trepidation. He smiled, "Good, you have understood the concept. It will come easier the next time. We both have identical copies. You will use the same page for the first message." He looked down at my family ring, the seal of the Macgregors. "As an added precaution if you would seal it with your ring then I know it has not been tampered with." He leaned back.

"Is that it?" It all seemed far too simple to me. I had expected something more complicated.

He smiled contentedly, "Of course. You have done well. Now, rest for the remainder of the day." He waved his arm in the general direction of the stairs. "There is a room up there for you. Tomorrow you will leave for Copenhagen." He stood and shook my hand, "Welcome back to the service of France, Robbie."

As I was putting the book in my leather satchel he went to the map. I had not noticed it before. It was of Italy.

"You say your sponsor is at Gibraltar at the moment?"

"There were plans to send him there," I added vaguely.

"Good, if you hear anything about Italy, Sicily or the Iberian Peninsula when you speak with him then we need to know urgently."

I suddenly took a closer interest in the map. I saw Masséna's name and below it the names and numbers of regiments. I recognised the 9th Chasseurs. I saw an arrow leading to Naples. "I thought the Emperor had finished with Italy?"

"Italy yes, but the King of Naples and Sicily appears to harbour ideas about allying with Britain. Do not worry Robbie your old friend André will be more than a match for those overdressed peacocks. One regiment of cavalry and a battery of guns will soon bring them to their senses. So you see why we need knowledge of British intentions?"

"Of course. And Iberia; I thought Spain was an ally."

"She is but the British have an ally in Portugal and that gives them a foothold there. So far they have shown little interest in Iberia apart from their garrison on the rock but... Anyway, you will need rest. Good luck, my friend and take care. Do not get caught for the Emperor can do nothing for you."

That was nothing new. Our job had always been to take risks on the Emperor's behalf.

As Sergeant Sharp and I went upstairs the thought came to me that for all their Republican and egalitarian ideas, Sharp was always ignored because he was considered a servant. Nothing changed in France; just the man wielding the whip and now it was Bonaparte. France had exchanged one master for another.

Bessières had provided not only a carriage but a guard too. We were given papers which identified me as a diplomat travelling in the service of the new Emperor. The guard and driver had been provided with the funds for our accommodation and we had an easy time as we headed north. Sharp and I spent much of the daylight hours practising with the code. We travelled quickly through France for we had requisitions for spare horses. Once we had left the Batavian Republic and entered Denmark the journey was a little slower. Our guides were glad when they could deposit us at the quay in Copenhagen. They would be able to enjoy a leisurely ride back to France. I suspected they had not spent all of the money allocated to them as our accommodation and food had been basic at best. I did not mind. We had made quicker time than I had anticipated.

We took rooms close to the port so that I could arrange our passage. Unfortunately there appeared to be few English ships in port and the rest of the ships were avoiding England like the plague. The Emperor had let it be known that he disapproved of trade with his enemy and those on the Continent were in imminent danger of invasion should they transgress. I managed to find us a berth on a ship expected in the next couple of days from Newcastle. Sergeant Sharp was disappointed but I told him that we would easily be able to travel from there to London.

We spent the next two days exploring the town and the port. Nelson had upset the Danes some years earlier when he had burned their fleet to prevent it from falling into French hands. Had we spoken English we would have received some cold looks and harsh treatment. The attack still rankled.

We travelled on the 'Bluebell'; she was a Newcastle collier and the captain knew Geordie. Most people in Newcastle knew the irascible captain. It made the journey both pleasant and informative. The garrulous Captain Dunston happily chatted about the way the war had improved his livelihood. The British fleet could not get enough of the Baltic wood for their masts and spars and they, in turn happily, consumed the Newcastle coal. It was ironic that Napoleon's plan to isolate Britain had, in fact, made many of its citizens richer.

"I think Geordie will be in port when we get home. He was on his way back from London. He's doing well, mind. He and Betty have the finest furniture you can buy in Newcastle."

I smiled. Geordie's wife was always house-proud, quite literally. Geordie did not care what the house looked like but he cared what his wife thought and that was important. The captain would not take a penny from us. He was doing a fellow Briton a service was his view and that should be done without recompense. The men of the north were always fiercely loyal and patriotic. I had met the men of the Royal Scots Greys and they were a wild bunch. If the foot regiments were half as good then Napoleon had better watch out.

The 'Witch' was in harbour when we arrived and the Third Mate directed us to Geordie's house. As soon as the door was opened I knew that we would be treated like royalty. Betty squealed with delight and Geordie came running from the parlour with a pipe in hand ready to deal with whatever problem had frightened his wife.

She wagged a finger at him, "Put your eyes back in their sockets man! I'm not in any danger. It's Robbie, come for a visit."

I hugged her and kissed her on the cheek, "I hope we won't be inconveniencing you."

Geordie slapped me on the back. "Why no, you daft bugger and who is your friend?"

"This is Sergeant Sharp, from my regiment."

Geordie held out a ham-like hand, "Pleased to meet you, bonny lad. Any friend of Robbie's is welcome here." Without waiting for a reply we were whisked into the parlour.

Betty appeared with a jug of ale and three glasses. "Now you lads enjoy that while I nip down to the shop for a bit of something for tea."

"Don't trouble yourself on our account."

I saw the warning look in Geordie's eyes but it was too late. She had heard. "And it is no trouble to feed some friends. I thought you knew that! We aren't Londoners here. We give guests a good welcome!"

The northern folk were deeply suspicious of all those who lived down south and I saw the shocked look on Sharp's face. Geordie and I just laughed as she left the room like a typhoon.

"Now then what brings you here? Not that you aren't welcome any time."

"We were in Copenhagen and the only ship we could get was bound for Newcastle. I thought we might get a boat down south to London from here."

He nodded. "I'll be bound there at the end of the week you are more than welcome to travel with me." He raised his glass, "Cheers."

"Cheers."

"And what were you doing in Copenhagen I wonder?" He grinned and held up his hand, "Don't tell me because it will probably be a lie and we don't lie to friends. I suspect it was something to do with that fellow from London, Selkirk." He shook his head, "You want to watch yourself, Robbie. You are no cat and you dinna have nine lives!"

It was a delightful three days we spent with Geordie. We were treated like guests in a fine hotel and I could see the effect it had on Alan. He felt part of a family. He had gone from being the loner, isolated and unhappy to a confident soldier who now had real friends.

The weather was changing as we headed south to London. It was now late February and the cold had abated marginally. Perhaps it was the fact that we were not in the heart of landlocked Austria that made the difference but we both felt happier as we headed south towards London and Colonel Selkirk.

Colonel Selkirk never seemed to leave his office. We always found him there. He was delighted with all of our news. The codebook particularly intrigued him. We spent a whole day being debriefed and working out what I would say in my first report.

"You go back to your regiment and I will work on something. I'll pop down and see you and we will encode it and send it off." He rubbed his hands in delight. "For once we have the edge over Bonaparte." He clapped me on the back. "That information about Masséna and Italy and Iberia is priceless. Well done!"

"But sir, one thing has me confused. What can we learn about Bonaparte and his plans? I am here and soon he will realise that the information he is given is useless."

"Ah, but it won't be. The journey to these ports takes time. We will send him some information which will reach him too late and that will give credence to the rest of the stuff we send him. We will even send him some true information to reach him on time but it won't help him." He tapped his nose. "That is why we chose Hew Dalrymple to be the man you said was your benefactor." He leaned back, "As for learning about Bonaparte's plans... let us just say that this was not your last visit to the Continent." He saw my look of horror and held up his hand. "Oh don't worry, it won't be for some time. It may even be years but it is an option." He pushed over the bag of gold coins I had been given. "Here you two keep these, you have earned them. They won't be going in my report in any case." He smiled, "Buy yourself some property. Prices are low with the war and such. Believe me, they will rise."

"Thank you, sir."

I did take his advice and, after purchasing some items from Fortnum and Masons and writing a letter to Sicily I put the rest of the money in the bank and asked the bank to find me a suitable property in London. We booked seats on the mail coach and I took back two cases of Alpini wine for the mess. It seemed the least I could do for my comrades.

As we approached the Medway Sergeant Sharp asked, "Sir, what do we say to the lads when they ask where we have been? They will you know?"

"You tell them a version of the truth. You say we went to Copenhagen to sell wine to the Danes and then visited friends in Newcastle."

"But that wouldn't explain why we were away so long."

"I know but it is plausible and within a few days they will have forgotten that we were ever away. Try to keep to yourself for the first few days. That will help."

Poor Alan was in a worse position than I was. The other officers might be curious but good manners and Colonel Fenton would prevent too many awkward questions. The sergeant's mess was a different affair. I would need to speak with Sergeant Major Jones.

The duty sergeant recognised us immediately, "Good to see you, Captain Matthews. That was a nice long leave eh sir?"

I knew that he was fishing for information, "Just long enough, sergeant. We are both glad to be back. Have I missed much?"

"A couple of new officers, sir, and that is about it."

"Sergeant Sharp, take our bags to our rooms and then take the rest of the day to get yourself sorted out. I'll go and see the Colonel."

"Begging your pardon, sir, but the Colonel is on leave. It is Major Hyde-Smith in command."

"Thank you, Sergeant Glover."

The major knew my role as an agent of Colonel Selkirk as did Colonel Fenton. However the major was less opposed to my dual role. He was a younger man and could see the benefits for both the country and the regiment.

When I entered his office his face lit up. Garrison duty was boring and conversation and stories of foreign travel were to be relished. "Well, Captain Matthews I see you are back safe and sound. Hopefully in one piece?"

"Yes, sir. We had a couple of run-ins with some cavalry but we survived."

I knew he was desperate for more information but he was too much of a gentleman to ask. "Good, good. How is Sergeant Sharp?"

"He has found he has a taste for German food and beer."

"Ah, you were in Germany then?" There was a twinkle in his eye and I knew I had been indiscreet.

"Right sir, I am raring to get back into action what is new and what do I need to do?"

"We have some new officers, Captain Dunn and Lieutenant Selby. Your troop numbers have been made up and you are at full strength. Lieutenant Jackson has done a remarkable job. He has changed beyond all measure since the DeVere pair left. He has trained the new boys and they fit in well. Of course, Sergeant Seymour and Sergeant Grant have given him sound advice."

I stood. "If that is all, sir, I will get changed and then see to Badger."

As soon as I entered the stables I heard the whinny which told me that Badger still remembered me. He was a fine horse. He would never truly replace Killer, the horse who had been killed in Egypt, but I would not trade him for any other horse. I was just finishing inspecting him when Corporal Richardson, one of the farrier corporals came in.

"Don't you worry, sir. He has been well looked after. The lads from your troop came in every day to check on him and give him a treat, it's a wonder he isn't the size of a house."

That touched me more than anything. My troop, which had been a bunch of badly led and unruly rabble were now the best troop in the regiment and cared enough about me to look after my horse while I was away. This was the reason I would bring down Napoleon; I owed it to my men.

We were soon back in the rhythm of the regiment. Training and drills gave both meaning and order. The colonel returned and we found that there were no plans for our deployment. In fact, the colonel seemed pleased that we were not one of the many regiments who had been placed on half-pay. Our record in Pomerania and our services rescuing the civilians from France had ensured that we were well thought of.

By summer it looked as though we would have a tedious and predictable existence. And then Colonel Selkirk arrived along with a small fussy looking official. I had expected to be summoned to a meeting with the Colonel but I had not expected it to be in public.

When Colonel Selkirk had been in Colonel Fenton's office for over an hour I wondered what was afoot.

Sergeant-Major Jones put me out of my misery by summoning me. "Well sir, it seems they want you for the conference. Unless I miss my guess your troop is going to have a little action."

I shook my head, "It is hard to see where; unless they intend to send us to the West Indies." That was the fear for all regiments. A tour in the West Indies meant disease, drink and death. Few regiments returned from that hell hole with a full complement of men.

"I doubt that sir. As I recall you have some ability in European languages..." he was grinning as he let the sentence end.

I suspected that the Sergeant Major knew more about me than he let on but he was as much of a gentleman as either the colonel or the major.

The major was in the office with the others and there was a rolled-up map on the table. The air was thick with cigar smoke. I was relieved that both Major Hyde-Smith and Colonel Fenton looked happy. They hated my excursions as an agent.

"Ah, Captain Matthews. This is Mr Grimble from the Foreign Office. He is here to answer any questions you may have." The little man just nodded and continued scribbling in a notebook. Colonel Selkirk continued. "After this meeting, Captain Matthews, you and I need to have a little chat but Colonel Fenton will brief you on your mission." He smiled an innocent smile that made me suspicious.

Major Hyde-White stood and unrolled the map. It was Italy and Sicily. "Your troop is to be detached and sent to Sicily. It appears that Bonaparte has an army ready to invade Italy. It seems he is unhappy with the position of Naples. He either wants an ally or the kingdom. He does not want a neutral. Sir John Stuart commands the forces in Sicily. There are some Russian and English troops in Naples itself but you will be joining Sir John Stuart because he has no cavalry. Logistically it will be impossible to send the regiment but Colonel Selkirk has arranged a fast transport to get you and your troop to Messina." He smiled. Your knowledge of the area and your connections made you an obvious choice. You will leave this evening. The transport is already at Dover awaiting you. I am afraid that we can only send Corporal Richardson as support. You will have to beg steal or borrow anything else. The quartermaster is arranging as much as ammunition as he can gather as well as much spare equipment to be available for you but this is short notice." He flashed a look of disapproval at the two visitors. "But I know you are a resourceful young man and your knowledge of the language may well help. Any questions?"

I stared at the map. I had not expected this. A month ago I had been freezing in Austria and soon I would be baking in Sicily. "I don't think so."

Mr Grimble banged his notebook on the table. "You mean I have been dragged down here for nothing?"

I felt I ought to say something, "I am sorry, sir, I know Sicily and I thought that was all I needed." I searched my head for a question, "Who is in command of the French?"

"Marshal André Masséna."

Colonel Selkirk smiled, "I believe you know him, Robbie."

I nodded and Mr Grimble looked surprised. "You know a marshal of France?"

Colonel Selkirk laughed, "You would be surprised who my young friend knows. Well go on little man, tell him how many men and so on."

"Well, this is pure speculation and is based on a report from the captain of a naval frigate who captured some despatches."

"Yes, yes, get on with it."

The official shuffled and then opened his notebook. "There are a number of infantry regiments, light infantry regiments. He has Chasseurs à Cheval as well as Polish, Swiss and Italian regiments. We believe he has a battery of four guns. His total force is over ten thousand men."

"And how many does Sir John Stuart have?"

"Four and a half thousand with three guns."

The odds were stacked against us already. I smiled, "Thank you for that information, sir. Who is the general who will be leading the French armies?"

He looked up confused, "I have told you, Massena."

I shook my head, "He is in command of the whole force in Italy. There will be a general in command of the forces who attack Naples."

He looked at his notes and his surprised expression told me that he had the information. "General Reynier."

I nodded, "He commanded a division in Egypt."

This time the only one who was not surprised was Colonel Selkirk. Mr Grimble mumbled, "I can see why they have chosen you, young man. You are remarkably well informed."

Colonel Selkirk stood, "If there is nothing else then I need to speak with Robbie here and I am sure that there is much to do to get the troop moving quickly."

I knew that he would have annoyed my fellow officers by his rudeness but it was his way and he whisked me away.

"Where is your room?" I pointed to the officer's quarters. "Good, have your man stand guard."

Once alone, with Sharp outside the door, he sat on my chair leaving me to sit on my bed. "Of course, as you realise the information did not come from a frigate; you brought it. The only additional information we had was the make up of the force and the commanders. Knowing that Masséna was the commander made it easy to find out the rest. It has taken this long to confirm all of the information. Now, what do you know of this Marshal and General?"

"André Masséna is a cunning commander and cautious but he is favoured by Bonaparte and so great things will be expected of him. Reynier is a sound general but predictable."

"Good. Now we can use this to our advantage. When you reach Gibraltar I want you to send a message to Bessières telling him of the British expedition to the mainland."

I was shocked, "You want me to tell him we are attacking his invading army?"

"Think about it, Robbie. The force we are sending is small. You don't need to give away the numbers. It might even help as it might make him think we are sending a larger force than we actually are. The main thing is it gives you credibility so that when we want to deceive him he will swallow the bait."

"Very well."

"Good lad. Here is the information for you to give him. You will have plenty of time. It can take a month to get to Gibraltar." He smiled, "You might even get to see Our Nel again. His fleet is close to the straits at the moment." He suddenly looked serious, "Do not risk your life in heroics Robbie. You are more use to Britain as a spy than a Captain of cavalry. Stay alive and keep safe."

I shook my head. Colonel Selkirk was like a spider in the middle of an enormous web. Each tap on a strand was transmitted to him. As he left I reflected that I would soon be fighting my old countrymen again. This time I would be in uniform; I would be a Light Dragoon.

Chapter 7

The Indiaman we travelled on was called the 'Warwick Castle' and the captain was an ancient mariner called Captain Douglas. He was a good captain but he ran a tight ship and would suffer no breaches of discipline. The troop sergeants were hard-pressed to maintain order amongst the troopers. The trouble was that the troopers were excited. I blamed myself for that. As soon as they realised that we were the only troop to be travelling to Italy they began to invent fantastical adventures for us. The first night at sea I held a meeting with Lieutenant Jackson, the sergeants and the corporals. Since my days in the Chasseurs, I had always believed that every man who commanded in a troop should know as much as possible. I was aided by Sergeant Sharp who had become adept at reading my mind.

We used the officers' mess. As we were so close to the French coast Captain Douglas had every one of his officers on duty. We were travelling without escort and there were still French privateers. I had an hour to brief and inform my men about the coming campaign.

"Firstly I need to tell you all that I only discovered our mission a short while ago and secondly, I need you to impress upon your men that we are not engaged in some secret mission. We are heading to Sicily to join Sir John Stuart's force to repel a possible invasion by the French. The invasion may not take place. In that case, we will all enjoy the sun, fine food and fine wine. If that is not possible, I have to tell you, we will be the only cavalry available to Sir John and we will be faced by at least one regiment of excellent French cavalry." I allowed that to sink in before I continued. "What we carry aboard this ship is all that we will have to supply us. There will be no more supplies. If tack breaks then we repair it." I pointed to Corporal Richardson. "We have one farrier to shoe horses and deal with issues related to our mounts. There will be no remounts. Any horse which is lost means a man afoot."

Suddenly I had their attention. A cavalryman afoot was like a soldier without his gun.

"We need to look after our horses and our equipment. The quartermaster gave us as much ammunition as he had. We need to collect as much from the enemy as we can. I have been to Sicily." There were looks of surprise on their faces. "There is very little grazing. It is a rocky hot place with brown dried grass. We will have to use grain." I paused. "There will be no more supplies of grain forthcoming. I am telling you this because you need to impress upon the troopers that we have to live on our wits and forage as much as we can. As the only cavalry in the region, we will be asked to do the job of a regiment. That means that all of you will have to shoulder more responsibility. Mr Jackson and I may not be there to give orders. You will have to do that." I allowed that to sink in. I smiled. "I am confident that you will do well. I trust each and every one of you. Remember that. Any questions?"

Corporal Lows put up a tentative hand, "Sir, what language do they speak?"

I smiled, questions like that were easy to field. "Italian. I speak a little and I will give lessons for any who want them. We will make it at four o'clock each afternoon. Anything else?"

"Yes sir, how do we keep the men occupied? This voyage might take weeks. When we went to the Cape we had all sorts of problems."

"Good point Sergeant White. We spend as much time as possible each day training. We cannot use the horses for obvious reasons but we have the men and we can practise as much as we are able. Make competitions which test their fitness: push-ups, lifting weights, anything to keep their minds off the monotony." I could see them all nodding. They had brains and they could see the wisdom of my words. "Do not let the men drink. I know that the crew will have drink. Keep our men away from it and I want no trouble with the crew. Luckily we are a small number and it should be easy. We have the full complement of officers and NCOs. Each of us is responsible for a small number of men. Sergeant Sharp can help out. Any more questions? No, then go and help the men to get bedded down." I grinned, "Hammocks can be a bugger!"

Thankfully we had a stormy voyage through the Channel and the men were too preoccupied trying to retain the contents of their stomach to be either bored or troublesome. Due to the proximity of the French coast and their fleet we had to beat some way out to sea which added time to our journey but also ensured that the men had other things on their mind. When the wind and the waves abated they were ready for some drill and they were given it. They worked really hard and seemed to enjoy the break in routine. The sun was shining and I did away with the need for uniform. Most just wore their overalls. Some suffered from the sun but, on the whole, I think they enjoyed the experience.

The war was brought to mind when we saw the masts of the blockading fleet close to Cadiz. The narrow straits meant we had to sail close to the huge battleships. I think the wooden walls of the Royal Navy really impressed our men. They were a visible sign of our resistance to Napoleon. I had found Captain Douglas to be a mine of information once he had time to talk to me. He pointed out a massive three-decker with immaculate paintwork. "That, young man, is the flagship of Admiral Nelson!"

I strained my eyes to try to spot the diminutive figure but it was in vain. "I met him once. I even had a meal with him and Lady Hamilton."

The old seafarer was impressed, "Then you have an honour I would give my right arm for. So long as we have Little Nel then Britannia shall rule the waves and be safe from invasion."

Once we passed the fleet I knew that Gibraltar would not be far ahead and that I would need to have my message ready. Sharp and I had encoded Colonel Selkirk's missives many days ago. I just had to work out how to deliver it.

I approached Captain Douglas, "Sir, I have a question for you."

I had approached him when alone at the stern of the ship and he could tell from my voice and manner that discretion was required. "If I can answer, sir, then I will."

"I need a package delivering to Cadiz. How would I do that?"

He frowned and scrutinised my features, "Cadiz is in Spain and we are at war with them."

"I give you my word sir, as an officer and a gentleman that I am doing this on behalf of His Majesty's Government."

I did not need to imbue my voice with sincerity; it was there already for I was speaking the truth. He nodded, "I believe you. Bring me the package. When the water boats arrive I will see your package is delivered. It will cost a silver piece. Not for me, you understand, but the man I use does not do such things out of the generosity of his heart."

I smiled, "I understand. I will get both of them." I slipped down to my cabin and retrieved the package and the coin. Gibraltar was rapidly approaching.

The captain glanced at the letter and started. "A Marshal of France?" He hissed.

I smiled and nodded, "As I said this is not of my doing; I am merely the messenger."

He sighed, "I believed your story before and this confirms it. You are a deep one for one so young."

We did not enter the harbour but waited with other ships out in the straits. The water lighters and other bum boats hurried out to us. The Bosun stood at the side warding off the unwanted vessels and securing those who were permitted to approach. A couple of the captains boarded and I saw one, who looked to be Spanish in appearance, descend to Captain Douglas' cabin. When they emerged they both looked in my direction and gave me a subtle nod. My first missive was on its way to the Emperor.

We left in a convoy with two frigates and a brig for escort. This was before the total destruction of the French Fleet and there were still patrolling hostile vessels in the Mediterranean. We now increased our training. The bad weather was behind us and we would only have a week or so at sea. We used the time well. The men were tanned and fit. The voyage had done them good and they were eager for action. I was not sure what action that would be but I was confident that they would meet whatever challenges were put in their way.

As we skirted Malta and its British garrison I thought back to that fateful day when I had been sent to spy on the garrison and met the old Knight of St.John, the man who turned out to be a relative. I hoped I would see him when we reached Sicily for he was old. Cesar, in his letters, told me that my sudden appearance had given the old man a new lease of life but I also knew that no one could fight old age forever.

Lieutenant Jackson joined me as I watched the ship bound for Malta, head towards the British bastion. The island slipped further south as we spoke. "What do you think our role will be sir?"

"Scouting I think. We are too few for anything else. Perhaps we might have to discourage the Chasseurs."

I hear they are fine horsemen."

"They are and they are handier with their swords than our chaps. That is why I have had them practising with their carbines. They are better than the French musketoon and give us a slight advantage."

"You favour powder weapons then sir?"

I nodded vigorously. "I do indeed. That is why I have two on my saddle and two in my holster, as does Sergeant Sharp. We have learned that it gives you an edge in close combat."

"I shall have to get more then."

"With luck, they will come through combat. Remember we cannot afford to leave anything on the field. It matters not if it is British, French or Italian equipment, we take it and use it."

He shook his head and smiled, "You are the complete opposite of Captain DeVere."

"I will take that as a compliment."

"And it was meant that way. He cared not where anything came from. He just expected others to service his needs."

"Ah well, it may be in the way we were brought up. I was brought up to value everything I was given for I was given little. I was taught to look after what I had and it has served me well."

He nodded and continued looking out to sea. "As with your horse. Captain DeVere mocked you for caring for Badger yourself."

I laughed, "I know, he called me the stable boy."

"Did that not offend you, sir?"

"It might have done but that would have gained me little. It was his opinion and it was wrong. Besides stable boys are valuable themselves. Without them, our horses would not survive the rigours we put them through." I looked at him remembering Killer. "A horse will give its life for you if you have treated it well. What greater sacrifice can a beast make?"

The convoy docked at Messina. We were not far from Cesar's estate and Sir John but I had to concentrate upon my duties. We were the first ship to unload. It made sense as we had the horses. Luckily it was the Mediterranean and we were able to rig up a ramp and walk them off. There was little tidal movement here. We did not have to use a sling. The horses hated it. While one in four men looked after the horses the rest of the troop unloaded the stores that we had brought. I wondered how we would transport them.

Suddenly I was hailed, "Captain Macgregor! What the hell are you doing here in your fancy get up?"

I turned and saw Captain Dinsdale. He carried the Alpini goods in his ship. I was a half owner in the ship. I strode over to him and clasped his arm. "Good to see you, Matthew. We are to be stationed here."

A frown crept across his face. "I thought there was danger. The number of French ships has increased and they are becoming bold." He looked around at the men and horses. "Mind you, you cannot do much with these."

"Don't worry, we have other troops here. Are you outbound or inbound?"

"We sail tonight when we are loaded."

"Good. When you return I may have a task or two for you."

He rubbed his hands. "Intrigue again! Excellent."

I laughed. In another life, he would have been a pirate. "Tell me are there any wagons to be had?"

He pointed, "They are expensive but why not use your cousins? They have just unloaded my cargo and they will be heading back later on. Come on I'll introduce you to the wagon master."

The wagon master looked to be barely more than a boy. "This is Carlo." He nodded seriously, "Carlo this is Signior Roberto, the master's cousin." Carlo didn't react. "The man from Scotland, the soldier friend of Sir John."

That made all the difference and he grinned from ear to ear and pumped my hand up and down as though drawing water from a well.

"I have heard much about you."

I sighed. The stories of my life were always exaggerated, "I need to use the wagons to transport my men's equipment."

He nodded, "Of course. Shall my men load them or…"

"No, I will get my sergeants to do it. They know how it should be packed."

James and the sergeants had watched as I had gabbled away in Italian. I forgot that there was much about me that they did not know. "Sergeant Grant, have these wagons loaded with our gear." I put my arm around Carlo who swelled with pride, "This is Carlo."

It was almost comical watching my sergeants trying to communicate with the Italians. They would work it out. "Sergeant Sharp, bring our horses. We need to find out where we are to be stationed."

As he ran off Captain Dinsdale said, "I'll leave you to it then."

Before he left I said, "Is business good?"

"Excellent. You are becoming richer by the day."

"Have you thought about another ship?"

He looked surprised. "Can you afford it?"

"As you said I am a rich man and my expenses are small. If you wish to buy another and have a suitable captain then I will supply half the finance as before."

He gave me a shrewd look. "What do you know?"

"Let us just say that I think there will be a demand for good Italian wine for this Emperor is likely to make more enemies than friends."

"I will look into it."

Waving goodbye I shouted, "Lieutenant Jackson, take charge. I am going into the town to find out where our billet is to be found."

Messina is a bustling old town but I knew my way around its medieval streets. I had an idea where the consulate was to be found. I assumed that the Consul would have been kept informed about Sir John and his troops. It was hard to hide four thousand redcoats and three cannon.

I saw the Union Flag fluttering outside the grand white porticoed building. The two red-coated sentries were reassuring. We dismounted and they both stood to attention. "Sergeant Sharp stay with the horses." Turning to the two marines I asked, "Who is the consul?"

"Sir Charles Frere."

"Have you any idea where Sir John Stuart and the rest of the army might be?"

Although they both snapped a smart, "Sir, no sir!" I knew that they did.

I sighed. Inter-service rivalries bored me. "Very well. I'll do it the hard way."

Entering the building was refreshing as the interior was several degrees cooler than the hot street. As soon as I entered an Italian servant rushed up to me. His English was impeccable, "Yes sir. How may I be of service?"

"I am looking for either Sir John Stuart or the consul."

"I have no idea where Sir John is to be found but I will see if Sir Charles is free. If you would follow me."

He led me to a large double door and he disappeared inside. A moment later he reappeared. "Sir Charles will see you now. May I get you some refreshment?"

"An iced Limoncello would be appreciated." He raised his eyebrows that this Englishman would have such discerning taste. I entered the room, helmet in hand.

"Ah, Captain er... dashed awkward this." Sir Charles was old school diplomat. He was small and neat. His moustache was trimmed immaculately and there was not a hair out of place on his head. His desk was so tidy that it looked to have just been arranged.

"Matthews, sir, Captain Matthews of the 11th Light Dragoons. What is awkward?"

"Well Sir John was supposed to have arranged for your billet but when you did not arrive yesterday he took the expeditionary force for a forced march."

"Ah. And have you any idea where our billet is?"

"Off the top of my head, no. The camp is just south of the town but it is too small for your horses. I have no idea what he intended."

"Very well sir, then do I have your permission to make my own arrangements?"

"Well of course... if you think you can. I'll let you have Julio to interpret." He stood to summon the servant.

I waved my hand, "No need sir, I can speak Italian."

That totally flummoxed him. He sat down, "By God sir, you don't say. Remarkable." He recovered his composure. "Well, then Captain Matthews if you get the bill sent here I will arrange payment. Try to negotiate eh? Save His Majesty some money eh?"

I liked Sir Charles. I grinned, "Of course sir. I not only speak Italian I can barter like one too."

The servant came in with my drink and Sir Charles told me as much as he knew about the current situation. It did not add much to my knowledge but I enjoyed the chat.

As we rode back to the port I told Sergeant Sharp what had ensued. "I don't like that sir. It isn't right."

"No, I know but we will make the best of it."

When I reached the port the wagons were loaded and the troop stood by their mounts. Sergeant Grant and Lieutenant Jackson were standing beside Carlo. "We have a problem chaps. It seems Sir John has gone off on a forced march and we have nowhere to stay."

"Bugger!" Sergeant Grant had the ability, to sum up, a situation quickly.

"Quite." I turned to Carlo. "Carlo, do you know of a field close by here with water and some grazing? We need a camp."

"How close is close?"

"Within an hour's ride."

He beamed. "Then I will arrange for you to stay at the farm of Uncle Giuseppe. He lives not far down the road."

I was not convinced, "Horses smell you know."

He tapped his nose, "And that is why my uncle will let you stay there. Free fertiliser for his lemons and horses do not eat lemons do they?"

I laughed, "I suppose not."

As Carlo went to instruct his drivers I turned to my two companions. "It seems we are staying at Uncle Giuseppe's lemon farm. Get the men mounted. We will follow Carlo."

I rode next to Lieutenant Jackson who was bursting with questions. "Sir, how do you come to speak Italian?"

"Oh, there are many skills I have. Let us just say I enjoy learning."

We headed towards the area where Uncle Giuseppe's farm was to be found. We left the main road and headed up a narrow track. I worried that this might be too small and I began to work out how to explain that Carlo. We crested a rise and I saw the lemon trees. They were spread over a large area like a canopy. It was perfect. There was grass beneath and the lemon trees themselves would shade the horses. I just hoped that Uncle Giuseppe would be amenable.

The noise of our arrival attracted everyone from the estate. Before I was introduced I recognised Uncle Giuseppe. He was a larger and rounder version of Carlo. I saw Carlo descend and kiss the hand of his uncle. I nudged Badger forward and we reached the pair when their conversation had finished.

Uncle Giuseppe tried to speak in English, "Happy we are to meet you."

Carlo smiled and said, in Italian, "Do not worry Uncle, this is a relative of Don Cesar; he speaks our language."

The smile that lit up Giuseppe's face was as wide as the Bay of Naples. "Welcome Englishman. My nephew tells me you are here to fight the French pigs. I salute you." He grabbed me and kissed me on both cheeks.

"Thank you, sir. Are you sure it will not be too much trouble to put us up?"

"For our allies, it is worth the sacrifice," a sly look crept across his face, "of course there will be costs…"

"The British Consul in Messina will pay any expenses you might care to lodge."

His face darkened, "Pieces of paper? Pah!"

I almost panicked. Had I said the wrong thing? Then I remembered the bag of gold Louis given to me by Bessières. I brought out one golden coin. "Would this suffice?"

His face changed immediately. "I knew that you were a gentleman the first time I laid eyes upon you. Of course, this will suffice."

"Where shall we put the tents?"

He wandered off, caressing the gold and he shouted over his shoulder, "Wherever you like."

I smiled at Carlo, "Thank you, Carlo. I shall tell my cousin of your help." I turned in the saddle, "Sergeant Grant; find somewhere for the tents. Tie the horses to the lemon trees when they are watered there is shade enough."

And so we began our war in sun-baked Sicily.

Chapter 8

I sent Sergeant Sharp to inform Sir Charles as to our whereabouts. I would dearly have loved to contact Sir John Stuart but he had taken himself off. I hope this was not a sign of things to come. I did not wish to waste the time we had spent aboard ship training and so I led the troop on a patrol. I had an ulterior motive; I intended to visit my family. It would be a good way for the troop to get to know the conditions under which we would be operating. Within four miles of the camp, they were beginning to suffer. The heat and the humidity made them start to reach for water skins. I had discussed this with Sergeant Grant and, as the first man pulled the stopper he roared, "That man! Wait until you are given permission to drink!" They soon realised that you loaded with water before you began to patrol.

Carlo had obviously told Cesar and his family of my arrival on the island for we were spotted some way from the estate and Cesar, his wife and his children were waiting for us. The boys had grown and I could see the awe on their faces as the smartly turned out troopers halted in immaculately neat lines.

I dismounted and embraced my cousin and his wife. "It is good to see you, Roberto. When Carlo told us I was delighted. Sir John will be pleased to see you too."

"I cannot stay long. I am on duty."

"Of course but your men will take some food with us?" Hospitality was important to the Sicilians.

"Of course," I lowered my voice, "but do water the wine. These are Englishmen and they drink beer."

Cesar looked shocked and shook his head. "I am sorry about that."

"Lieutenant Jackson, have the men dismount and go with Don Cesar's man. The men will be fed." I saw the look of anticipation on the boys' faces. "Would you two boys like to look after Badger?" They nodded their pleasure and led him off. I caught Sergeant Sharp's eye and pointed to the boys. He smiled, he would watch over them.

The house was wonderfully cool and I left my helmet in the hall. I knew where we were going. Cesar led me to the room at the rear which looked out on the garden. It was Sir John's favourite spot.

"I will see to your men." He smiled, "It is good to see you again cousin." He left me alone with the old knight.

Ever the gentleman he tried to rise as I entered. I hurried to his side. "Sit down Sir John. I am still young and fit."

He smiled, "As I was once. Let me look at you." I stood back and he nodded his approval. "You look fine in that uniform and you have filled out. They have made you a captain?"

"Yes, sir. I command a squadron although I have only brought a troop here."

"And we are pleased that you are here for we have heard rumours of French armies preparing to attack us." He shook his head, "The Neapolitans are brave but then so were the Maltese and they are no match for the French. It is good that you have come." He gestured me forward. "I fear I have not long to live. I can feel the cold hand of death creeping ever close and I think it is fate which has brought you here."

"Nonsense you will outlive us all."

"And you know that is not true. I am a warrior and soon I will join my companions. I have lived long enough. But I am glad to see you again. It is such a long time since you left. You are often in my thoughts." He gave a cough which seemed to cause him pain. I poured him a glass of wine. He drank it down and smiled. "You should know that in my will, I have left all to you and Cesar equally."

"You did not need to do that."

"I know but it is my choice and Cesar is quite happy about my decision. Your connections have increased our wealth anyway. I want my Scottish family to benefit too."

We spent a couple of hours chatting. It was good to catch up. I told him of some of my adventures. I knew that he could keep them a secret. He did not seem at all surprised. He just kept smiling and chuckling at some of the incidents I described. I realised we had been there too long and then I had to take my leave. It would not do for Sir John to arrive at camp and find me and the men gone. The looks on the men's faces showed that they had been royally looked after. Even dour Sergeant Grant had a happy face.

As we rode back James said, "What lovely people sir. They made us feel like family. The men were quite touched. And the food…"

"I know James. Different from what we are used to but good for you."

That night the camp was a happy relaxed place although the return to rations did not please the men and I resolved to source some local ingredients. Salted pork in a hot climate was a recipe for disaster. It would be better in the long run to eat the food which was grown locally.

It was at noon the next day when my problems began. The men were just finishing digging their latrine when one of Sir John Stuart's staff arrived. He had the arrogant look of someone who had had a commission purchased and then found the easiest billet he could. He was barely civil to me.

"Sir John asks that you present yourself as soon as possible to his headquarters."

I waited and then snapped, "Sir."

His eyes widened and he gulped, "Sir."

"Good at least you have recognised my rank. Let us move on. Do you assume I am a mind reader?"

"No sir." he looked confused and I noticed the grins on James' and my sergeants' faces as they watched his discomfort. We were in undress but he was in full uniform and baking in the noon day sun.

"Then would you care to tell me where the headquarters is? Or perhaps I should wander over the island and hope that I manage to trip over it."

He had obviously not thought things through and I dreaded to think what he would be like in combat. "Er, I could wait for you sir, and take you there."

I smiled but there was no warmth in the smile. "That is dashed civil of you, sir."

I did not offer him any refreshment. I thought that half an hour in the hot Sicilian sun might make him reflect on his manners. "James, best bib and tucker."

"Sir."

"Sarn't Grant, take charge and keep them busy." I lowered my voice, "I think our freedom is about to be curtailed."

He shook his head sadly, "I know sir and me and the lads were just getting used to this little billet."

As we rode along the quiet country road, the Sicilians had sensibly decided to stay indoors whilst the sun blazed down, Jackson and I remained silent as we followed the young aide. I could sense his frustration as he rode before us. He had arrived full of arrogance and his bubble had been burst. He now had two officers following him and no one likes that.

The huge camp was outside of Messina on the western side. Sir Charles had been quite correct; it was unsuitable for horses. The small area of ground which could have been used for grazing was taken up by the twenty-four horses of the horse artillery. I assumed that Sir John and the other officers would have had horses and it would have been impossibly cramped to force another hundred or so mounts there. The smell from the horse lines and the badly dug latrines assaulted our noses when we were half a mile away. It was no wonder that the commander had left the camp, even for a short while.

We reined in next to a command tent. The young lieutenant handed his reins to the guard and scurried inside. James and I dismounted but held on to our reins as we took in the camp. It was well organised and it was neat but I would not have chosen it for my base. There was no shade at all and you learned, in this part of the world, to grab whatever shade you could.

When the lieutenant emerged he had regained his composure and had a smug smile upon his face. "Sir John will see you now captain. Er Lieutenant, just the captain."

I hated games like this but I kept my stoic expression and handed Badger's reins to James. "Could you find some water and some shade for Badger eh?" I lowered my voice, "See what you can find out." I winked and James smiled.

"Will do sir."

I entered the tent and found that Sir John was alone. He wore a plain blue frock coat. He was a neat little man but, as I later learned, his size determined his character. He was one of those little men who seem to resent everyone who is taller. His pinched and pasty face glared at me.

"Well Captain Matthews what have you to say for yourself?"

I was at a loss. What had I done that was wrong? "I'm sorry sir. What have I done to offend you?"

"Going off like that without waiting to speak to me!"

"Sir, the Consul told me that this camp was unsuitable for my horses and advised me to find another. I did so. I tried to find you but Sir Charles did not know where you had gone."

"You could have waited here. There were no other troops around."

"With respect sir there is neither shade nor grazing and my horses have just had a month on board a transport. I wanted to ensure that my troop's mounts would be in the best condition possible for whatever task we have to perform."

"Hmn." He shuffled papers around. In my experience that was always a sign that someone was buying time. He looked up, his sharp eyes wide in triumph. He obviously thought he had another point to score against me, "And Lieutenant Stuart tells me that you are miles away on a farm!"

That explained the Lieutenant's attitude. They were relatives. "Sir, we are only half an hour away from here and the campsite is perfect for my horses."

"And how much is it costing us eh? We have to live within a budget."

I smiled, "It is costing the army nothing, sir." I paused, "I have incurred the expense."

He was really taken aback at that. I wouldn't tell him that the money actually came from Napoleon; that would be far too difficult to explain. He seemed mollified. "Well don't get too comfortable. I expect to have the force moved across the straits to Calabria. We are just waiting for the French to make their move. We do not wish to provoke them. Until then you can stay on your farm but I want you here each morning for an eight o'clock briefing with the other officers."

If he thought that would upset me he was wrong. "Sir, might I ask how you see the cavalry being used?"

He slammed his pen down, "Well a troop is neither use nor ornament to me. You are not enough to be used offensively so what do you think you can do?"

He was not as stupid as I had first thought. He was putting me on the defensive. He was trying to make me defend my troop. "We can scout and we can screen. The French have a Chasseur Regiment and they are good but I believe the 11th Light Dragoons are better."

"Do you indeed. And have you fought the French before?"

"Yes sir, in Pomerania. We held the French cavalry off to allow the Hanoverian Army to escape. The Prince Regent was very happy with our performance."

His mouth opened and closed like a fish and then he said, "Dismissed. I'll see you in the morning."

After saluting I left. I saw James and the horses. They were talking to the gunners. I walked over to them. They were laughing as I approached. "Ah Captain Matthews, this is Captain Sillery who commands this battery."

He held out his hand, "Damned pleased to meet you. I see we are both in the minority eh?"

"True but I suspect that we will have an effect beyond our numbers."

"Damned right." He put his arm around my shoulder and led me to one side, "I see you have met the little man?"

"Oh yes. I have been suitably admonished."

What for?"

"Not camping here."

He burst out laughing making some of the infantry officers turn and stare at us. "But this is bloody useless for horses. Ours are getting worse by the day!"

"Ask if he will let you bring them to the farm. The grazing is good and there is shade."

He shook his head, "He does things by the book." He smiled slyly, "Still we can take them for some exercise and it will get us away from this damned oven."

"I think we will be here until the New Year you know. I can't see the French attacking in winter. The roads will be awful and it will suit our allies, the Neapolitans."

"Oh don't say that. We will not survive another two months of this." He waved a hand at the wagons. We haven't even any drivers for the wagons. They forgot to send them their orders. I have no idea how we are going to get the wagons across the straits."

"I may be able to help you there. Do you have funds for drivers?"

"Of course. There is a set rate for hiring civilian drivers if official ones are not available. I control that not Sir John."

"Then your problem is solved. I can get you, reliable local drivers."

"Really? That is damned good of you. Things are looking up."

"Well, I had better be off. I am back tomorrow for an eight o'clock briefing."

"You poor sod. That is a living death."

The cycle was set with the daily briefing. There was never anything new and I soon gleaned that our commander was terrified of making a mistake. The only break was in late October when we heard of the wonderful victory at Trafalgar; a victory which was offset by the tragic loss of Nelson. He had been, for me, our only hope against Napoleon. Although the French and Spanish fleets had been destroyed and we ruled the waves again I would have traded it all for Nelson still alive.

That day apart we had our briefing and the soldiers paraded and marched to no avail. My men just exercised in the cool of the morning and early evening. Sir John seemed to think he was in England and they worked in the heat. Had I been in charge then I would have based myself closer to Naples. When Masséna came it would be faster than General Stuart could picture. I had fought against the Italians before; they were brave but they had second rate equipment and third rate leaders. However the pattern was set and, I daresay, might have continued in the same fashion had King Ferdinand not sent a messenger to Sir John in early January. The message must have arrived at night for, at our daily meeting, he held the missive before him.

"I have been informed that King Ferdinand wishes to confer with an officer from this force. It seems that the forces we had in Naples, General Craig and the Russians have been withdrawn and that leaves us as the only allied soldiers in Southern Italy. I daresay he wants to use us in some way." He glanced at Lieutenant Stuart, "Unfortunately I do not speak Italian and he has stipulated that we need an Italian speaker. Do we know of any officer or sergeant who can speak their language?"

All faces turned to me. Sir John had virtually ignored me since my arrival and the lieutenant had obviously not mentioned that skill. Captain Sillery had told the others of my linguistic abilities and they had all profited by my negotiation for wine and foods. I was very popular.

Captain Sillery coughed, "I believe, Sir John, that Captain Matthews is fluent in Italian sir."

The news did not please the General who flashed an angry look at his young relative. "Hmm. If you went, sir, then who would command the cavalry in your absence?"

"Lieutenant Jackson is more than competent sir and has my complete support."

"Very well then take yourself and half a dozen of your men. There will be a transport waiting for you in Messina tomorrow." He glowered at me. "I want a complete report of what you are doing."

I gave him an innocent look. "Every day, sir?"

"No, you buffoon, weekly!"

The other officers hid their smirks and I left. This was good news. I was bored and craved excitement. Perhaps the court of King Ferdinand would provide that.

I selected Sergeant Seymour and asked him to find four troopers. James was both disappointed not to be coming and pleased to be given command. "I shall just go and see my cousin. Sergeant Sharp will pack my things. We leave at first light."

Cesar told me to be wary of King Ferdinand. "He is our king, I know but he is not like you, Roberto. He is impulsive. Be careful." He hesitated, "I have friends at court and they tell me that he relied on the soldiers that the British and the Russians stationed in Naples. Now that Bonaparte has defeated the Austrians…"

"He has beaten the Austrians?"

"Did you not hear? He marched his men to Ulm and they captured that city and all the men and then he marched towards Austerlitz where he defeated the Russians and the Austrians. They are calling it the battle of the Three Emperors. So you see Robbie, your French friend will be able to turn his attentions towards those who turned against him. Our king! The Queen is also the daughter of the Austrian Emperor and your friend Bonaparte will not miss an opportunity to humiliate the Austrians still further. Here we are safe for he needs ships to capture Sicily and your victory at Trafalgar protects us but on the mainland? Take care."

Sir John said much the same thing but our parting was more personal. We hugged and I felt sadder than at any time since Jean and my mother had died. I had enjoyed my bi-weekly visits for chess and conversation. It was our last meeting. He died three weeks later. He had lived to the age of over eighty and he was ready to die. It was we who were not yet ready to say goodbye to that fine old man who was a relic of a bygone era. I, for one, wished we could live by those values once more.

Chapter 9

Lieutenant Stuart was waiting for us at the harbour. He looked tired but I suspected he had been given the task as some sort of punishment. He saluted, "Here is a letter from Sir John for King Ferdinand. This is your ship."

I looked up at the smiling face of Captain Dinsdale. "How on earth…!"

"Get your tackle on board and I will tell you."

"Thank you, lieutenant. I will send reports as directed."

As we headed north, our horses safely berthed below decks, I stood with Captain Dinsdale and my two sergeants. "The thing is, Robbie, I am English and so I get all the trade from the Consul. They don't like to speak the local language. They think they are being robbed and so they hire me. It works out very well… for both of us."

"And you rob them!"

He grinned, "Got it in one. But as you share the profits then so do you. Well, I have been told to take you to Naples. Is that still the orders or have you some ulterior motive?"

"No, Matthew, for once my mission is above board. We will enjoy the voyage. How long will it take?"

"Could take a week if the winds are wrong but more likely it will only be a couple of days. You and your lads can enjoy themselves."

Although the weather was cool, by Sicilian standards, the weather was clement and it was a pleasant voyage. During that time I briefed Sergeants Sharp and Seymour. "I think we will be operating here as a troop sooner rather than later so keep a map and remember what we see. We have the luxury of peace at the moment but when the French come it will be in a hurry."

"What are were expected to do with this king then?"

"I have no idea. I think he will just want the reassurance that Britain will come to his aid if he decides to snub the Emperor."

Sergeant Seymour did not look convinced, "I don't think we can do much with one troop of cavalry and three poxy six pounders."

He was right. As a force, it was not much but it was all that His Majesty had deemed fit to be sent. I would have to learn diplomatic skills.

Naples was a huge bustling city nestling under the brooding shadow of the mighty Vesuvius. There appeared to be no order in the harbour and the whole maelstrom was a scene of chaos. The smaller ships and boats looked to be like seagulls mobbing the larger ships. Captain Dinsdale was obviously practised in the art of navigating such chaotic waters and we were soon tied to a stone quay. While my men offloaded the horses and equipment Matthew took me to one side.

"I wouldn't count on these Neapolitans too much. They are fairly useless and you will have to live off your wits. If you need someone to come back for you then leave a message with the harbour master. We have slipped him enough coins over the years for him to owe us many favours." He shook my hand. "Take care Robbie although you have the uncanny ability to step into horse shit and come out smelling of roses."

I shook my head in mock indignation, "A fine way to talk to your partner."

"It is because you are my partner that I can talk to you this way."

We led our horses along the quayside. Our uniforms and our mounts forced people to stand and stare creating a passage towards the town. I guessed that we would head for the Royal Palace. I vaguely remembered it from my visit all those years earlier when I had met the late lamented Nelson. I wondered how the lovely Lady Hamilton was coping with the loss of the love of her life. The memory of that fine lady triggered other memories and I glanced to my left to see if I could see Carlo, the old fisherman who had helped Jean and me all those years ago. He was nowhere to be seen. Perhaps he too had died. I began to feel morbid as all the good people in my life seemed to have passed on.

When we emerged from the chaos of the harbour we entered the equally chaotic town. "Mount lads, otherwise some of these locals will have the buttons from your uniforms."

Once above the mass of humanity, we could see the fluttering flags which identified the Royal Palace. We kicked on. The Neapolitan Royal Guards were easily spotted for they wore a very bright and gaudy uniform. The ones selected for the palace, however, appeared to know their job. The muskets were in perfect condition and they bore themselves like professionals.

"State your business!"

If the sergeant was surprised when I spoke Italian he did not show it but he became less aggressive. I showed him my credentials and he sent for the officer of the day. While my escort was sheltered beneath a marble portico I was whisked into the presence of the King and Queen of Naples along with their military commander General Count Roger de Damas.

The king was a serious-looking man but, perhaps because of my cousin's warnings, he looked to me to have shifty eyes. His wife, Queen Maria Carolina, was everything one might expect from a queen. She was beautiful and she looked thoughtful. I was surprised at the youth of the general. He looked to be of an age with me. I later discovered that he was seven years younger and he was French. He too was the son of an aristocrat but, unlike me, he had not fought for Napoleon, only against him.

The Queen did the speaking. "We understand that you speak Italian."

I nodded and added, impetuously, "And also German."

She smiled and said in German, "Ah so you know where I was born."

I bowed, "Yes, your majesty."

She reverted to Italian, "You are unusual for an Englishman."

I smiled, I was enjoying our conversation, "That is because I am Scots, your majesty."

King Ferdinand said irritably, "Get on with it. The French are almost at the border already!"

The Queen patted his hand, "You will have to excuse his majesty he was less than happy when General Craig and the Russians left last week. Now, what can General Stuart do to help us?" She smiled at General de Damas, "Although I am sure that our dashing General de Damas will be more than capable of defending our borders."

The young general almost simpered.

I was not convinced about his credentials. I looked at the king as I spoke. "If you were to request his presence then I am sure he would be able to bring his three guns, four thousand infantry and the rest of my cavalry."

General de Damas spoke for the first time and his Italian was accented as I expect was mine. "How many cavalry do you possess?"

"A troop."

He snorted in a derisory fashion. "We have sixteen squadrons. Your troop will not make any difference."

I stared at him and saw him properly. He reminded me of many of my father's friends. They were arrogant with a total belief in themselves. "And have they fought the French before?" I kept my voice as calm as possible.

"No, but I have!" He snapped petulantly.

"Where?"

"In the Vendee when we tried to restore the king."

That told me all that I needed to know. Even against the early Republican armies, the émigré forces had been useless. "Well my troop has fought the French before now and more importantly we have defeated superior forces of French cavalry so do not underestimate us because of mere numbers."

He looked a little less confident. The queen smiled at me, "Well then Captain, when can we expect Major General Stuart and his men?"

I was not sure that he would come but I had to be the diplomat. "I will send one of my men back to Sicily with a message and I think they could be here by February." I was making that up but it seemed a reasonable time scale.

The king's shoulders sagged, "By then it may be too late." He stood and wandered off. The general followed him leaving myself alone with the queen and her guards.

She stood, "Come and walk with me in my lemon groves." Leaning on my am she took me through a small side door into an enclosed lemon grove. Even though it was winter there were still lemons to be seen. "It is sheltered here and even in January we enjoy the rays of the sun." She sat and patted the seat next to her. "You must understand that my husband, the king, fears the French Emperor. He has defeated the Russians and the Austrians and we are under no illusions. Despite what General de Damas says our army is no match for the French war machine. Your army could have made the difference." She stopped and looked at me, "Would you stay here until we have a better idea of what may happen?"

I bowed, "It would be my pleasure. General Stuart made it clear I was to do all that I could to aid you."

She clapped her hands. Although middle-aged she was still a beautiful woman and at that moment she looked like a young girl, "Splendid. I will arrange for you to stay with my guards."

"And if you will excuse me I must send a message to my general."

However, we had no sooner entered the reception room than King Ferdinand appeared. "You there, captain. I want you to take me to Sicily to meet your general."

"But your majesty I have no ship and I have promised to protect the Queen."

He glared at me and then the Queen. "You will stay here when we might be invaded at any time?"

"It is our duty to stay and share the hardships of our people."

"Pah! Stuff and nonsense. It is our duty to ensure that our line continues." He looked back at me. "Then give me your messenger to guide me to this Major General."

"Yes, your majesty."

I went to my men. They looked up expectantly. "It looks like the French are about to invade." They nodded but showed no concern. "Sergeant Sharp, you have a few words of Italian, I want you to take the King to Major General Stuart. Tell him that the Queen has requested that my patrol protects her."

Alan was not happy, "But sir, my place is with you."

"No Sergeant Sharp, your place is where I decide and you have more linguistic skills than the rest. You know that. You can leave your horse here. Impress upon the general that the French are on the doorstep. It is his decision."

Sharp's shoulders sagged, "Sir."

"Follow me."

By the time we returned the King and his retinue were ready to go. "This is Sergeant Sharp. He speaks one or two words in Italian."

"Good. Tell him to pick up that valise and follow me."

I told Sharp who picked up the bag and joined the king who wasted no time in getting to his carriage. Sharp put the valise in the back and then King Ferdinand pointed to the seat next to the driver. "I think you are an extra guard." I held his carbine while he climbed up.

"Don't do anything daft, eh sir?"

"You know me Sergeant Sharp."

"That is what worries me."

The carriage and the King's escort had no sooner left than General de Damas and another troop of cavalry rode up. "I have told the Queen that I need to rejoin the army." He leaned down from his horse. "She has only her personal guards and your men. You will need to protect her."

He did not wait for an answer but led his men out of the gate and, as they closed again, it suddenly felt deserted. There were just the two guards on the gate that I could see. I had to take charge and take charge quickly.

Sergeant Seymour had my four troopers all ready. "We will be billeted in the barracks. Bring the horses and I will find out where they are."

I returned to the two guards at the gate. "The Queen has asked us to stay and protect her with the rest of her guards. We are to share your barracks."

98

"I am Sergeant Benito Marciano. There are just ten of us left."

I felt my heart sink down to my boots. Fifteen of us left to protect the Queen; it was not enough. "Where are the barracks?" He pointed to them. They were just behind the main building. "Good, I am Captain Matthews and I have fought the French before."

He nodded, "You look like a man of action. My men will not let the Queen down."

"I never doubted it for a moment."

While my men went to the barracks I returned to the queen. She was speaking with a small man who looked remarkably like a priest or a clerk. He had inky fingers.

"Captain Matthews, this is Alberto; he runs the palace and he is the most important man in the whole building." He smiled and nodded. He was like a puppy eager to please. "He will show your men where the barracks are."

"I know where they are I spoke to Sergeant Marciano. He is the senior officer now."

"You are resourceful; that is good. Now is there anything else that you need?"

"It would be handy to know when the French are close. I assumed that the General would let me know that but he has left too."

Her smile showed that she was not surprised. "Do not worry Captain Matthews; they will fight." She turned to Alberto, "Where are the French?"

"They are still in Rome I believe." I looked at him in surprise and he shrugged, "I deal with the deliveries and the drivers and deliverymen are such gossips. They keep me informed. It is better than having a network of spies."

Even as I nodded I realised that I ought to send word of this to Colonel Selkirk. "Good. Now I must see to my men and then deliver a message to the port."

A look of fear appeared on her face, "You are leaving too?"

"No, your majesty. I gave you my word that I would stay and I am a man of honour. I just need to deliver a message that is all."

The sergeant had not unsaddled Badger and I quickly mounted him and galloped towards the port. The King's departure had acted like a catalyst and the port was thronged with people attempting to flee the city. Had I been on foot then I would not have been able to force my way through. I saw Captain Dinsdale's ship. It had not left although he had four of his biggest sailors stopping people from boarding.

I handed Badger's reins to one of them. "Keep him facing the ship. If anyone approaches him he will give them a kick!"

The sailor grinned, "Good!"

I ran up the gangplank and Matthew came to meet me. "Do you want to embark too?"

"No, we are to protect the Queen. You saw the King leave?"

He pointed to the large frigate bearing the colours of Naples about to leave the outer harbour. "They came down like a bat out of hell. Did I see one of your lads with him?"

"Aye. Listen I need a message getting to Colonel Selkirk in London. "

"Give it to me and I will make sure it gets to him."

"I haven't written it yet. Let's go to your cabin." As I wrote I told him all that I knew. "The French are coming and I think that Naples will fall. The soldiers they have are not good enough. I am afraid that you will be restricted to Sicily. Thank God that we are there."

I'll tell Don Cesar and the rest of the captains. We can profit from this news. Thank you, Robbie. But how will you get out?"

"When the time is right we will leave and head down the coast. We could try to get a boat in Sorrento or failing that head down to the straits."

"I'll pass the word for ships to watch out for you." I handed him the letter. "You had better watch out Robbie. I think you are in danger of losing one of your nine lives!"

When I reached the gangplank there was no crowd. The sailor handed me Badger's reins. "You have a good horse here sir. Two good kicks and he cleared the quay in no time."

Captain Dinsdale hauled in the gangplank and cast off even as I was mounting Badger. By the time I reached the palace, I could see him heading south-west to Sicily. At least the colonel would know what was going on. But I now had to protect a Queen and ensure that she did not fall into Masséna's hands. It would not be easy.

Chapter 10

I had no idea what intelligence we would have and so I held a meeting with Sergeant Marciano and my men. It was tiresome having to translate everything but it needed to be done. We all had to have the same information.

"We must be ready to leave at a moment's notice. I am not sure if we will be able to get a ship and so we will assume we have to go to either Sorrento or another port. If we have to we will ride to Reggio."

Sergeant Marciano looked appalled. "But that is a long way!"

"About three hundred miles by my calculation. The alternative is to hand the Queen over to the French."

I saw his jaw stiffen. "Then we will have to do this."

"I want our bags packed and ready at the stables. Benito, how many extra horses do we have?"

"Probably ten."

"Does that allow for some of the Queens's servants coming with us? She will probably need them."

He shook his head, "Probably only three or four."

"Then one horse has spare weapons. One has spare food and the last one blankets. It will be cold at night."

Once again Benito showed his shock. "The Queen must have a roof over her head."

"And we will try to get one but if we cannot then we sleep where we can. Make no mistake, Sergeant, we will have to be as fast as an eagle and as cunning as a fox if we are to outrun the French. If I had my way we would leave now but the Queen seems to think that she owes the people her presence."

"She is a good Queen and a fine lady."

"That I do not doubt but it will do us no good if she is captured. Sergeant Seymour, you and the Sergeant here gather what we need at the stables. I will go and see the Queen."

"But sir, I don't speak Italian."

"Then start to learn and use sign language." I knew I was being blunt but we had no choice in the matter. I found the Queen.

"Ah Captain, you need to learn to rest you have not stopped since you arrived."

"We have much to do your Majesty." I steeled myself. "We will need to think about leaving Naples should the French come."

She set her lip, "We will leave when they are at the gates."

That was what I had feared. It would prevent us from leaving by ship. I knew that when the French came there would be a mad rush for whatever ships were left in the harbour and the Queen's status would avail her nought. I could see that there was no point in arguing and so I made the best of a bad job. I sighed and launched into my prepared speech, "Very well then if I am to protect you I need some information. Firstly, your majesty, can you ride?"

She smiled, "Of course, I am Austrian. Have you never heard of the Spanish horses of Vienna?"

"Good. Can you ride as a man?"

"Yes."

"How many of your people would you wish to take?"

"All of them."

I shook my head. "You can take seven and they must all be riders. If we are to wait until the French are knocking on the gates then we will have to move faster than French horses and that is not easy."

She touched my hand. "I can see that you are doing this for the best. I will choose seven and they will be able to ride."

"You will have to take as little as possible."

"The Crown Jewels?"

I smiled, "You may take them in lieu of dresses."

She laughed and it was a lovely tinkling laugh, "I shall wear clothes such as you, Captain Matthews. If I am to ride I will be comfortable."

I was relieved. "Good then tell your people and I will see my men. The moment the French arrive, we leave!"

She smiled a young girl's smile, "Of course, Captain Matthews."

Exasperated I returned to my men. "Sergeant Marciano, I want you to take me to the northern border. I want to see how long it will take the French to get here." He hesitated. "I am just doing what your Queen wishes. The more information I have the more chance we have of getting the Queen to safety."

He nodded and strode off to pass his instructions on to his corporal. "Sergeant Seymour, let the men rest. They have worked hard today."

"No more'n you sir. Sergeant Sharp will have my bollocks if owt was to happen to you."

"Don't worry. The French are still in Rome and Masséna will be enjoying the city. We have a few days yet. Feed the horses up and make sure they are looked after."

"What about a ship sir? Won't that be the quickest way out?"

"It will but I doubt that there will be many ships in a week's time. They are like rats leaving a sinking ship."

The Neapolitan Sergeant returned, "Let us ride, my friend."

By the time we returned I was much happier. The narrow coastal road would slow down the French advance and we would have time to escape. Of course, all it took was one fast regiment of Chasseurs to be sent ahead of the rest and we would be caught; we would be riding with the Queen and her courtiers. They would not ride as fast as French cavalry.

Every day we expected the news from the frontier that the French had arrived. The fearsome Sergeant Marciano had impressed upon all the guards along the border that failure to inform us of the arrival of the French would result in his displeasure. It seemed to have the desired effect. We just had to wait. The good news was that the horses recovered well from their short sea voyage and they ate well from both grain and grass. If the Queen had any riding skills at all then we stood a chance. I had already planned for our escape with my men. Although there were only five of them I knew that I could rely on them. They had discovered an arsenal of weapons and we were all now equipped with four pistols in addition to our carbine. That gave us twenty shots at the enemy. I was convinced that we could slow them up. Sergeant Marciano and his troopers could guard the Queen. We would stop the French or at the very least slow them down.

In the event, it was the end of the first week in February when the news came that a French column had been sighted. God alone knew what the Neapolitan army was doing. The passes to the north of Naples were perfect for slowing down an enemy advance whilst the two Neapolitan armies were waiting south of Naples. It made no sense to me. As I had predicted news of the French arrival preceded the guards from the border and the road to the port was soon thronged.

"Your majesty, the French are less than a day away and your people are fleeing by sea. We must leave now or we will be caught."

There was urgency in my voice and I saw resignation on her face. Alberto was the only man to accompany us with just four women. It gave us a couple of spare horses. When they reached the stables the Queen went to a beautiful white mount. I shook my head, "No, your majesty. You ride Sergeant Sharp's horse."

"But mine is the fastest horse in the land."

"But has he had guns fired at him? Has he had to ride all day and all night across rough ground? This horse is not afraid of guns and he can carry your tiny weight to the ends of the earth and back. I will be happier if you are riding him. One of your ladies can ride your horse. Mount... please."

I saw the shock on Sergeant Marciano's face while my men barely hid their grins. They did not know the words but they could tell what I was saying. She nodded and mounted. I was pleased that she wore breeches as did her women. In fact, the one who looked most ill at ease was Alberto.

I said quietly to Sergeant Marciano, "Detail a man to watch Alberto. I fear he will fall off."

Suddenly there was the crack of muskets. "Benito, lead them away. My men and I will buy us time."

As the Neapolitans galloped towards the Sorrento gate I whipped Badger around and headed for the north gate. We reached the gate, which was still locked and saw no sign of the French but I knew they were coming. The sound of the muskets had told me that. We dismounted and hid behind the wall. We each had a carbine and two loaded pistols. There was a flurry of shots and I saw some Neapolitan soldiers running towards us. They were pursued by French Chasseurs. As I had expected the French cavalry had deigned to use firearms and were sabring the fleeing troops. It meant that they were focussed on the ground close to them.

"Wait for it lads. At fifty yards let them have it. Carbine first and then the pistols." I was counting on the shock factor. These cavalry were not with the main column. They were the scouts. They had overextended themselves.

"Fire!"

As soon as the carbines fired we were blind and so we emptied our pistols into the grey murk of the smoke. "Let's get out of here." As we mounted and were above the smoke I saw that we had emptied eight saddles and the others had retreated. They would approach warily and that had bought us valuable time.

We wasted no time in heading for the Sorrento gate. The road we were taking led us away from the narrow coastal path and it tracked through the hills which ran inland from the sea. To my horror, I saw them walking their horses as though out on an afternoon ride.

Sergeant Marciano knew that he had let me down from my murderous expression but the Queen just smiled. "Your Majesty, until we are at least twenty miles from here I want us to canter or even gallop. If your ladies cannot manage it then we will leave them."

I am not sure she had been spoken to like that before but she shrugged and said, "Very well."

She was a good rider and I was impressed by her seat. "Joe, take Trooper Cartwright and lead the way. I'll bring up the rear with the other two lads. Keep up a good pace until we reach Sorrento. Hopefully, there will be a boat there."

I kept glancing over my shoulder to see if we were being pursued but I could see no sign of the green uniforms. There was just a prickle at the back of my neck which told me there were horsemen following us. I had been to Sorrento once before but I had sailed to Naples and I did not know the road well. I kept hoping that I would see the port around the next bend in the road but I was disappointed each time. Finally, the road suddenly swung around a headland and I caught a glimpse of Sorrento in the distance. I had not looked at a map before but now I saw that it was virtually a dead end. The cliffs rose high on the southern side of the bay. We could be trapped there.

"Trooper Rae, you and the boys stay at the back I need one of the Neapolitans to do a little job for us."

"Sir."

I kicked Badger on and we overtook the riders at the rear. I rode next to Sergeant Marciano. "Benito, send one of your boys down to the port. If there are no boats we will head for Salerno."

"Yes, Captain," he smiled, "sensible."

I reined Badger in and allowed the others to overtake me. "Anything?"

"No, sir." Trooper Rae pointed ahead, "We'll have to rest soon sir. Our horses can run all day but these Neapolitan horses, well sir, they are like a bunch of nags." He pointed at the Queen's white one which was sweating profusely. "Even the Queen's!"

"You are right but we need to put as much distance as we cane between us and the French."

"Will they follow sir?"

"I have no doubt that they will question those at the palace and find out that the Queen has fled. They will want her. Yes, Trooper Rae, they will come."

He was right of course and, just two miles up the road we were forced to stop when one of the Queen's ladies slipped from her mount. She was not hurt but she cried a lot and the others joined in. I made the best of it, "Give the horses some grain and drink a little of the water. Sergeant, any sign of your man?"

"No Captain Matthews, but he will be back soon."

As we waited I looked at the road. It twisted and turned and was treacherous in places. We would have to travel a little slower for a while.

"How are you, your majesty?"

She grimaced, "It is some years since I rode so hard and I am no longer a young woman but," she smiled, "I am Queen Carolina and I will bear it."

"Good. With luck, there will be a boat in Sorrento and your ordeal will soon be over."

Even as the words came out of my mouth our hopes were dashed. The trooper sent to investigate Sorrento galloped up shaking his head. "The harbour is empty. Nothing bigger than a fishing boat, Captain."

That decided me. "Sergeant Marciano, you and your men lead. We will head to Salerno. How long will it take us do you think?"

He looked downcast, "We will be lucky to get there by night."

"Then we had better be lucky for that is where we will be staying tonight. If you hear firing then it means the French have caught us. Keep the rest going. Do not stop for us. Understand?"

"Yes, sir."

The Queen had heard all. "Do not take risks, my Scottish friend. If I am caught then we will negotiate something."

I shook my head, "You do not know the French. Your capture would take the heart from your people. I will get you through."

"I believe you will."

"Now go."

I let them get some way ahead. "Load your pistols." This was the first chance we had had since the attack at the palace to reload. I wanted the six of us to have as much firepower as we could. Once we had loaded we trotted along the trail. I could see the beautiful bay of Sorrento below me. I wondered if Old Carlo, the fisherman who had helped me before still fished from there. I had considered his boat but he could only have taken four of us and I knew that the Queen would not abandon any of her people. We would either all survive or we would be captured. Chance, in the form of the accident, had made us all rest at noon and that had helped us. Horses and riders were slightly fresher. The sea air kept it a little cooler than it might have been and I began to hope that we might make it.

Our hopes were dashed when Trooper Rae warned, "Riders behind us sir."

I looked ahead and saw that the road crested a rise and disappeared. I watched as the last four Neapolitans dropped over the other side. "We will ambush them on the other side of the rise."

The road helped us by twisting away to the left. I saw the last three riders vanish into the tree-lined track. "Tie your horses to whatever you can. Sergeant Seymour, take three men to the left. Trooper Rae, you come with me."

I tied Badger to a scrubby and stunted old olive tree. I had no worries. Badger would not stray. I heard the hooves as the French cavalry thundered after us. They were not galloping but they would have good horses and they were eating up the road at a steady pace. Their leader did not have to take lady riders into consideration. I caught a glimpse of their shakoes as they began to rise towards us. We were all well hidden and the Tarleton helmet blended with the rocks better than one might have hoped. I counted on the fact that they thought we would keep on running. They would not expect an ambush.

"Wait until they are close. The bugler and officers will be at the front. I want them dead. "

From the noise of the hooves, it was a full troop of cavalry. We could only hope to slow them. Our brief rest had allowed them to catch up. Perhaps their horses were tiring. I shook my head; I was clutching at straws. I had to do this one piece at a time; ambush them and then try to escape. I knew that as soon as the first shot was fired Sergeant Marciano would know what was happening and they would hurry on.

They came along in a column of twos. I saw the captain and bugler leading the column. I gave a wry smile as I saw their queues and moustaches. It was like looking at my old regiment. I had no time for sentiment. I was now a British soldier.

"Fire!"

The carbines all barked. The troopers drew their pistols but I reloaded my carbine. The wall of smoke was thicker on Sergeant Seymour's side but the air was clearer on mine. I aimed at the sergeant who was rallying the men. My ball took him in the shoulder and he fell from his horse. I drew my pistol and fired. The column was in disarray. The riderless horses were milling around and, with their leaders dead or wounded, the troopers were looking for someone to make a decision.

"Get mounted, draw your swords. We are going to attack them."

To their credit, none of my men questioned my suicidal order. I wanted the French to think that there were more of us than there actually were. I led the way with Rae next to me, boot to boot. "Charge the 11th!"

The men whooped and hollered as though we were a regiment and we charged through the smoke. I saw a surprised trooper who had dismounted to give comfort to the wounded bugler. He stared at me as I sliced down and split his face open. Badger knocked a horse to the side as I skewered a second trooper. I saw the green uniforms begin to flee. I stabbed at the back of one man who slipped from his horse.

"Halt!" I sheathed my sword.

I turned to count and saw that we had suffered no casualties. There were four riderless horses. "Grab those horses and let's go."

As I turned the sergeant I had wounded began to rise from the floor. He held his pistol with his good arm and it was aimed at me. In one motion I drew my own pistol and fired. The brave sergeant's head disappeared. All that were left were the dead and the dying. Nine officers and troopers had fallen. I hoped that their deaths would buy us at least an hour.

I was delighted when it took us almost an hour to catch up with the others. It showed that Sergeant Marciano had obeyed orders. There was relief on their faces as all six of us rode up. They had all stopped when they saw us. The Queen looked concerned, "We heard the shooting and when you did not come…"

I smiled, "We had the advantage of surprise your majesty but that will not last. We have four spare horses. If any of our mounts are suffering we can replace them. Lead on Benito there are still a hundred cavalry chasing us."

I was relieved when we saw, in the distance, the lights of Salerno. We had seen no sign of pursuit for an hour and I knew that the French would struggle to make good time, in the dark, over such a treacherous road. What worried me more was the fact that I had seen neither hide nor hair of the Neapolitan army. Where had de Damas taken them? The road we had just used was perfect to slow down the French. Their artillery and cavalry would be useless. As I had shown, with just six men, a much larger force could easily be stopped. I wondered why the British and Russian soldiers had been withdrawn. With twelve thousand men Naples could easily have been held. It had to be politics. I decided to ask the Queen when we halted.

The town had a wall and a barred gate but Sergeant Marciano soon gained us admission. They were only militia on the walls and there were less than forty of them. They would not halt the French. Had we so chosen, we could have driven them from the walls. The mayor was delighted to have the Queen but I also saw fear in his eyes. Like me, he knew the attraction of the Queen to an invading enemy.

We took over the house of a noble who had fled to Sicily when the French had crossed the border. While food was prepared I went around the men and horses with the two sergeants. I wanted to know if there were any weaknesses. There were not.

Sergeant Marciano insisted on providing the pickets that night. "No Captain, you and your men have taken all the risks. We will watch tonight. It is not honourable to let others do all the fighting for you."

My men stabled the horses and saw to their needs. Their welfare came before ours.

The Queen had spoken for a long time with the mayor. When I entered the dining room she rose to speak with me. "You look tired Captain Matthews."

I shook my head, "I am a soldier. I will be fine."

"You did well today. The sergeant told me what you intended and I could not believe that you would survive. You have done this sort of thing before?"

"A few times."

"Then I am hopeful that we will defeat the French if there are more men like you."

"Tell me, your majesty, did you discover if there were any ships in the harbour?"

"None big enough for all of us."

"My men and I do not matter. Are there any big enough to take you and your ladies away?"

"You think I would leave those who fled with me? I have responsibilities too. And to answer your question there is nothing bigger than a fishing boat in the harbour. Everyone fled." She smiled wryly, "Sicily will be so overcrowded soon that it might sink beneath the waves."

I realised I needed a map. "I must go and get a map."

She restrained me. "No, you will eat. Alberto, go and find the Captain a map."

Happy to be doing something useful again the little man trotted off and I was forced to sit with the Queen and her ladies. I felt guilty. I should be looking to the needs of my men. The Queen seemed to read my thoughts. "The two sergeants seem quite competent and they will get food for the men."

"But they don't speak each other's language."

She laughed, "Then they will learn won't they."

I reluctantly sat down and, as I began to eat, realised that it had been many hours since I had eaten. I was ravenous. The Queen seemed amused by my appetite. She waited until I had finished and then said in Austrian, "Someone said you could speak the language of my birth. Would you mind if we conversed in that language for a while? It has been some time."

"Not at all." She asked questions about me and my men. I had to be very careful not to tell her the total truth about myself. When Alberto returned with the map she reverted to Italian and said, "You are an interesting man, Captain Matthews. You have told me much and yet not all. Are all your countrymen so interesting?"

"As with all nationalities, some are and some aren't."

Alberto's little head bobbed up and down as he laid the map out on the now cleared table. "It is the best one I could find."

I looked at the coast from Salerno to Reggio. "Are there any other ports along the way?"

Alberto shook his head, "Little fishing villages."

"And do we know your majesty, where your army is?"

She looked angry for the briefest of moments and then shrugged, "Like you Captain Matthews I hoped that we would have met them but I have no idea."

I looked at the map. We had about a hundred and fifty miles before we came to the next big town, Cosenza. That would take two or perhaps three days. Then there was a short hop of sixty miles or so to Reggio. We could do that in one day.

The Queen saw my frown. "What is the problem, Captain?"

I noticed that her hand was on mine again, "Call me Robbie, your majesty."

She said the name tentatively, as though tasting it, "Robbie. Yes, I like it. What is the problem, Robbie?"

"I think it will take three or four days of hard riding to reach Reggio. The French will be looking either for you or your army. We will need to push on and I am not certain that your people are up to it."

I must have offended Alberto for he stood up as straight as he could. "I may not be a soldier like you, Captain Matthews, but I can do my duty as can the Queen's ladies. If her majesty can endure the pain of the saddle then so can we."

Queen Carolina patted him on the hand, "Brave little Alberto."

"I am sorry, Alberto, I never meant to question your honour. If you ask my sergeant he will let you have some saddle soap for your saddle and," I lowered my voice, "olive oil is very good for your seat too."

He brightened, "Thank you. I should have thought of that myself."

I excused myself and went to find the other soldiers. "We will be pushing on to Reggio on horseback." I saw the looks on their faces and nodded, "I know; it will be hard. We now have four more horses. Benito, see how many more you can get. We will take as many supplies as we can. I hope we can find places to sleep. I don't want to take tents; that is assuming we could get them. Joe, make sure we have as much ammunition as we can get our hands on. Check the saddlebags of those Chasseurs' horses. Most troopers keep spares. There may even be a couple of pistols for the Neapolitans." That was everything I could think of.

"Sir, get some rest. It will do us no good if you collapse on us."

"Thank you, sergeant, but, until we reach Sicily, I don't think any of us will get much rest. By the way, how is the language coming on?"

He grinned, "I speak a little Italian now and Benito here speaks some English."

"Good morning Capitano." Benito seemed proud of his English phrase.

I laughed, "It is evening but well done!"

After I had checked the perimeter and made sure that there were guards at all the gates I returned to the room I would be sharing with my men. They were all asleep apart from Sergeant Seymour. "At least we have food sir and you know the lads. So long as they have a full belly then they are happy."

He was right. I knew that I was lucky in that the men chosen by the Sergeant were not the type to get drunk as soon as they found some booze. They had drunk wine, along with the Neapolitans, but it had been in moderation.

As I rolled in the blanket I said, sleepily, "We just take this one day at a time Joe and hope that we have a little luck on the way." He might have replied but I didn't hear it; I was out for the count.

Chapter 11

I awoke well before dawn and sat bolt upright. Something had disturbed me. I shook Sergeant Seymour. "Something woke me. I'll take a quick look around. If I shout then get the lads up."

"I'll get them up anyway. It can't be long off dawn."

"Right."

I put on my tunic and drew my sword and a pistol. I went to the southern gate first and the Neapolitan there, who I was certain had been dozing, said he had seen nothing.

"Keep your eyes peeled."

When I reached the northern gate Sergeant Marciano was there. "Anything wrong Benito?"

"One of the men thinks he heard hooves along the coast road."

"Get the men and the Queen up. We'll make an early start. I'll go and check the town gate."

I went to the stables and saddled Badger. Sergeant Seymour joined me. "Get the men fed and the horses saddled. I am going to check the main gate."

I quickly galloped the couple of hundred yards to the main gate. The Mayor was there along with ten or so of his militia.

"What is it?"

"One of my men thought he heard horses. He might be wrong."

"I think he is right. Call out your guard. I will take the Queen away from you but I need you to hold them for a couple of hours. Can you do that?"

I saw the doubt on his face and, when I glanced at the ancient muskets his men held, I had to agree with him. But his backbone straightened. "We will do our best."

"Good man. Anything will help. I'll just go and fetch my men but I will be back."

By the time I reached the house, everyone was up. "Your Majesty, the French are here. As soon as you have eaten Sergeant Marciano will take you out of the south gate. My men and I will be right behind you."

"We won't let you down," she paused, "Robbie."

It felt good to hear my name spoken so softly. "Joe, get the lads. We eat on the hoof."

He handed me a hunk of bread wrapped around some ham and cheese. "Here sir. Eat now."

By the time we reached the gate again, there were thirty militia lining the ancient worn walls. "Right lads, spread yourselves out. We are going to make the French think that there is a regiment here. When I say 'Fire' keep firing until I say otherwise."

We listened as dawn slowly broke. Soon we heard the unmistakable tramp of feet and hooves on the road. They had infantry with them. I turned to the Mayor. "Tell your men to wait for my command before firing. It will be better."

It was a company of Light Infantry who accompanied the Chasseurs. As soon as they saw the walls and the men on them they halted. "Everyone get down."

The walls were ancient but they were almost two feet thick in places. The company of Light Infantry deployed into line and fired. Their officers were good for they gave us three volleys in case we were foolish enough to raise our heads. The walls protected us. I risked a glance over the parapet and saw that they were deploying into a column ten men wide and the Chasseurs were readying to charge.

"Everyone up." The line of Neapolitans joined my men. I saw some of the muskets wavering. They might not hit anything but I wanted the noise and the smoke of as many guns as we could. Our carbines had a maximum effective range of a hundred yards and at eighty I shouted, "Fire!"

I emptied my carbine and all four pistols. I reloaded my carbine three times and fired. It was impossible to see much because of the smoke.

"Cease Fire!"

The Neapolitans began to cheer as though they had won the war. "Sergeant Seymour, get the men mounted."

As the smoke drifted away I saw the huddle of a dozen or so blue bodies which showed where we had struck them. One or two were crawling back along the road. The rest had retired a suitable distance. They would be cautious now and we had bought some time.

"Thank you, Mayor, I shall tell the Queen of your bravery. Do not waste their lives. An hour will be sufficient."

He nodded, "It has done the men good to chase the French away," his tired old eyes told me that he knew the truth, "even if it is only briefly."

Leaving the militia to maintain some sort of front we galloped towards the southern road. The French would regroup and they would try to pick off some of the men of the town. They might, hopefully, even wait for some artillery. Whatever the outcome I had bought us an hour. We now had to use it.

We spurred our horses on and caught up with the Neapolitans. They had learned their lesson and did not hang around. The women no longer moaned and even Alberto seemed a better rider after two days in the saddle. We needed no words; we just rode on through the February morning. We had all been fed as had the horses. I made sure that we stopped every couple of horses. Each time we did so I placed two of my men a mile or so back to give advance warning of any pursuit. I assumed that it would take an hour to make the town surrender and then they would search for signs of the Queen. That might take another hour and then they would pursue us. They must have travelled overnight and would be tired. We would make much better time. The rests I allowed the horses and riders would be beneficial in the long run. We had to keep going and avoid any unnecessary delay.

After half a day of travel, we suddenly dropped from the high mountains and narrow passes on to a wide valley. The road was the Via Adua and we made good time. The bad news was that there few settlements of any description. As dusk approached I sent two of Sergeant Marciano's men to find anything; a barn or a farmhouse, it didn't matter which.

We were in luck. They found a farmhouse just off the main road. We headed up the track. The owner came out with an old blunderbuss. I do not know what he thought he would do against twenty armed soldiers but he ordered us from his property.

The Queen stepped down from her horse, although in her trousers and with her hair beneath a hat it was hard to recognise her regal qualities.

"I am Queen Maria Carolina of Naples and we are fleeing the French. We seek shelter and supplies."

I thought that would have sealed the deal but it did not. He shrugged, "When the bandits stole my goats where was the King then? It is as with many things. You only talk to us when you are in trouble. If the French are coming then we will need all the food for ourselves."

I saw Sergeant Marciano reaching for his pistol and I restrained him. I nudged my horse forward. "In that case could we buy some accommodation for the night?" I pointed at the barn built into the hillside, "And some food perhaps?"

I thought he was going to refuse but I took out a gold Louis and flipped it into the air. There was enough light from inside the house to make the spinning coin sparkle as did the farmer's eyes. He reached to grab the falling coin but I was quicker.

"Now you greedy little farmer, this buys us accommodation, firewood and food. You have one chance to accept. I have twenty men behind me who are angry enough to kill you and all your family, take your food and burn your hovel to the ground." I smiled, "So what will it be?"

He nodded and held out his hand for the coin, "You are welcome sir. Whatever I can do to help her majesty I shall do."

As we led our horses to the barn, Sergeant Marciano grumbled, "Miserable little swine. You should have let me kill him, sir, rather than waste your gold."

"The Royal Family will need as much support as they can get, Benito. Word would have spread had we killed them. This way the word will spread down the valley that we have money and we will be welcomed."

The Queen nodded as she passed me, "I can see why they sent you on this mission Captain. You are a thinker. I will repay the gold when we reach Sicily."

I nodded, "If not it does not matter."

"You are rich then?"

"I have money but gold does not interest me."

"And neither does killing. You are an enigma, Captain Matthews, but you have enlivened our journey somewhat."

The Neapolitans brooded and fumed all night about their countryman. I tried to explain it to them. "I would imagine, Benito, that this is a quiet part of the world. I would even predict that none of you has ever been here before. To the farmer the Kingdom of Naples means nothing. If Napoleon Bonaparte conquers this land it will make little difference to him. You are from Naples where the King and Queen are ever-present. You have a link to them. This farmer does not even know who they are."

The Queen had been listening, "You are right, Robbie, we should have left the palace more. If we are to defend against invaders we need the whole country behind us."

I nodded my agreement to that sentiment, "For me, I would like to see the army a little closer. They obviously did not come this way so where are they?"

For the first time since I had met her, the Queen lost her air of confidence. "I do not know. The King put a great deal of faith in the young Frenchman. He is passionate and he has fought the French Army."

"True. But I would prefer to put my faith in a man who had fought the French Army, and won."

Those words hung in the air for the rest of the evening and I began to regret saying them. The truth had to be told. Both my mother and father had taught me that. My mother had a saying, '*Speak the truth and shame the devil.*' It was a good axiom to live by. I could see the Queen and Benito pondering my words.

The farmer must have realised the value of the coin I had given him for he was effusive the next morning. He even gave us some homemade sausage and a ham to take. It still did not endear him to the Guards but the Queen oozed sweetness. As we headed towards Cosenza I reflected that the French would have taken the ham and the sausage but at least the farmer would be able to bury the coin until they had left.

Our party of courtiers were becoming hardened to a life in the saddle and even Alberto stopped complaining. We rode faster. When we used up our supplies we changed horses so that the burden was borne by them all. We reached the walled city of Cosenza at dusk. The gates were closed but the sight of the Royal Guards and the presence of the Queen ensured that they were opened. Here there was a small garrison under the command of a lieutenant. He was keen to show his willingness to serve the Queen. Sergeant Marciano and I found it more than a little amusing. He reminded me of many of the young British officers whose father's had purchased a commission. I dreaded to think what the French would make of him. He told us that the Neapolitan Army had passed through and were somewhere south of us.

We slept and ate well. We were protected by the thick walls of the town and a garrison, however small. The Neapolitan Guards actually achieved a full night's sleep. Before we left, the next morning, we were able to replenish our ammunition. The lieutenant was keen to escort the Queen but she told him he would be doing his country a greater service by defending Cosenza. The look on his face showed that he was looking forward to the prospect.

As we headed down the last stretch towards Reggio Sergeant Marciano asked me about the wars in which I had fought. I had to be very careful to restrict my descriptions to the battles fought for the British. I had fought Italians before.

I told him of the Pomeranian campaign and the rescue of the prisoners from the Pas de Calais. He nodded as I spoke of the charges, ambushes, retreats and battles. "That is why we need your army. I have fought in one small battle. I did not even get to draw my sword or fire my weapon. I am a fraud."

"No, my friend, you will get your chance. Besides your task is to protect the Queen is it not? You will not have to fight in battles." He had not thought of that and I saw him ruminating for the next few hours.

Perhaps complacency had set in or we thought that we had outrun danger but, whatever the cause it was nearly our ruin. Not long after Pizzo, the road twisted and turned down a narrow and steep-sided valley. We were well spread out and there were two of Marciano's men at the fore with the women behind. Suddenly there was a fusillade of shots from the hillside. One of the soldiers and a courtier were pitched from their saddles. Muskets began to pop all along the valley. I saw the puffs of smoke which indicated a marksman. There were many of them.

"Dismount and take cover." There were enough rocks to find shelter and I was certain that the attackers would avoid hitting the horses. They were too valuable to kill. I drew my carbine and dropped my reins. Badger would not move until I told him to.

Once behind a rock, I took a bead on some smoke. The attacker made the mistake of trying to reload while still crouched. I saw the top of his head appear and then his arm. It was only sixty yards away and I blew the top of his head off. I could see that my men were hitting their targets but the Neapolitans were not. We had to get closer. The Neapolitans did not have carbines and they would be wasting powder if they just used their pistols.

"Sergeant Marciano, leave four men to guard the women, the rest follow me. We are going up to get them." He shouted his orders and I said, "Sergeant Seymour, we will lead this attack. Trooper Rae, watch our backs in case the ones on the other side try anything."

"Sir!"

"Now!"

I had reloaded while talking and we sprinted from cover. Multiple moving targets are hard to hit and we were helped by three muskets all firing at one of the Guards. Even though musket balls buzzed above our heads the smoke from their own guns hid us from them. The balls flew ever higher. Suddenly I saw a man to my left. I swivelled my carbine and fired from the hip. He was two yards away and he was cut in two. I dropped my carbine and drew my sword and a pistol. A huge bandit leapt at me with an enormous axe in his hand. I fired my pistol and his face disappeared.

"Come on lads, these are bandits!" I repeated it in Italian and I heard Sergeant Marciano roar at these evil men who had threatened his queen. Another bandit came at me swinging his musket like a club. He was above me and it was a mistake. I ducked as I lunged forward and stuck my sword right through his body. I heard muskets from behind us.

"Back to the horses lads, they are attacking Rae."

I turned and ran down the slope. I was lucky not to slip. If I had then I would have broken a leg for certain. I saw that two of the Neapolitans left to guard the Queen had been cut down whilst the other two were fighting desperately to save their own lives. The Queen and her women were gathered with Alberto before them. Even as I watched the Queen fired a pistol and a bandit fell dead.

Trooper Rae was trying to fight three men. I drew my second pistol and shot one of them. The second turned to face me. He held a cutlass in his hand. It is a savage and clumsy weapon; I twisted the tip of my blade and then jabbed forward. My sword entered his throat. The blood blossomed and bloomed like petals in the wind. Rae finished off his opponent. I saw that he was wounded. "How is it?"

"A scratch sir. Get after the Queen, sir."

As the four of us joined Sergeant Marciano to hurry to the Queen's side the last of the bandits fled. My men continued to shoot at them with their carbines and three more fell. We had won but the Neapolitans had lost four men and two of the women had died. There were some with minor wounds but the Queen, thankfully, was not among them.

None of the bandits lived long enough to talk. The Neapolitans took their revenge on the wounded ones. I suspect they treated them better than they would have had the women not been there. It was a brutal end to a savage and unexpected encounter. We had suffered more damage from the Queen's countrymen than her enemies. It was ironical.

"I am afraid we will have to bury the dead quickly your majesty. They may return."

She nodded, "Leave the scum for the carrion." I saw a hard side to the Queen. She could be ruthless when she chose and she had been coolness personified when she had shot the bandit.

We moved fast with fewer people to guard and I put two of my men at the front and the rear. We might have spotted the ambush had I employed the same tactic before. Trooper Rae had just a scratch along his leg. It bandaged well and the bleeding stopped. No one was more relieved than I was to see the lights of Reggio and the Straits of Messina hove into view. We had made it. I was not certain how but we had been extremely lucky.

The walls of Reggio were manned and the Guards there took it upon themselves to escort us. We descended through the streets and I saw the port. There were ships in Reggio harbour. There were even Royal Navy vessels. The Queen and her Guards were taken by the Guards we met to the Governor's Palace. They were beside themselves with worry. I was eager to return to my troop but I felt we had to say goodbye.

The Queen handed me the reins of Sergeant Sharp's horse, "You were right, he was the best choice of a horse. And now we will give you our thanks, Ladies, Alberto." The Queen and her ladies all stood before us and curtsied. Alberto gave a small formal bow.

"Captain Matthews, you and your men have done a great service to the Kingdom of Naples and Sicily. We will never forget it. Now is neither the time nor the place but we will reward all of you." Then she walked up to me and kissed me on the cheek. "Thank you, Robbie," she whispered in my ear. They all departed inside, the Governor giving us a smile and a nod of thanks.

Sergeant Marciano and the remains of his Guard all stood to attention and saluted us. I returned the compliment. He came over and shook my hand. It was a firm handshake. "I have learned much from you and I have seen a little of real war. All of us will be better soldiers in the future."

"And we were honoured to serve with you. I dare say we will run into each other again. Stay safe Benito. The Queen needs you."

We rode to the harbour. "Well sir, that was exciting. I thought we were done for a couple of times."

"You know what they say, Sergeant Seymour, it is always darkest before the dawn. In my experience when you have nothing left to lose decisions are somehow easier."

When we reached the harbour there were three Royal Navy vessels in the bay. A Midshipman and a shore party stood at the top of the steps. He snapped to attention. He took in our dirty, blood-stained uniforms and our horses which looked the worse for wear. The bosun with him suddenly whispered in his ear. His eyes widened, "Sir, are you the one who rescued the Queen? I mean is she rescued? Did you manage it?" I saw the bosun give a disgusted shake of the head.

I smiled and nodded, "Yes Middy, she is safely delivered to the Governor's palace."

The look of happiness was replaced by a look of horror. "But sir, we were told to take her directly to the ship."

I sighed, "Well at the moment she is making herself presentable. How about taking me to the ship and I will report to your..." I hesitated, "Admiral?" The bosun nodded. "Sergeant, take charge. Rae, you come with me. We'll get your wound looked at by the ship's doctor."

As they rowed out I spied the name of the hundred gunner battleship, she was 'Britannia'. "Were you at Trafalgar then?"

The bosun snorted, "The ship was sir but Mr Graham here only joined us last month."

"I hear Nelson died?"

The Middy nodded and the bosun said, "A great loss."

"I met him you know, some years ago up the coast at Naples. He was a good man and very witty."

I saw the respect in their eyes, "Then you are a lucky man sir."

"I am that bosun, I am that."

We were met at the entry by a lieutenant, "I am Lieutenant Pullen."

"Captain Matthews. I have just escorted the Queen of Naples and delivered her to the Governor's palace."

He looked relieved, "The admiral will be pleased. Follow me."

"I have a wounded man here would it be possible to have your sawbones look at him?"

"Of course." He nodded to a petty officer.

The man put Rae's arm around his shoulder. "Come with me son. The doc will have you sorted and we'll see about a drop of rum for you too."

I was quickly ushered into the Admiral's sumptuous quarters. They were a total contrast to the tiny cabin Jonathan Teer had on the 'Black Prince'. The lieutenant said, "This is Captain Matthews. The Queen is with the Governor."

The Admiral stood and came to shake me by the hand, "Damned fine show, sir. We had given you up for lost. The Frogs are all over Naples. Well done, sir."

The captain said, "Thank you snotty, we'll take it from here." He poured me a glass of something amber as the Lieutenant reluctantly left. "Here you are sir, have a drop of brandy. I am Captain Bullen and this is Rear Admiral the Earl of Northesk. Take a seat and tell us your tale."

Two refills later and my tale was told. "So you see sir, the Queen will need to be dressed properly. She travelled in men's clothes from Naples and she will want to look her best."

"Of course, of course. She'll be safe in the town will she?"

"I think we outran the French and there should be a couple of Neapolitan Armies north of here. Still, it would be better to get her to her husband."

The Admiral nodded, "Rum thing that. Husband leaving his wife alone. Not sure what my wife would have made of that. Still Italians and all that." He raised his glass, "To you sir, you did well. You are as a game as a sailor and I can't say better than that."

"Thank you, sir, but I prefer the back of a horse."

"Quite, quite."

"What happens to us now then sir?"

They looked at each other. The captain spoke. "Well, of course, all things being equal we would board you and let you rest but you seem to have the ear of the Queen. We would like you to persuade her to come with us."

I sighed. I thought I could get back to my regiment. "Very well sir but we will need to take our horses back. Will there be a problem."

Captain Bullen shook his head, "Of course not. It is only a short voyage to Messina. They can stay on deck. I know how horses hate to be below decks."

"Then I am relieved. With your permission, I will return to the palace and request the Queen's presence here. It will probably be the morning."

"We will tie up at the harbour. I think it is deep enough."

And so I returned to the land. Trooper Rae had the best of it for he stayed aboard 'Britannia' where he was feted by the Navy and asked for the tale of our flight. We had to make do with the barracks but I knew it would just be one more day and I could hand the Queen over. The responsibility was just a little too much.

Chapter 12

As I had expected the Queen wanted to appear her best but she surprised me by sending servants down to clean the worst of the dirt from our uniforms and providing clean shirts and underwear. It was a small thing but it showed her concern. When we rode to the ship I didn't feel as dirty and dishevelled but, compared with the Queen, we were.

As soon as we saw Messina I began to relax. The frigate had been sent the previous night to warn the King of his wife's arrival. We were greeted by a huge crowd of soldiers, dignitaries and ordinary people. As Captain Bullen confided in me, the whole island had been waiting with bated breath for their popular queen to arrive.

After the Queen and her entourage had landed we began to prepare to disembark. We waited patiently for the Royal Party to move off but an officer came for me, "His majesty wishes to speak with you, Captain Matthews. "

I led Badger down the gangplank. It is a good thing he was a surefooted beast for a fall into the sea would have been embarrassing. The king strode over to me and there were tears in his eyes. "My wife has told me what you have done for us. I owe you everything. We will visit with you and Sir John so that I can properly show my appreciation."

"There is no need, sir, I was just doing my duty."

He looked at me seriously, "No sir, you performed above and beyond the call of duty."

It seemed to take forever for the party to move off but that gave my men the time to leave the ship. Suddenly I heard a voice, "Captain Matthews!" It was Sergeant Sharp.

"Here's your horse, Sergeant Sharp, and it has been ridden by the Queen. She appreciated her."

"I am glad you are back sir. Sir John wants to speak with you immediately."

I had hoped for some time to change uniforms. "Are we still in Giuseppe's?"

Sharp grinned, "Yes sir, there was nowhere else suitable."

"Good, Sergeant Seymour, take the men back to the camp and I will go with Sharp here."

As Sergeant Sharp led me to Sir John's headquarters I asked him about the troop. "Mr Jackson is a good officer sir but Sergeant Grant doesn't let anyone get away with anything. They work well together."

"Ah, so you didn't miss me then?"

He laughed, "I didn't say that. We were all worried. We knew that all the ships had left Naples and wondered how you would get back. No one thought as how you would ride all the way... with a Queen!"

"She was a strong lady, Alan. She has steel in her backbone."

As we entered the camp every eye was on us. Captain Sillery strode over, "Well you have made me a guinea or two."

"How?"

"I bet the infantry officers that you would get back with the Queen and not lose a man. Well done, sir."

Sir John came out of his tent to greet me. He was actually smiling, "Congratulations, Captain Matthews. Exemplary behaviour." I wondered what he would have said if I had obeyed his original orders and returned directly to Sicily but I just smiled and nodded. He put his arm around my shoulder. "Your knowledge of the mainland, as well as your linguistic skills, will be invaluable. Tell me what do you make of the Neapolitan Army?"

"Hard to say, sir. They disappeared but the worrying thing is they have an émigré commanding them. He is younger than I am and managed to disappear with ten thousand men."

"Oh dear. That does not sound good. Well, the King wants us to take our little force over to the mainland." He paused and held the decanter over a glass. I shook my head. "What do you think of returning there?"

"Actually sir, the land to the south of Naples would suit a small force. There are many passes and narrow valleys to hold up the French. It is not cavalry country and that is for sure."

"And yet you have acquitted yourself well."

"I improvised. My men are very handy with their firearms and, as I said the steep valleys aided us. The horse artillery is light enough to move along the narrow passes and block them off. British infantry could hold up one of Masséna's divisions quite easily and cause all sorts of trouble."

"You have given me confidence. Well, we shan't be leaving for a while. I will be planning with Colonel Kempt but we will keep you informed. Now rejoin your chaps and well done, Captain, well done!"

As we rode back to Giuseppe's farm I wondered about Lady Luck. I had ridden my luck and things could have turned out so differently. Had the Queen been lost then I have no doubt that I would have suffered a court-martial and not even Colonel Selkirk would have been able to help me.

"Well, sir, what do you want to do first?"

"A bath and a clean uniform!"

"I thought you might say that. Corporal Richardson managed to get hold of a tin bath with a hole in it. He repaired it for you."

"Both of you shall be rewarded."

"Don't be daft sir, we are all glad to do it."

We had a whole week of a normal camp life. The daily briefings were now every three days. That was mainly due to the demands made upon Sir John Stuart by the Neapolitans. It suited me. Badger recovered as I did along with the men who had accompanied me. We heard of the French advances in Naples and the privations inflicted upon the populace. Masséna's army was underfed, underpaid and lacked clothes. There was nothing new there. They simply took it, by force from the Neapolitans. I wondered if the farmer had hidden his gold piece. Or was he one of the ones who ended dead and all that he had hoarded, taken. Of the Neapolitan Army, we heard little save that it was in the region of Calabria close to Morano Calabro. It was a good defensive position but it did little to threaten the French whilst the people were suffering. That was not my problem. I just had to ensure that the troop was in the best condition it could be. I immersed myself in the minutiae of independent command and, surprisingly, found I enjoyed it.

At the end of the first week, Sir John commanded that I present myself and my troop at the Palace in Messina. The town had changed since the arrival of the Royal Family. It was now arrayed in bunting and the flags of Naples and Sicily. The populace seemed to take pride in the fact that their rulers had sought refuge with them. The town had been cleaned up and there was an air of optimism. All those who had fled the French had gathered there and accommodation was at a premium. The Sicilians were happily taking the money from these rich refugees.

As we approached the gates I saw that the guards stationed there were now the King's Guards and I wondered where Benito and his men had been billeted. I guessed that they would still be close to the Queen's side.

There was a raised dais in the square before the palace and on three sides were Neapolitan and British infantry. I wondered where we should go and I halted the column. Sergeant Marciano and the remains of the patrol appeared at my side. He was in his finest uniform and grinning. "Sir, please ask your men to place themselves behind your British infantry. Except for you and the others who rescued the Queen; you are to come with me. You are to be honoured."

My heart sank. I hated fuss. I turned to James. "Lieutenant take the rest of the troop and line then up behind Colonel Kempt's men. Sergeant Seymour, the ones who rescued the Queen are to come with us." The men detached themselves from the troop as a grinning Lieutenant Jackson led them off.

Sergeant Benito rode ahead of us and he lined his men up before the dais. I could see, at the front, the King and the Queen as well as Sir John Stuart. The ones on the front row looked to be the Government and officials of Naples and Sicily. However, behind them were seated some of the important families of Sicily and I saw Don Cesar and my family. They waved and smiled. They looked both proud and pleased in equal proportions. At least they would get something good from all of this.

When we were in position a band played the Neapolitan National Anthem and then the British. Everyone clapped and cheered. The King stood and began his speech. This was a political event, I could see that immediately. He spoke of the treachery of the French and the evil nature of their soldiers. He seemed to relish reeling off their atrocities. Each one was greeted by a scowl and a murmur of disapproval from the Neapolitans. He finished with a rousing sentence about how we would drive the French back from whence they came; there was a huge patriotic cheer and a thunderous round of applause and he, the Queen, Sir John Stuart and four officials walked from the dais towards the line of waiting soldiers.

Sergeant Marciano said, from the side of his mouth, "Sir, we dismount."

I nodded, the King was not a tall man and we would have towered over them had we remained on our horses. "11th detachment, dismount!"

The men's Italian must have improved for they were ready for the order and we stood to attention by our horses.

The party halted and the King began again. He looked at us but he addressed the crowd behind him. "The men before you are the future. They have shown what Neapolitans and their allies can do. Even though outnumbered they defeated the French and they delivered Queen Maria Carolina to the arms of her husband and her nation." There was another huge cheer. Everyone seemed to have forgotten that she had been deserted by her husband and left alone in a palace. "We have created a new medal for this occasion; the order of Queen Carolina. Each of these brave men will receive the medal from the hand of the Queen." There was another cheer. The Queen began, as I had expected, at the Neapolitan end of the line. She put the medal around the neck of each trooper and kissed each him lightly on the cheek.

When she reached me she looked at me and said, "Tell your men that the medal also comes with a gold piece as a reward." She smiled, "It seems to be the price we pay for freedom."

She returned to her husband's side. He began again, "However one man deserves special recognition. Captain Robert Matthews led this tiny band of men with courage, honour and intelligence. It was through his efforts, aided by the brave men of the Queen's Guard that they were able to evade and fight off not only the French but those bandits who prey upon travellers. We are to make him a Knight of Sicily. Come forward, Captain." Benito took Badger's reins and I saw that he was grinning.

I walked forward and stood before the king. The Queen gave a subtle nod of her head. I knelt. He took his sword and touched me lightly on the shoulder. "Rise Don Roberto of Messina!" He then placed a chain with a medallion upon it around my neck. I guessed that was the Order of Sicilian Knights. There was a huge cheer from both the assembled soldiers and the people of Messina.

The Queen said, very quietly, "You can rise now, Robbie."

As I rose there was more cheering. The King kissed me on both cheeks as did the Queen. Sir John Stuart was smiling but he just shook my hand. "Well done sir."

I felt a fool standing there; I was like a puppet being operated by others. I had no doubt that this was a symbolic gesture to make up for the fact that the Neapolitans had fled before the French. Had their army remained then the whole escape might have been unnecessary. The garrison at Gaeta still held out and showed what determined resistance could achieve. They were making much of what was, in effect, nothing. I had only done what I had been doing for years. Sir John nodded and I strode back to my horse. As I did so I saw that Sergeant Marciano now wore a captain's uniform. I nodded at it and he grinned and said, from the side of his mouth, "This was my reward."

The Royal party went indoors, the stand emptied and the people joined them. The troops all marched off and we stood there in a line. I saw my men looking at their medals. "There is a gold piece goes with that too, lads." Their faces brightened even more. I glanced over my shoulder and saw that my troop still stood on the empty square.

I was about to order my men to mount when Alberto came running out. "Captain Matthews, Captain Marciano, you are to join the party inside."

I looked at Benito. "What about our men?"

"They can go back to their camp I think. My men will be going to their barracks. They now have the day off."

I turned and shouted, "Lieutenant Jackson!"

James, along with Sergeant Grant and Sergeant Sharp rode over. "Yes, sir."

"It seems I am wanted inside. Take the troop back to the camp."

"Yes, sir." He hesitated, "Sir, what was all that about?"

"The men all received a medal."

"And the kneeling?" He was grinning and enjoying my discomfort.

"I am a knight of Sicily."

His eyes widened, "Sir Robert then?"

"Don't be daft," I snapped. It is still Captain Matthews and the title means nothing."

Sergeant Sharp said, "I'll wait with Badger, sir."

"Thank you Sergeant Sharp."

I strode, with Captain Marciano behind Alberto. He had to almost run to keep ahead of us. "What have you heard of your army?"

"They are dug in close to the road we took to Reggio." He sighed, "It seems I have had my war. I am to remain here with the Queen. Still, I have my memories." He seemed wistful about the ride south.

When we entered the ballroom there was much clapping and cheering. Total strangers told me what a hero I was. A glass of something was placed in my hand and then the party started. I could not understand it. They were treating the incident as a major victory and yet it was the opposite. We had fled with our tails between our legs.

Don Cesar and his family found me. They were bursting with pride. "Don Roberto! You have brought great honour to our family."

I shuffled my feet and blushed. "It is purely honorary, you know that."

Cesar shook his head, "No my cousin, you have a place on the council of knights. There are only fifty of us. It is an important job."

"But I am a soldier. I go where I am ordered."

"But the war will not last forever and you now have somewhere where you can rule. You have enough money to buy a fine estate to go with your title."

I was not sure but this was no place to argue such matters. We spoke of Sir John and his death and they asked me of my journey. We were interrupted by Sir John Stuart. "I am sorry to take you away from your friends, Captain, but the King wishes to speak with you."

I explained this to Cesar who nodded, seriously. "See, you are now the counsel to the king. Our family has great honour; thanks to you."

The King, Queen and a General were standing away from the rest. Sir John took me to their side. The Queen turned to a courtier and retrieved something. She handed me a gold coin. It was the same size as the gold Louis but it had the portraits of the King and Queen upon it. "My debt is repaid."

"Thank you, your majesty, but there was no need. I was happy to be of service."

Sir John said, "Enough of that. Now I need you to translate for me. I am not convinced that the chap they had was translating my words exactly."

"I may struggle with some of your words, sir. I just learned the language when I stayed on the island."

He threw me a curious look but continued, "I need to know where the Neapolitan Army is and where the French are."

It was a tortuous conversation as I listened to Sir John, translated, listened to the Neapolitans and translated again.

"Sir John wishes to know where your army is and what their intentions are."

"They are in Calabria and they are preparing to defeat the French. What are Sir John's intentions?"

"I am awaiting reinforcements and orders from England." As I translated that I shot a look at Sir John but he gave nothing away. I wondered why his force was still safely ensconced on Sicily when they could be helping the Neapolitans.

"Could you not send a force over to the mainland?"

"Until I get orders it would have to be a token force. Perhaps half of Captain Matthews' troop."

I translated it as directed but my heart sank. I did not mind taking my men but half would do nothing. However, it seemed to please the Neapolitans. Their faces lit up and the King clapped me on the back. It was a stretch for him. "Excellent. You will find General de Damas. This will drive the French from our land!"

The Queen put her hand on mine. "Be careful, Captain."

Sir John led me from the room when he discovered that it had met with their approval. "We have a couple of transports permanently moored in Messina. You will be able to travel to and fro easily. A pity though; your language skills came in very handy." It was on the tip of my tongue to ask him why he did not make more effort but I knew it would fall on deaf ears.

"The men I took with me, Sergeant Seymour and the others have some Italian. They might be able to help you." I shrugged, "It is better than nothing."

He nodded, "Good, good and who will you take?"

"I will take Sergeant Grant and Lieutenant Jackson. Both need to see the lie of the land." I stared at him. "I assume we will be landing the force in Italy, eventually?"

I knew I had gone too far when he stopped mid-stride, "Do not be impertinent, Captain. Do not let your recent success go to your head. There are politics involved here. Believe me, I will take the rest of the troops when I deem it right and proper until then you will be my eyes and ears."

I sighed, "I am sorry sir. I meant no offence. And when should I return?"

"I will leave that to your judgement. So far you have shown that you can be relied upon to act appropriately. I pray it continues."

"So do I, sir. Just one more thing; do I have to be under the orders of this General de Damas?"

"Good lord no! He is French is he not? No Matthews, you make all the decisions. I trust your judgement."

"Well, I will take my leave and leave on the morrow."

"Good, good and er, congratulations on your title. That will come in handy."

I could not see how but I smiled and nodded. Sergeant Sharp saw me and trotted over with Badger. "Well, sir, where to?"

"Back to the estate and then get ready for another foray into Italy. We are taking half the troop to help the Neapolitans."

He actually seemed happy at the prospect. "It will be good to be back in action. Sitting on my backside doesn't suit sir. By the way, sir, what do I call you now?"

There was the hint of a smile playing on his lips. "Don't you start." I snapped. "It is just an honorary title."

"That may be sir but that Sergeant Marciano and the Neapolitan lads seem to set great store by it."

"Well, spread the word that I don't want it mentioned again."

The camp was buzzing when we returned. Giuseppe, in particular, was excited about the medals the men had received and my title. After Sharp had taken Badger away he took me to one side. He held the Gold Louis in his hand, "Sir, I feel I cannot take this. You are now a great man honoured by our King and Queen. I could not take payment."

I closed his fingers around the coin. "You will take it Giuseppe and there will be another one when we leave. And I have to tell you that I am taking half the men with me tomorrow. We will be away some time."

He nodded, "Then tonight we celebrate. I had planned on killing some suckling pigs anyway but now we will make it a real Sicilian send off!"

I asked Sharp to bring the sergeants and corporals to my tent. I firstly told them of the feast, "Keep an eye on the lads. The last thing we need is for them to be too drunk tomorrow."

James asked, "Why, sir?"

"Because Lieutenant Jackson, I am taking half of the troop with me to Calabria."

There was a mixture of excitement and worry on their faces. Who would be left behind? "Joe, I am leaving you and the four lads who rescued the Queen here." He looked like he was going to complain and so I held up my hand. "Before you object I have made up my mind. The five of you excelled yourselves and you will all be mentioned in my report. The troopers will all be in line for a promotion soon. You have seen Calabria. The other non-coms haven't. They will need to because we will be fighting there sooner rather than later. Lieutenant Jackson and Troop Sergeant Grant will be with me and you will be in command. It will be good practice for you. You want to be Troop Sergeant too don't you?"

"Yes, sir."

"Good, then this is your chance." He sat down, mollified. I added, "Oh, by the way, General Stuart will be using you and the other lads to translate so make sure your Italian is up to muster."

His face fell. "I knew it was a mistake learning the bloody language."

"The rest of you; we learned that we need plenty of ammunition. We have no spare horses yet so we will have to carry it all. I am hoping we can get some remounts in Italy although we didn't see any."

The next hour or so was spent in the detail of the detachment but they all seemed happy enough. I let Sergeant George Grant choose the sergeants, corporals and troopers who would accompany us. He knew them all far better than I did. Once that was done we all enjoyed ourselves at the feast. The Sicilians had excelled themselves and the food and drink flowed. I was able to sit and watch it all, as though detached.

I was pleased to see the sergeants keeping their eyes on those who were taking too much advantage of our host but it was a good send-off. The only part I did not like was the attention I gained from the Sicilians. They all wished to see the seal of office I had been given and they all insisted on calling me, Don Roberto. It was not easy. I suspected that my mother and father would have been pleased and I know that Sir John MacAlpin would have thought it right and proper. I was a clan chief, albeit a Sicilian one. At least that would be behind me the next day when I left for Calabria.

Chapter 13

Reggio now had marines guarding the port and the battleships there promised that we had an escape route from Calabria should we need one. Having been denied a crossing recently I wanted that reassurance. The intelligence we gleaned from the locals was that the General was somewhere south of Naples and, in all likelihood, close to Cosenza. We had the advantage that I knew the roads and we were able to push on hard. The weather had returned to the wintry winds of a few weeks ago. March looked to be coming in like a lion, all roaring winds and biting cold.

The bodies of the bandits were now spread over a large area. The animals of the night had enjoyed the feast. The stone mounds which marked the dead courtiers and soldiers were in stark contrast. They would be there forever and become part of the landscape. As we passed the farm where we had stayed I saw that the building was still intact. The French had not reached it yet. We were forced to find shelter north of Cosenza. I had hoped to find a camp but I found nothing. We camped in the freezing valley bottom and ate cold rations washed down with hot bouillon. James and I shared one of the small tents. I envied the troopers eight to a tent. The steaming bodies would keep them warm. It was as cold as I could remember it in the tiny tent. I was stiff and cold when I awoke and a cold shave did nothing to improve my humour.

We rode through the high pass and we were shivering. We had no greatcoats. We had not needed them in Sicily but here in the high passes, we did. Sergeant Grant observed, "I thought Italy was like Sicily all warm sun and wine."

"We are in the high mountains Sergeant and it is only March."

"I know sir but it is definitely a bit parky!"

It was late in the day when we spotted them. I was about to make camp when James smelled wood smoke. As we crested a rise I saw the campfires of the left-wing of the Neapolitan Army. They were in the wide valley bottom some twenty miles north of Lagonegro. I wondered if the General was heading towards or from the French.

139

We were not challenged as we rode through the camp. I found that disturbing. The camp itself was not organised well; there appeared to be little order. Most worryingly of all there were more militia units than regulars. The lack of uniform and consistent weapons easily identified them. They looked almost like the bandits we had encountered. The regulars would find it hard enough to stand against the well-drilled French but the militia would be fodder for the guns and the cavalry.

I saw the Neapolitan flag and the white flag of the Royalist French. "George, see if you can find somewhere to camp." I pointed to the west away from the other units. He nodded glumly. "James, Alan, come with me."

General de Damas still looked like a boy. I had expected him to look the part of a general now that he was leading ten thousand men. He did not. He did, however, looked pleased to see me.

"Ah, Captain Matthews. Are the King and Queen safe?"

"They are both in Sicily and I have been sent to find you." I handed over the letter which had been delivered to the ship just before we left."

"Sir, sit, I am sure one of my men will bring refreshments." He began to read. I was not hopeful that we would be served anything and so I just waited. "He looked up at me. "You have done well Captain or should I say, Don Roberto."

"Please, I did nothing." I leaned forward. "Now what can you tell me, General?" I was careful to use his title. I suspected his ego needed the reassurance. "Have you met the French yet?"

"No, not yet. I have arranged to meet with the rest of our army under Marshal Rosenheim. We are to rendezvous at Cassano all'Ionio."

I looked at James; we had passed that not far north of Cosenza. "That is many miles from here. Where are the French?"

He shrugged. "I am not certain but I need to slow them down and allow the Marshal to reach the rendezvous."

"With due respect, General de Damas, you need to get to the rendezvous and prepare your defences."

He smiled patronisingly, "Do not fret my dear fellow. Masséna is busy besieging Gaeta and that is far north of Naples. If he has men heading south it cannot be many. We will be able to hold them up."

"Sir," I used the term but I felt no respect for this boy, "find out where the French are first and ascertain their numbers."

He became increasingly irritated. "We have managed to do well enough without your interference. We will continue with my plan." He smiled, "You must be tired after your long ride. Join me and my staff for dinner."

It was useless arguing with him. I stood. "Very well, General, I will see to my men."

He had a look of surprise on his face. "Can't your sergeants do that?"

I took a deep breath, "Yes sir, but I like to do it too. Now if you will excuse me."

James could tell that I was angry and he wisely kept his counsel. We found the men. Grant had taken them up a small farm track leading to an abandoned building. It looked ancient but it was on slightly higher ground and there was a stream nearby. It was a better campsite than the ground lower down. "I know it is some way from the others sir but it will make a good camp."

"Don't apologise, Sergeant, it is perfect. Get some food on the go eh? The Lieutenant and I are invited to dinner with the General."

I suspected the sergeants thought that would be a better meal than the hard, cold rations they would have to eat but I would have preferred it. I was not looking forward to listening to the pompous young aristocrat boasting about his plans. I knew what the French army and, Masséna, in particular, were capable of.

We reached the main camp and saw that the General had a long table and the senior officers of all the regiments were there. There were thirty men around the table. From their uniforms some were regulars but many were militia. The General welcomed us as heroes. "Here are the men who rescued our Queen, our gallant allies, the British."

I could see that they had all been drinking heavily and the cheering was raucous and boisterous. It was more like a boys' outing than a campaign against the French.

"Here, sit next to me, Captain." I sat between the General and an officer in a heavily gilded militia uniform. He had the look of the some of the bandits we had had to see off in the high mountains. "This is Colonel Giorgio Sciarpa, he commands my rear guard."

The colonel grinned, revealing yellow stained teeth. It was not an attractive sight. I smiled. "You will have your work cut out when the French come, Colonel Sciarpa. They move swiftly."

He stabbed at a piece of lamb with his knife and began chewing. Unfortunately, he then began speaking and I had to try to avoid the bits of lamb fat and meat which hurtled from his mouth as he spoke. "We have not seen them, Englishman. Besides," he gestured with the wicked-looking knife at the mountains which rose from the valley bottoms, "the land here helps us. They cannot outflank us and we will hold them."

I remembered the muskets the bandits had used. "How fast can your men load and fire?"

The question puzzled all of the officers around me and the conversation stopped. Sciarpa halted with meat poised to enter the cavern that was his mouth, "What do you mean?"

"If I timed your men while they were firing, how many musket balls would they fire in one minute?"

He shrugged, "One perhaps two."

"The British infantry can fire three a minute easily and, when they need to they can fire four or five a minute. The French use light infantry who can run, drop and fire from the ground. They are called Tirailleurs. In the time your men take to fire one volley they would be upon you."

I watched their faces as they digested that information. I could see that it was no surprise to De Damas but he had omitted to tell his men about that. "Perhaps, Captain Matthews you might find the French for us tomorrow and then Colonel Sciarpa will have a better idea of what is to come his way."

I did not relish the prospect but it was better than suddenly being attacked by the French Vanguard. Sciarpa would not hold them up for long. "Very well sir."

"I do not need your men Captain for I have four cannon but I will be interested to see if your men are any good."

I ignored the insult. "What time will you break camp in the morning, sir?"

"We should be moving south by ten."

I think my mouth opened and closed like a fish but I regained my composure. "My men and I will leave before dawn."

The whole table laughed and Sciarpa snorted, "Then you are a fool Captain for it will be dark. My men and I will be at Lagonegro. We will build a defensive position there."

That did not inspire me with confidence; the village in question was just three miles down the road. Colonel Sciarpa was not moving far. I stood, "I will see you there Colonel. We will take our leave now General we have an early start in the morning."

As I walked back I explained to James what had been said. He had understood a little of it and, like me, could not understand the lack of urgency amongst the officers. "We will need to be on our toes tomorrow James. This is not cavalry country and we will need to be able to get out of danger as quickly as we get into it."

We rose, the next day, to a totally silent camp. We packed our tents away and walked our horses through the snoring, sweating Neapolitans. The lack of security was appalling. We saw neither pickets nor vedettes. We saw evidence of where they should be from the tethered horses but they appeared to be sleeping. Once clear we mounted, "Sergeant Grant, send a good corporal and a trooper half a mile ahead. I want early warning of the enemy."

"Sir."

The road twisted and turned and began to rise from the valley bottom. I remembered the road from our journey south. If the French had light infantry ahead of them then they would see us before we saw them. I hoped that they would use their cavalry. There was a vicious wind blowing from the north and I felt chilled to the bone. The sky was mercifully free of clouds and we would

have neither snow nor rain. That was the only element in our
favour. We passed through the village the rear guard would be
using. It looked to have potential but I had no confidence in the
leader.

We stopped at noon and fed the horses with grain and ate some
cured meat. Giuseppe had provided us with a large quantity of such
dried meat. Some was venison and some was ham. It was
appreciated by the men. The road dipped a little and twisted to the
right. I was standing on a rock chewing the dried meat when I saw
a flash of blue. I immediately dropped to my knees.

"Stand to! French!"

My men calmly mounted their horses and drew their carbines.

"Sharp, bring me my look-see." He handed me my telescope
and, taking off my helmet, I slithered forwards across the cold
rock. I focussed on the spot I had seen blue and was rewarded by
the sight of French Tirailleurs moving in a column up the road.
They were in two lines and they were on the opposite sides of the
road. They were leaving space between them which meant they
had cavalry ready to gallop through them when they spotted an
enemy. I estimated that they were less than half a mile away. They
would be upon the rear guard by dawn the next day at the latest.

I dropped down from the rock. "French infantry. It is their
army." I looked up at the sky, it was still clear of clouds. "We will
wait and see more of the column but be ready to leave the minute I
say." As I clambered back up the rock I saw the men checking
their carbines and pistols. If we were surprised then it would be the
French who would get the shock.

I saw the light infantry move along the road followed by a
squadron of Chasseurs. Then I saw the solid columns of infantry.
This was the advance guard and the soldiers I had seen already
could scatter the men Sciarpa commanded.

"Let's ride. I think that the colonel will have his hands full by
morning."

The ride back was easier for the wind was behind us. We
trotted along the road knowing that the French Infantry could make
almost as good time as we could on these mountain roads. It was

getting on for dusk when we saw the defensive works built by the colonel. They were not a deterrent. Sciarpa had just dragged a wagon across the road. His four artillery pieces were clustered on both sides of it. They could be easily flanked. The two thousand militiamen he had appeared to be just camped behind the primitive breastwork. Had we been French cavalry then we would have slaughtered them already.

The Lieutenant at the barrier grinned at me. I wiped the smile from his face with my words. "Lieutenant, there is a French column a mile or so down the road. I would get your men at their defences."

The smile left his face and we rode through the barrier. Sergeant Grant gave a derisory laugh, "We could have jumped that and what idiot puts his guns that close together?"

He spoke for all of us. We had fought alongside and against artillery pieces. Correctly placed they could be lethal but badly placed they could lose you the battle.

"Lieutenant, get a camp erected and some food on the go."

James looked surprised, "We are staying?"

"You want to abandon them then?"

"Well, no sir, but shouldn't we get them pulled back? There are too many French."

"It is too late for that. These people do not move quickly. If they were caught on the road then they would be slaughtered. They have a chance here, slim, but a chance all the same. We will do what we can to help them but I will not risk our men for these fools."

Colonel Sciarpa was sat at a table eating with his captains and majors. He smiled at me as I rode up. "Yes, Captain?"

"There is a strong French column. They are less than two miles away. Infantry, cavalry and artillery."

He paled. "But…"

"Call the men to arms."

"We have only just begun to eat!"

There was no arguing with logic like this. "If you and your men wish to eat I would suggest that you take your food to the barricade and eat there. I would also suggest you send a rider to the general. He will need to be informed. The French may not be here until morning but they could arrive in the next hour or so."

It was as though he had not thought that he would be called into action. He nodded, "Yes, that is a good idea." He turned to his officers. "You heard the Englishman. Go!" As they ran off in all directions he asked, "Will they come tonight?"

"They will probe for weaknesses. If they can they will attack but, if not, they will wait until they have their whole force ready and they will attack in the morning." He nodded. "Make sure your men have clean muskets and plenty of ammunition. They will need it. Your officers will need to be firm."

"When the French come they will send in their light infantry. They will swarm like flies. They will not stand in straight lines and shoot at you. Your officers must wait until their men cannot miss and fire volleys. If they do that then you and your men have a chance. But the quality of your officers will decide the outcome of this action."

His back stiffened. "They are all loyal and they will defend this pass with honour."

I somehow doubted that honour would help them over much but I nodded and rode to the camp. The men had fires going and were boiling some of the snow which had gathered in the crevasses of the mountains with bouillon and dried meat. It would be warm and sustaining.

I gathered the sergeants and Lieutenant Jackson around me. "After we have eaten I want one man in four to take the horses down the valley about half a mile. The rest of us will be along the barrier. I am not certain that their pickets will be able to do much. I want our eyes and ears to warn us of an attack."

Sergeant Grant nodded, "They'll send some of their light infantry tonight. Try to slit a few throats and disable the guns."

"You are right Sergeant Grant. Hell, they might even attack tonight but I suspect they will wait until morning. Their column will be strung out all along the road."

I heard the militia grumbling as they took up their positions. There were a lot of men and they were just covering the middle four hundred yards. The flanks were unguarded. I went to Colonel Sciarpa, "You need to spread your men out more. They can be flanked."

He shook his head and smiled. "They will not come tonight and my men will have to sleep at their posts. They will be warmer and we can spread out more in the morning. Do not worry, Englishman, you have done your duty. I am grateful."

Exasperated I sought out Lieutenant Jackson, "Take half of the men and cover the left flank. If I were the French I would try to infiltrate that way. I will do the same with the right flank. Take Sergeant Grant with you. I will keep Jones with me. Listen for the bugle call but, if you think you are going to be overrun then get out of there. Understand?"

"Yes, sir."

I led my men away. With seven horse holders staying with the horses, that left just twenty men each to guard the flanks. I hoped it would be enough.

When we reached our position, a rocky patch of rising ground with some large boulders and scrubby bushes, we saw the unmistakable blue of the French column. They had arrived. The Neapolitans began to jeer the French. It was foolish; they were too far away and it would not bother them anyway. Still, if it bolstered their resolve then so much the better.

"Sergeant Dale, divide the men into pairs. One sleeps and the other one watches. You and Bugler Jones form one pair. I'll take Sergeant Sharp. I think they will send men tonight to test us. They might crawl up close in the dark."

"Right sir."

"First or second watch Sergeant Sharp?"

"It's up to you sir."

"Right then I will sleep now. Wake me in two hours."

It was freezing cold and the ground was hard. I just had my cloak and a blanket and yet, as soon as my head touched the ground, I was asleep. I dreamt but the dream dissolved into nothing when I was suddenly woken by Sharp. "Is it that time already Sergeant?"

He whispered, "No sir. Dick heard something. It might be the French." I was going to ask a question when he added, "The lads are all awake."

"Good." I grabbed my carbine and primed it. Peering out in the dark I could see nothing but my eyes were not yet accustomed to the dark. I used my ears as I allowed my night vision to return. I could just hear the snores coming from the militia. I hoped that the colonel had impressed upon his men the need to keep a good watch.

Suddenly I saw a shadow move about a hundred yards or so in front of our lines. Our slightly elevated position gave us an advantage for we were looking down on the valley. Once I had seen one Tirailleur I soon saw the rest. There appeared to be about a company in strength. They were small quick men who were adept at this sort of thing. They were too far away for us to guarantee a hit. I did not need to give orders to my men. They would know what to do.

Corporal Jones sidled up to me, "Sergeant Dale reckoned you might need me, sir."

"Good man. When I start to fire then give the call, stand to."

"Yes, sir."

I noticed that he had his carbine ready. He would join in the firing when his call was done.

The shadows had gone to ground. I assumed they were slithering along on their bellies. The quiet of the cold night was broken by one scream and then another. They were amongst the militia. I aimed at a crouching shadow and yelled, "Fire!" My carbine cracked and the bugle sounded. A line of flashes erupted next to me. As I reloaded I saw a line of flashes on the opposite side of the valley; Lieutenant Jackson had kept his wits about him. The shadow fell and I aimed at a kneeling shadow with a musket. He too fell. Our fire was beginning to take its toll. Suddenly there was a ripple of musket fire along the front of the militia and I saw the shadows begin to run away. When they had gone a hundred and fifty yards I shouted, "Ceasefire." The bugle sounded but the militia kept popping away and wasting powder. The target was out of range and too small to hit with their muskets. We had, however, driven them off. The militia cheered as though they had won the battle.

"Right Sharp. Get your head down. I'll wake you in two hours."

He knew me too well to argue and he was soon snoring. Trooper Jones went back to the sergeant and I watched. I could hear the moans of the dying Frenchmen. The moaning did not last long for a militiaman would creep out and there would be a scream of pain and then silence. Soon the silence of the night returned.

I managed a couple of hours sleep and then it was dawn. I summoned Jones. "Sound, 'horse holders'. We might as well keep our horses close by."

As the notes rang out in the valley I saw that the French soldiers had been stripped naked and mutilated. It was a mistake. The French would wreak vengeance on the militia for what they had done. I heard the French bugles and drums. It would not be long now.

"Sergeant Dale, get the men fed and I will see the colonel."

Colonel Sciarpa greeted me warmly. "You see Captain. We drove them back." He nodded his approval. "Your guns were effective. Thank you."

"I'd save your thanks for later. They are coming. Do your gunners have the range?"

I could see that he had no idea from the blank look on his face. "They are good gunners."

I looked at the ancient four and six-pounder cannon. If they had not marked the range then they would waste shot but it was too late now for a lesson. "Good luck colonel."

"We do not need luck, Englishman. God is on our side and the land will help us too. You will see the French driven back over the pass believe me."

I rejoined my men and Sergeant Sharp handed me a mug of bouillon and a piece of bread. He nodded towards the militia.

"Some of the Neapolitans sent this over. Seems they liked our guns last night."

Looking at the position of the bodies it was obvious that we had killed most of the attackers. I turned as the hooves of the horses thundered and skittered across the rocks. We now had the means to escape if we had to. I was confident that we would need to. James would need his wits about him on the north side of the valley. At least he had George Grant with him. He had a calm head on his shoulders.

I took out my telescope. Reynier was sending four battalions of light infantry and the light infantry of the foot regiments. It was like a swarm of ants. Reynier was being clever. It was the perfect attack against artillery. Behind them, I saw two regiments of Chasseurs preparing to follow. Neither target would be easy to hit. I just hoped that the Neapolitans had plenty of canister and case shot.

The cannons began firing far too early. The hard ground meant that the balls bounced and moved off line easily. Any hits would be lucky. With only four guns it was easy to approach the Neapolitan lines especially as the guns were firing independently. I saw a handful of Frenchmen fall, each death greeted by a cheer of victory. Still, they came on. The Neapolitans opened fire with their muskets at two hundred yards range. It wasted powder and clogged the guns. The rate of reloading and the lack of volleys also meant that the firing was ineffective. The light infantry raced forward and stopped at a hundred yards. They began to kneel and fire. They were aiming at the gunners.

I shouted to Jones, "Sound open fire!" The strident notes echoed off the valley walls. I aimed at a sergeant a hundred and twenty yards away. He fell clutching his arm. Soon my men were trying to pick off the officers and sergeants but the damage had been done. The gunners fell like flies and the ones who remained took shelter beneath their guns and behind their caissons.

Suddenly I heard the drumbeat of the pas de charge. The four battalions of infantry roared and leapt forwards. The militia had no response. Many of them had clogged guns, others were in the process of reloading while others panicked and fired too high. I saw the Chasseurs riding to support their comrades. I watched in horror as the Neapolitans began to flee down the road. The battle was over and they had lost.

"Jones, sound fall back."

As the bugle called I grabbed Badger's reins from Sharp and hauled myself in the saddle. I fired one last shot from my carbine and then clipped it to its sling. "Fall back." We had the advantage that we were on the side of the valley. The militia found their way clogged by equipment, tents and their comrades. We trotted along the side of the mass of fleeing soldiers. I saw them throw weapons to the ground in their panic to escape. It was a disaster. Four guns had been lost already and the French had barely lost a man.

Our horses soon overtook the leading elements and I headed for the road. I was relieved when James joined me. "Any casualties, Lieutenant?"

"Corporal Lows was hit by a chip of rock but he can still fight." He gestured over his shoulder with his thumb. "Disaster eh?"

"And it is not over yet." As I watched I saw the Chasseurs fall amongst the militia. It was a light horseman's dream to chase fleeing men. I saw Colonel Sciarpa struck in the head by a sabre. His inert body was trampled by the horses which followed.

"Skirmish line. Let's discourage them." We formed a wall of horseflesh and the militia milled around our flanks. When the Chasseurs were just fifty yards away I shouted, "Fire!" I emptied all four pistols in the blink of an eye. The road was filled with smoke but the Chasseurs were halted. "Jones, sound fall back!"

Even as the bugle sounded and the men began to retreat I saw one Chasseur, luckier and more foolhardy than the rest had made it through the wall of lead. I drew my sword and charged forward. I remembered the sabre that my opponent used. It was not a good weapon. As he slashed at my body I hacked at his sword and it shattered. He held the broken hilt, with a surprised expression on his face and as I back slashed at him I felt my sword cut to his backbone. Before his comrades could react I joined my men in the retreat.

Chapter 14

Although we watched for pursuit we saw none. Occasionally we were overtaken by militia who had acquired horses but there were fewer of those the further south we went. The two thousand men of the rear guard had been merely militia but their numbers might have made the difference when the French finally caught up with the Neapolitan army. I do not think that they suffered calamitous casualties but they had lost their guns and they had lost their cohesion. Naples was all the weaker for that.

I was relieved to see that the general had a good defensive position. Campotenese had to be approached through a narrow valley. The escape route, however, was also a narrow gap. I saw as I drew closer, that the general had built three redoubts and filled the valley with lines of men. I saw nine battalions in his front line and his cavalry just behind. The cannon could fire over the heads of his men. It was a good position. There was however a major drawback which Bugler Jones spotted. "Sir, there are no men on the mountainsides. It will be like Lagonegro all over again."

"Yes Bugler, I had noticed that but some of these troops are regulars. The front line looks strong. I do not think this army will fold as easily as the one we just left."

"I think you are being optimistic, Lieutenant Jackson. If the French artillery gets to work then those redoubts will not last long and they have now captured four more guns. Anyway, I need to report to the General. Lieutenant, find somewhere for us to camp. I'll go with Sergeant Sharp and find General de Damas."

After many questions I found the General inspecting his redoubts. "Where is Colonel Sciarpa and his men?" His face showed that he knew the answer to his own questions already.

"Dead at Lagonegro."

If I had slapped his face I could not have had a more dramatic response. "And his men? How many survived?" His voice was quiet; almost as though he didn't want the answer.

"At least three hundred are dead and the rest just ran. If you are lucky then some of them may find their way here. He lost your guns too."

"What happened?"

"He made the same mistake you are making. He did not protect his flanks." I pointed to the hills and mountains surrounding them. "The French Light Infantry attacked where he had no men. There are no men there." I was being as blunt and explicit as I could be. Perhaps I should have been more diplomatic; it did not sit well with the young general.

De Damas coloured. He waved an angry hand towards the mountains. "The land protects us. No one save a goat could get over those mountains could they?"

I nodded, "They could and if they can then the Tirailleurs and Voltigeurs probably will."

He began chewing on his fingernail as he stared at the mountain. "We have no troops trained in that sort of thing."

"You must have some local men who work in the mountains. Use them."

"It is too late. I assume the French are pursuing you?"

"Yes but not too closely."

"They will attack tomorrow then. It is too dark to send them tonight and tomorrow will be too late." There was a certain amount of logic to his statement but it would be worth the try to send a few hundred militia into the mountains. Having seen their performance in the line they would be better serving in their natural habitat. "What happened … in detail I mean."

"The French tried a night attack which we beat off. The next day they sent in four battalions of light infantry with cavalry support. Your colonel tried to kill them with ball and it was wasted. Then the militia fired too early. When the light infantry began to pick off the gunners the guns stopped firing and the cavalry advanced. Once the light infantry got to work the militia collapsed and the cavalry charged. The colonel fought until the end but the men were not good enough. It was a waste of men."

He nodded, "Hindsight is a wonderful thing, Captain Matthews, it always gives you a perfect view of events but we have to deal with the situation in which we find ourselves today. Hopefully, the Marshal will reach us soon; if not then we will have to fight a long day tomorrow until he arrives." He smiled at me. "I have no doubt that he will come and we will share in a great victory. If you would use your men as you choose tomorrow then I would appreciate it."

I nodded, gratefully, "As we are mounted and have carbines, I will keep us mobile to fill gaps. Where will you be sir?"

"I will be here so that I can see the battle unfold before me and react quickly."

I left him. He was well-intentioned, that much was obvious, but he had no idea how to fight the French war machine. He was like the British when they fought the colonists in America. He wanted his enemy to stand in straight lines and trade volleys; last man standing. That was doomed to failure on two counts; firstly the French Tirailleurs would swarm all over the field and not present a solid target and secondly because his men had neither the skill nor the discipline to trade volleys. Napoleon was about to capture Italy and there was nothing I could do about it.

Lieutenant Jackson had excelled himself. We had a whole field to ourselves on the other side of the village. Already fires were going and Sergeant Grant had managed to acquire a couple of huge cooking pots. He pointed to the hills. "Sir, I took it upon myself to send Trooper Sands and Trooper Cooper up into the hills to get some game." The two men were natural hunters. "I thought the lads might like a change from dried meat."

"Well done, Sergeant Grant." I turned to Sergeant Sharp. I gave him a handful of silver coins. "See if you can get a few bottles of local red wine. Just enough for a bottle for the stew and a swig for each of the troopers. They have earned it."

"Right sir."

Defeat, even when it is not of your own doing, leaves a sour taste in the mouth. No one likes to run; least of all my men and I wanted them to know that I was proud of them. Perhaps the taste of rough Italian wine might take the taste from their mouths.

We ate well with a stew containing a whole menagerie of animals. I deemed it best not to inquire too closely about their provenance. There appeared to be some particularly small bones. They did help to pick the meat from between our teeth. The wine was rough but made wonderful gravy for the stew. The mouthful of wine each made the men feel as though it was special. As we were so far behind the front line I knew that we would not need to have pickets out and the men had a good night's sleep; the first since we had landed.

The French appeared at nine o'clock in the morning. They were hard to see for the wind was blowing snow from the mountaintops into the faces of the waiting Neapolitans. The weather would not suit them. They hunkered down behind barriers rather than watching for the enemy. Reynier was just using light infantry. They made no attempt to close with the Neapolitans. They just spread themselves in a long line facing the waiting battalions. I had the men mount and be ready for action while I sought the general. He seemed pleased. "They have not attacked yet. The Marshal still has time to get here."

"I would still send men to the mountains."

He handed me his telescope. "Look for yourself. They are devoid of anyone; French or Neapolitan."

"They could be on the far side."

"You are clutching at straws. Listen, Robert, I appreciate your efforts but I have a feeling that today we will halt the French here and begin to drive them back north."

I returned to my men. I ordered them to dismount; there was little point in tiring out our horses. We had no idea what the day held. "We are waiting on the French."

Sergeant Grant had a bone from one of the animals we had eaten in the stew and he gnawed on it like a dog. He used it to point out features. "The thing of it is sir, we can do bugger all here. It is too narrow and hilly. This is not cavalry country. Those French light infantry, now they impressed me. They were good shots and they were fast. If I was the general I would worry about them."

I nodded glumly; it did not make me feel any better that my sergeant had spotted the same weakness in our disposition as me. "I know. Keep your eyes on the mountains. If you see blue then let me know."

The French attack began at about three in the afternoon. A brigade of French infantry with drums beating began to march forward. I heard the crack as the Neapolitan cannon fired. It was hard to see from our vantage point but I heard little to indicate that they had caused much damage.

Suddenly Sergeant Dale shouted, "There sir, on the right and behind us. French infantry."

I grabbed my telescope and peered in the direction of the mountains. Sure enough, there were French light infantry hurtling down to attack the right flank and the rear of the Neapolitan army. British soldiers could turn and fight two enemies; I had seen them do it in Egypt. These half-trained militiamen would run.

"Lieutenant, send a rider to warn the general. The rest of you mount up. Let's see what we can do."

The problem we had was that we had to go around the town. It would take some time but it would bring us up on the rear of the French. It would give us a slight advantage. I just hoped that the right-wing would hold until we got there. The houses before us hid the conflict from view but we heard the collective groan as the Neapolitans were attacked from the front and the flank.

"Draw sabres!" The sound of a hundred sabres was like the hissing of a giant snake. As we turned the corner we saw the French falling upon the Neapolitans who were fleeing. We could do little but we had to do something.

"Charge!" The strident notes of the bugle made the French turn. I saw the horror on their faces as they saw the column of horses and steel.

Light infantry hate cavalry. We are their nemesis and so it proved. We fell upon them and they were facing the wrong way. Their shakos gave them no protection and their tattered uniforms even less. They were cut to ribbons. I almost felt sorry for them until I saw the demoralised Neapolitan army fleeing west. We rode

and killed until the horses were too tired. I halted the line. I
suddenly saw the French infantry battalions marching resolutely
towards us. Their muskets would make mincemeat of us.

"Jones, sound the retreat. Fall back."

I allowed most of the troopers to pass me and then Sergeant
Sharp and I followed. Sadly I saw four empty saddles gallop
passed. We had not emerged unscathed. As soon as we were out of
danger I ordered the column to halt. The loose horses were
recovered and the men primed their weapons. We were not out of
danger yet.

I turned to them all so that they could hear. "We will head for
Reggio. The pass will be filled with the refugees from this battle.
We will force our way through but do not hurt any of them. They
have been through enough. Follow me."

It was difficult but I forced my way through the maelstrom of
humanity trying to escape the French. The Chasseurs sensed
victory and were pushing hard. Badger, luckily, was a very patient
horse and did not react adversely to the knocks he suffered as we
gradually worked our way through the crowds. Our task was made
easier when the French began firing on those at the rear of the mass
of humanity. Those near us threw themselves to the ground and the
press eased slightly. As the narrow defile darkened we found
ourselves clear of the largest crowd.

We slowed to allow our horses to recover and I debated what
we ought to do. A large part of me wanted to ride as hard as I could
for the coast and board one of our ships. On the other hand, there
were a large number of Neapolitan soldiers who might be saved to
fight another day. I compromised. "Lieutenant Jackson, Sergeant
Grant, come here please." They approached, "How many dead
George?"

"Looking at the empty saddles there must be four although
some may just be wounded or prisoners."

I looked him in the eye. He was being an optimist. "Let us
assume they are dead for the moment. Who were they?"

"Hargreaves, Simpson, Wake and Thomas."

I nodded. It was important to have the name and picture the man. They were all good men. "Now we could push hard to the coast. It would take us two days of hard riding. What I want to do is to take it slower and see if we can help any of these Neapolitans to get to Sicily and fight again."

"That's risky sir, with respect."

"You are right to question me, James, and it is risky. I am taking a calculated risk. I think that we will have warning of the French; even if that warning is just a mob running away from their weapons. So long as we keep ahead of the main group of soldiers we should be safe. If we can I want to give the French a bloody nose and slow them down. It worked when we rescued the Queen. There is no reason why it should not work again." This time they both nodded. "George, is there anyone wounded?"

"Just Corporal Lows, sir."

"Right send him with another trooper to Reggio. The navy needs to know that there will be refugee soldiers heading their way and I want a ship holding for us. Make sure he understands that."

"Don't worry sir, Arthur is reliable. He will be annoyed to be missing the action but he will get the job done. Don't you fret."

We got off the road when it was well past dark. We set up a cold camp in a small valley close to the main road. A stand of trees hid us from the main road but we could hear the pop of muskets and the occasional scream of death. We shared the picket duty. I split mine with Lieutenant Jackson.

When dawn broke I saw that we were close to the sea. It was a wide plain and, in the distance, I could see a small town which looked defensible. I stored that information for future reference. The morning also brought a string of soldiers. I was delighted to see that many of them still had their weapons. It looked like one or two officers had managed to keep some of the men together. It was from them that I discovered that the Marshal's army had also fled in the face of fierce French forces. There were no Neapolitan soldiers now, in Calabria, save for the besieged garrison north of Naples. I asked one colonel about the bay. "What is that called?"

"Gulf of Sant'Eufemia."

I told all the officers the same thing, "Head for Reggio and the Royal Navy." We even added to our number. A few troopers, travelling alone or in pairs found us and begged to join our company. They wanted the protection of our guns and a chance to fight back. It seems our name preceded us. In addition, they were hurt at the magnitude of the defeat.

When we were a day from Reggio I had a hundred and fifty assorted cavalrymen at my disposal. We had taken to riding along the two edges of the road to allow the infantry to pass between us. I was taking a turn, with Sergeant Sharp, at the rear. Suddenly I heard, "Captain Matthews!"

I turned and saw Trooper Wake helping a wounded Trooper Thomas. "11th Halt! Sergeant Grant, to the rear."

George Grant was an unofficial doctor and he galloped to join us. "Now then Harry, what is it?"

"I got a bayonet in me leg sarge. It hurts like buggery." We cut his breeches and saw that the wound was poisoned. "That looks bad, sarge. Will I lose me leg?"

"Not if I can help it." He looked up at Sergeant Sharp. "You have a good nose. I want a dead animal." Alan gave him a curious look. "We need maggots. Bring me as many as you can get." When Alan left he said to me, "The maggots will eat the dead flesh. It will smell but he will live and he won't lose the leg."

Some of the other troopers gave them a drink and some food. Trooper Wake pointed behind us, "Sir, there is a squadron of Chasseurs and they are only a couple of miles back."

"Right. Sergeant Dale, detail a couple of men to look after these two. I want them getting to Reggio as soon as we can. Lieutenant Jackson, I want half of the men dismounted and hidden behind those trees on the two sides of the road. When they are in position come back here I have another job for you."

Sharp returned with a squirming mass of maggots. "Lovely, give them here." A horrified Thomas watched as they were wrapped beneath a bandage. "There that will do. "Smith, West, bring two spare horses and get these two lucky lads to Reggio."

"But sarge, I can still fight."

"No you can't; now be a good pair of lads and obey orders."
Helping his wounded comrade Trooper Wake went to the two
horses. "Right sir what now?"

"I am going to try to hurt the Chasseurs. I will keep all of the
volunteers and half of our men. When the French see us I am going
to pretend to flee. When they pass between you and Sergeant Sharp
you keep firing at them. We will then turn and charge them." Grant
nodded, "You all right with that Sharp?"

He grinned, "Yes sir."

"Good, join your men. Lieutenant Jackson, I want us to pretend
to be scared. When the French see us I will get Jones to sound
retreat. We will ride for a hundred yards and then turn and charge
them. I want you to explain that to our men. I will talk to the
Neapolitans." As soon as I explained it I had no worries. They
were cavalrymen and the chance to get back at the enemy appealed
to them. They liked the idea of tricking the French. I stressed that
they had to obey orders and they all seriously agreed. I hoped that
they would.

We had barely got into position when I heard the thunder of
hooves and the familiar sound of a French bugle. "Sound retreat.
Don't ride too fast!"

The Chasseurs must have thought their birthday and Christmas
had all come on the same day. They hurtled after us oblivious to
the potential danger of an ambush. All that they saw was a bunch
of stragglers. No one had stood up to them yet and it was unlikely
that the dispirited horsemen before them would either.

As soon as I heard the thunder and crack of the carbines and
muskets I roared, "Charge!" and wheeled Badger around. My
sword was out and my blood was up. I had run enough.

Badger leapt forward as though he too was eager to get to grips
with the French. There was a cloud of smoke where the French had
been. Four of them had evaded the ambush and I saw the horror on
their faces as they saw the wall of steel and horseflesh charging
them. I took the head of the first one and James the man next to
him. Three troopers from the Princess Regiment killed the other

two. Then we were in the smoke and amongst them. There was confusion but we had the element of surprise.

A major threw himself at me. I flicked my wrist and his sword slid away. I punched him on the side of the head and he reeled back. As he did so I stabbed him in the throat. I sensed a movement to my left and I leaned back. The blade cut some buttons from my tunic. I drew a pistol and fired at point-blank range. The man's head disappeared. The rest of my men had stopped firing now and were busy hacking and chopping at the French. The Chasseurs could not cope for they were assailed on all sides and they fled leaving horses and dead troopers littering the road.

"Sound recall!" We could not afford to go running off after the survivors. "Collect weapons, balls, powder and horses and then let's get down the road. Sergeant Dale, take four men as a rear guard. I want to know as soon as you see any danger."

"Sir!"

We had been lucky. We had a few wounds and six of the Neapolitan cavalry had died when they had continued charging past the recall but that was a small price to pay. The Chasseurs had left far more of their men dead. It took ten minutes to collect all that we could. "Saddle up and let's head for Reggio."

We were a weary band of horsemen when we finally limped into Reggio. The men we had sent back awaited us with the Indiaman which had brought us across. Marines guarded it to prevent other refugees from claiming a berth. A lieutenant from 'Britannia' was with the marines. "Thank God you made it sir. We were getting worried."

I pointed behind me. "There will not be many more. I do not think the French will be too close yet." I smiled, "We let them know there were British troops in Italy and discouraged them." I watched as more Neapolitans were allowed aboard one of the other transports. "How many have you taken off?"

"So far almost two thousand. It was a good job you sent the message when you did. We were able to bring more ships over." He lowered his voice, "So Italy is lost."

"I am afraid so and the men you have seen are all that remains of their army."

"Good God!"

"Quite. And now, lieutenant, I will get my men aboard the ship."

Chapter 15

This time there was no reception party for us. This was no dramatic rescue or victory to be celebrated. This was a disaster. True we had pulled many men from the jaws of defeat but we had barely hurt the French. I suspected that we had probably killed as many men as the whole of the Neapolitans and their army. I wondered what had happened to the general. I had seen no one above the rank of captain on the retreat to Reggio. Was he a prisoner or was he dead like Colonel Sciarpa?

The ships had been arriving in Messina for days and the initial shock and interest had waned. We disembarked to an empty quay. "Lieutenant Jackson, take the troop back to Giuseppe's. I will report to the General. Sergeant Sharp, come with me." As we rode through the quiet streets I asked Sharp about his first experience of independent command. "Well Alan, how was it commanding men on your own?"

"I was worried at first but once we got started it was fine. A real change eh sir?"

"How do you mean?"

"Well sir, when you first saw me in the inn I was like a frightened little rabbit; I was scared of my own shadow. I'd like to thank you, sir. You have made me a different person."

"No Alan, I have just helped you become the man you were meant to be. We all have different roads to take. Yours just took a little longer to reach your destination." I reflected that but for Jean, Albert and Pierre I might have taken a different direction too. Everyone who touched us affected us in some way. I suppose that was why I was the officer I was. I knew that even a casual word from me could have a profound effect on someone else. I had learned to choose my words carefully.

The sentry at the camp entrance snapped his heels together smartly and smiled at me. "You had us all worried again sir. The General will be glad to see you."

The General was in his tent and I was ushered in immediately. He gestured to a seat and poured me a glass of brandy. I told him of the events of the past few days. He shook his head, "A total disaster. Couldn't have gone any worse." He looked up as though suddenly aware of the implied criticism. "Not you, of course. If you hadn't sent the message then we wouldn't have got those troops off. They might not be much use but at least we have a couple of thousand men to begin to build an army." He leaned back. "I had been ready to take my men over but now…"

I nodded, "The pass and town could have been held but General de Damas made the mistake of assuming that the French would be put off by mountains." I drank some of the brandy. It burned as it went down. I was not used to spirits. "May I speak frankly sir?"

"Of course."

"The Neapolitans are brave lads. I gathered some of their cavalry on the retreat and they fought as well as my lads. The problem is that they don't seem to have any training. They are all for show. They have dirty muskets and they can barely fire two rounds a minute. If you want my suggestion, get the king to agree to let some of our sergeants drill and train their men."

"That is a good idea. We will not be getting any reinforcements soon. This is a forgotten war. England is not being threatened from here and the politicians are trying to save money, as they always do." He suddenly seemed to notice my appearance. "You look tired. Get back to your camp and take a day or so off. It will take me time to come up with a plan for his majesty. If you could write a report then I can send it to England." He stood as I did.

"You will have it by evening sir."

He leaned across and shook my hand. "By the way thank you for Sergeant Seymour. He translated quite well. I have Lieutenant Stuart learning the language now." He shook his head, "It is about time he started earning his pay over here." He smiled, "I have even learned a couple of words too. It's funny; they seem to think it is a good thing. They are strange these foreigners."

As I rode back to the camp I wondered what he would say if he knew that I was a foreigner.

We spent the next two days in camp. The horses needed recovery as did the men and I had reports to write. I also had mail.

There was a letter from Colonel Selkirk. It had some misinformation for me to use in my next report for Bessières. I had almost forgotten that I was still working for the enemy. I used the time given to me by the General to encode my second report.

I was summoned, three days after my return, to Messina. I took the opportunity of visiting the port. I found Captain Dinsdale's ship in port but he was not on board; he was at the estate. I left a message with the deck watch that I would return to see him in the evening.

General Stuart had convened a meeting with the senior officers. Along with Captain Sillery, I was the most junior there but, ironically, the only one who had fought the French or had any experience of Calabria. Lieutenant Stuart was at his side with pen and paper, taking notes and there was a map on the wall.

The General stood and smiled, "Could I mention, before we start, the sterling service performed again by Captain Matthews. His action was the only positive point in the whole debacle of the recent retreat."

There was a rumble of approval and smiles from the other officers. Captain Sillery patted my back and said, "Well done. Next time I shall come with you!"

"Now I have been asked by both Horse Guards and the King of Naples to begin to plan for a return to Calabria. Gentlemen, we are not ready yet. We need more information about the terrain and the disposition of the enemy. Captain Matthews has suggested that we use our sergeants to train up the Neapolitan soldiers who fled Italy. There are now three thousand of them. I think that this is a good idea. I would like one sergeant from each of the three branches to be sent to me tomorrow. They will be detached for a month." I heard a murmur run around the others. The General held up his hand. "That should tell you that I do not intend to do anything for at least a month." I sensed the frustration around the room. The rest of the force had been cooling its heels for months now and they had another month to try to occupy their soldiers.

There was a hubbub of noise and the General rapped the map irritably with his hand. "Gentlemen!" Quiet descended. "Captain

Matthews, would you be so good as to come here and point out the
route you took when you retreated and give us your views on the
terrain. Yours are the only eyes which have seen the land and we
would all value you your opinion."

I walked to the front and stood next to the map. "This is a land
filled with tiny valleys and high mountains. Unless you have
mountain guns of good horse artillery it will take you forever to get
anywhere. It takes forever to get from one place to another. Reggio
is a handy port for Messina but not for anything else." I pointed to
a spot some hundred miles north and close to the narrow part of the
country. Here is a better base for operations, the Gulf of
Sant'Eufemia. The lower part of Calabria; the toe can be cut off..."

Before I could go any further a marine lieutenant burst in, "Sir,
the admiral sent me. It is urgent."

I could see that Sir John was irritated but he waved at the man,
"Go on then. Tell me."

"Sir, the French have occupied Reggio!"

Every eye swivelled towards me as though I was some sort of
fortune-teller. Sir John said, "Thank you, lieutenant. You are
dismissed."

"Well, gentlemen that makes things interesting. At least we
know where we stand now; alone. Carry on with your assessment
Captain Matthews."

"The French are still besieging a city in the north of the
country, Gaeta, and they have limited men available to control
Calabria. They will be spread out thinly. There is a plain here. We
saw it when we escorted the Queen south. It makes movement
easier and then the narrow passes around the plain," I pointed with
my finger at each one, "give us the option of moving in many
directions and keeps the French guessing where we are."

I quickly sat down before I could be asked any further
questions. Colonel Kempt stood, "An excellent assessment." He
strode to the map and jabbed a large finger at the plain. "What we
need is more intelligence about the French here. Since the captain
rode through, the French may have fortified the area. We cannot
land where French soldiers are dug in. Can't be done!"

"Perhaps we could send in a frigate?" Colonel Cole obviously felt he ought to make a contribution.

Sir John shook his head, "It would only be able to report on the coast and we need to know what sort of defences they have inland. No, we need eyes on the ground."

It was uncanny. Every face turned towards me.

Sir John smiled, "I think there is only one person for this task. How many men would you need Captain Matthews?"

I sighed, "Just four, sir, including me."

"Good. You have a month but I suspect it will not take you that long. We will send you in a frigate or some other small ship and land you at night. It will take me a day or so to arrange that. Should give you plenty of time to organise your troop eh?"

"Sir, with respect, a sloop or a brig would be better. Frigates tend to be high profile and the Navy never has enough of them. The boat which drops us would need to come back regularly at particular times in case we need picking up." Sir John's face was blank. "Sir, they have Reggio and I would need to return to Sicily."

The penny dropped, "Quite. I can see we have the right man for the job. You have thought this through well and quickly too." I did not tell him that I had done this sort of thing before and knew the pitfalls and problems that might present themselves.

"And it might be better if we did not travel in uniform."

"A little risky, Captain Matthews. If you are captured you will be shot as a spy."

"As opposed to being kept prisoner by a half-starved army. I think we will take our chances in civilian clothes."

"So you will be asking for volunteers?"

"That is the way I work, sir."

"Extraordinary." He shook his head. "Well, you do as you think best and I will try to get you a sloop."

Riding back I mentioned our mission to Sharp. "Well, you have one volunteer sir, me."

"Are you sure, Alan?"

He laughed, "The first time we did this sort of thing I was petrified but the more times we do it the more confident I get. You'll need to have two more men who can speak a bit of Italian."

"That will restrict the number of potential volunteers."

In the end, it didn't. I had twenty men who all swore that they could speak Italian if not like a native then as near as made no difference. Sergeant Seymour was very keen but I pointed out that he would have to train up the Neapolitan cavalry. He looked like he might argue, "Listen, sergeant, the very qualifications you say you have for this mission are exactly the ones I need for the Neapolitan cavalry. Sergeant Grant's Italian isn't good enough yet and so it has to be you."

I also chose Troopers Rae and Cartwright. Trooper Rae's wound had healed and they had both shown themselves to be level headed. I rode to my cousin Cesar's house and took some of my old clothes. He found some others for my three men. I handed him the report for Colonel Selkirk and asked it Matthew Dinsdale could drop it in at one of the three ports.

He smiled, "That will not be a problem. He has found a ready market for our goods in those ports. He just has to avoid the customs officials. This Continental blockade works in our favour." He took the letter and placed it in his locked chest. "What will you do for horses, Roberto?"

"I don't know yet."

He took a piece of paper and a pen. He began to draw a simple map. "The place you are landing is roughly here?" I nodded. "Then about two or three miles inland, on a small ridge is the village of Maida. One of my old friends and business associates lives there. He has a villa overlooking the town." He handed me his spare signet ring, the one formerly worn by Sir John. "I should have given you this before; you are joint-heir. Show this to Vincente and he might be able to get you some horses." He smiled, "You may have to pay…."

"Don't worry I have funds."

"You should not be using your own money."

I laughed, "It isn't!"

Two days later I was summoned to Sir John Stuart's headquarters. "We have a sloop for you, the Heron. She is captained by a young lieutenant who seems keen for action; name of Hill. I believe he is related to General Rowland Hill although why he should join the navy is beyond me. You have him for three weeks. He is waiting for you right now in Messina harbour. I could not manage to persuade the Royal Navy to let me have it for longer. It seems they are in great demand. I only managed to get it for three weeks when I said it was for you. You have made somewhat of an impression on the admiral." He handed me a bag of silver coins. "You may need to cover some expenses over there. Try to keep an account eh?"

As I headed back to Giuseppe's farm I could not help contrasting the two systems. Bessières gave you a generous amount of money to get the job done while the British gave you pennies and expected you to account for each one. If we ever defeated Napoleon it would be because of the calibre of the men and not the pay.

I was not worried about French spies watching us leave and reporting. They would have no idea where we were going. Our goodbyes were brief. There was nothing more to tell either Lieutenant Jackson or Sergeant Grant. I left my Austrian sword in my tent and took a French one we had captured. I also took two French pistols. We rode to the harbour escorted by the four men who would return with our horses. Corporal Richardson led them. "Make sure Badger eats well and gets plenty of exercise."

"Don't you worry, Captain Matthews. He is a pleasure to look after. I envy you. He is the best horse in the regiment" That was the biggest compliment he could pay.

Lieutenant Hill must have been watching for our arrival. He waved us on board. "You must be Captain Matthews?"

"Yes Lieutenant and you must be Hill."

"Let's get you below and we can cast off." He looked at our uniforms. "Are you going ashore dressed like that?"

I laughed. "No, we will change once we are underway."

I had almost forgotten how small sloops and brigs were. We were given the Lieutenant's cabin, the largest on the boat and we still had to take it in turns to change. Sicily was a dot on the horizon when we reached the deck. The First Mate was steering. He was an ancient sailor who looked old enough to be my grandfather. His features looked to have been chiselled out of oak. The Lieutenant, by contrast, made Lieutenant Jackson look old.

He grinned when he saw me appraising him. "Don't worry sir. I am old enough! I just look young."

"Sorry, Mr Hill; that was rude of me."

"Not at all. I get it all the time."

"Someone told me that your father is a famous general."

"He is, Daddy Hill."

"Then why the Navy?"

"If I had joined the army I would never have known if I was treated well or badly because of my father. The Navy is different. I am viewed as a sailor and judged accordingly. Is your father in the army?"

"My father never served in the British Army or the Royal Navy. I am the first."

"Then you have done well to achieve so much without a sponsor." I kept silent; Colonel Selkirk was my secret. "Tell me is it true that you rescued the Queen of Naples and had to fight through a French Division?"

I laughed, "Don't believe everything you hear. I did rescue the Queen but there was only one squadron of French Cavalry chasing us."

"Still... exciting eh?"

"You could say that. Now let's get down to details. You know that you will need to return to the place you dropped us?"

"Yes sir but they didn't say how often."

"Every three days should be sufficient. If you come after dark we will try to be on the beach at midnight. We will signal with a lamp. We will flash the light three times with a pause between, three times."

"Nine flashes?"

"That's right. We will count to a hundred and repeat. If you are there then just flash three times. We will see it. Do not wait more than an hour. If an enemy ship comes and you are in danger then flee."

"Don't you worry Captain, since Trafalgar the French had nothing bigger than a rowboat south of Toulon. That is why Sicily is as safe as the Isle of Wight at the moment."

"Good, then everything is in order. You can store our uniforms for us until we return."

He looked a little embarrassed, "Er, what if you haven't returned after three weeks?"

I saw the First Mate watching and listening. I said, flatly, "Then we will either be dead or captured and in these clothes that amounts to the same thing."

"Oh. And I thought that this was going to be an exciting adventure."

"It will be. It is just that there is a great deal of risk involved. How long will it take us to get there?"

"We are a fast little boat. We could be there by nightfall. If not we will wait offshore." He pointed to the masthead pennant. "The wind is with us. Bigger ships would take a couple of days and a convoy, three days. I will try to get you there as soon as possible."

I nodded. I was glad that I had asked for a sloop now. "We will go below if you don't mind and I will consult our map. We all need to memorise it."

The four of us stood in the cramped captain's cabin. "The map stays on board the ship. You need to memorise it. We will have to remember what we see and, when we return, we will add to this map with any details." I explained the signalling system. "If anything untoward happens to me then Sergeant Sharp is in charge and I want the three of you to get back with the crucial information." They looked dubious. "That is an order! This mission is more important than any one man."

I took out the bag of coins given to me by the general and I divided it up between the three of them. "Here are some Italian and French coins. Use them if you need to. While we are together I will pay for any necessities but we may be separated." I looked at them all in turn. "You have been chosen for your linguistic abilities but, more importantly for your ability to think for yourself and not panic. They will be vital over the next week or so."

When we were changed I checked the weapons we would have. I made sure they each had a couple of knives as well as a short sword. We had no holsters in the civilian get up but we each jammed one in our belts. We looked more like pirates than soldiers.

We spent the next couple of hours poring over the map. I felt happy that I could draw it again from memory. "Now we will head for this Maida place and try to find a villa and someone called Vicente. He may be able to help us. If not then we will be walking."

I heard the call of 'Land Ho'. "Well lads let's go on deck. We are here."

The air was wafting warm breezes from the shore and the land was in darkness. As we stepped on to the deck I saw the setting sun behind us. I turned to see the last rays touching the beach of the deserted Gulf of Sant'Eufemia. Once again we were stepping into the lion's den. This time, however, we were without the protection of a uniform. I hoped I was doing the right thing.

Chapter 16

Lieutenant Hill took us as close as he could get to the beach and the four sailors only had a few hundred yards to row. The sun had set some time earlier and the land surrounding the beach was pitch black. Then one of the sailors who rowed our boat said, "Don't you worry lads, Mr Hill is a good 'un. He won't let you down. We'll be here when you need us."

Lieutenant Hill obviously had the loyalty of a crew and that was no small achievement in one so young. Sergeant Sharp and I had been dropped on a hostile shore before now but the other two had not and I saw them draw closer together as the boat, and our friends disappeared into the dark.

"Right lads, follow me."

We trotted across the sand and up the grassy slope which led to Maida. I had taken a rough bearing from the ship but I assumed we would soon smell the wood fires of the town and the people who lived therein. Maida was the only sizeable town in the area and would be a good indicator of the presence of the French. If they had occupied it then we were in trouble. Once we left the beach then movement was easier. I found a rough track which we followed. Once we reached the solid ground we made good time. The track wound beyond the river towards the ridge ahead.

Suddenly we heard voices and I waved the men behind some wild olive trees beside the road. We huddled close to the ground and listened. They were French voices! They appeared to be approaching from the track to our right. We could not see them for the undergrowth and the dark. I slipped my stiletto out in case it came to a fight.

"Jean, get a move on; you lazy bastard."

"I hope the next house has more money and jewels. That last one was as poor as a church mouse."

"Do not keep complaining, Marius. We now have some decent shoes, full bellies and those last women weren't bad."

"I'd rather have money and jewels than soft skin. I want to end this war richer than I started it!"

The voices disappeared. From the noise of the feet and the time it took to pass us, I guessed that there were six men. I assumed that they were soldiers. One question was answered already; there were French soldiers in the area. Another question, more important, remained: how many were there? If these six were the only ones then it would not be a problem.

I waited until I was certain that they had moved away. Trooper Rae said, "They were French soldiers sir. I saw the uniform and a musket."

"Right, we have to go carefully now." As well as my sword and my pistol I also had a stiletto I had taken from a dead bandit in the Apennines some years earlier. I checked now that it was tucked securely into the top of my boot. "I want no noise. If we have to deal with any Frenchmen then use knives or your swords."

We moved more slowly now that we knew the enemy was closer than we thought. At the back of mind was the worry that these soldiers did not sound to be under anyone's control. That could be dangerous for everyone. It also meant that they might be alone and that would help us.

We heard the screaming before we saw the house. It was obviously the last, or the first, house in the town. We crouched behind a low wall which ran around some sort of garden and peered at the open door. The windows were also open and we heard screaming from within. There was shouting too and we heard men's voices. Suddenly there were two shouts of pain and the men's voices stopped. A woman ran from the house. Two French infantrymen ran after her. They thrust her to the ground and one of them began to rape her. I felt Trooper Cartwright begin to rise and I restrained him and shook my head. When the animals had finished they dragged her inert body back inside and slammed shut the door.

I stood and signalled for the men to follow me. It was a harsh reality but the six men were occupied and that would enable us to move quicker. Cesar had said the villa we sought overlooked the town and so I headed up a street which climbed from the rest of the town. There were few houses and they all seemed shut up for the night. I wondered why no one had come out at the sound of the screams and the shouts. It seemed strange. Slightly above us, I saw a white wall and behind it a large building. This had to be the villa we sought. The wall was finished to a higher standard than any we had yet seen.

It appeared to be silent but the faint smell of wood smoke suggested occupation. Even more important was the smell of horse manure. Whoever it was had horses. I would happily pay for them but, if I had to, I would steal. I waved Rae and Sharp to go one way around the building while I took Cartwright, around the other.

There appeared to be just one gate, at the front. The wall was high but would not deter someone determined to gain entry. We met the other two at the back of the property. The hill rose steeply from the rear of the shrubs where we sheltered. Sharp pointed, "There are stables around there and there are horses within. I heard them."

"Good."

"Sir, why didn't we help that woman? There were only half a dozen of them."

"Cartwright, do you think for one moment that I enjoyed just walking off?" He shook his head. "We might have been able to take six men silently, but I doubt it and who knows how many others there were. If we get the chance we will deal with those six but we need to know as much as we can first. Understand?"

Looking contrite he nodded, "Sorry sir."

I looked at the wall. It looked easy enough to climb. "Rae, Cartwright, give me a boost over the wall. Sharp you follow me."

I put my feet in their cupped hands and they hoisted me to the top of the wall. I lay flat along it. I could see that this was an overgrown part of the garden. It was a large walled area and the rest looked to be well kept. Lady Luck had brought us to this perfect place to enter unseen.

The house looked to be thirty yards away and the back was in darkness. As Sergeant Sharp joined me at the top of the wall I pointed to the building and then rolled down into the scrub. I slipped down the wall and made my way to the back door.

Suddenly there was a shaft of light as it opened. I froze and hoped that the others were hidden. A man's head appeared. He looked around and then turned back inside. "I can see no one, Don Vicente…"

As the door closed I felt a sense of relief wash over me. This was the right place. We had some luck at last. I signalled for Rae to go around the side of the house and watch. I sent Cartwright to the front. With Sergeant Sharp watching my back I was ready to enter. I had not planned on doing this just yet but the presence of the French in the village meant that we needed somewhere to hide. It was a risk but one which we would now have to take.

I tried the handle of the door and it moved easily. Pushing it quietly open I slipped inside. It was the kitchen of the villa and I could see light emanating from rooms deeper in the house. I kept my hands away from my weapons as I moved forward. I could hear voices to my left. I headed down a cool corridor and the voices grew louder. It was an argument about the noises in the village. One voice was telling someone to stop panicking.

The door where the conversation was taking place was open. I took a breath and stepped in. There were two men; one was the older man who had peered from the doorway and the other was a well dressed and well-fed man in a silk robe. They stared at me as I entered. I took in that they had no weapons and I spread my arms to show that I came in peace.

"I am Don Roberto of Sicily and I have been sent by your old friend Don Cesar Alpini."

There was a pause and then the older man leapt at me in an attempt to punch me. By Italian standards he was tall but I was bigger. I stepped to one side and pushed him slightly so that his momentum made him crash to the floor.

"I have come in peace. There is no need for this. If you want me to leave I will do so."

The other man snapped, "Antonio, behave yourself." The big man began to rise. Casting me hateful looks. He looked at me. "How do I know that you come from Don Cesar?"

I showed him my right hand with the ring. He nodded, "However, you could have killed him and taken his ring."

I smiled. "In which case, I could kill you just as easily." I saw the fear on his face. I held up my hand. "But you are safe. Let me see what other proof could I offer? Ah, I know. Did you ever visit his home?"

"I have been there many times."

"Then you know that he shared the house with Sir John, the Knight of St.John." He nodded and looked a little more relaxed about me. "I am the relative of both men."

He smiled, "You said, 'shared'; has anything happened to Sir John?"

"It saddens me to tell you that he is dead."

"I am sorry for your loss and you are welcome. Antonio, get some refreshment for our guest." Antonio gave me a glare and pushed past me to go to the kitchen. "You must excuse Antonio. He has cared for me for many years. Tell me, you are not Sicilian, are you? I can tell from your accent."

"No, I am half Scottish."

"I thought so. Then why do you dress yourself with a borrowed title?"

"It is not borrowed. The King and Queen bestowed the honour upon me for a service I performed."

His face lit up, "You are the one who rescued her Majesty from the French. Even here in this little backwater, we heard the tale." He pumped my hand up and down. "As a loyal Neapolitan, can I thank you, sir? That is why my servant was worried, he had heard French voices."

"He is correct. We saw them too. There are at least six soldiers and they are pleasuring themselves with the women of the town. I have three men outside. They are watching for the French. "

Just then the front door opened and Rae and Cartwright burst in. "Sorry about this sir but the six Frenchmen we saw are heading up the road. I think they are coming here."

Antonio came in with his hands aloft followed by Sergeant Sharp who held a pistol to his back. "Sorry sir, he tried to punch me!"

I looked at Don Vicente. "Well? Do we fight or hide?"

"I am an important man I will be safe. You and your men hide in the dining room." He pointed to a door which led off from the main room. "I will get rid of them."

We ducked into the room. I did not close the door but left it ajar. "Sorry, sir. He caught me unawares."

"Don't worry Alan. It will be fine. All of you, get your weapons ready. Don Vicente may have confidence that his position will save him but I am not certain."

There was a banging at the door which suddenly crashed open. "What is the meaning of this?" I heard a strangled scream and then Don Vicente shouted, "Why have you killed my servant? He..."

There was the sound of a blow and crash and then I heard French voices. "What was he jabbering about?"

"I don't think he liked what you did to his friend."

"Couple of old queers. Well, lads, this looks like our billet. Search the place. We might as well make ourselves comfortable before the other lads get here. Once the officers spot this they will claim it for their own."

"That means we will only have it for a couple of days."

"Flat nose, you are a moron! We will have cleared all the good stuff from the village by then and hidden it. We just need a few days. When this war is over we will be rich men. Now search the rooms. I am going upstairs to find the bedrooms. These rich men like to keep their stuff there."

"What do we do with this one? Slit his throat?"

"Nah we might need him to tell us where the stuff is. Flat Nose, you watch him. The rest of you search the house."

I tapped Sharp on the shoulder and motioned for him to stand behind the door. I stood on the open side. A French soldier entered. Rae grabbed his gun and I put my hand across his mouth and slit his throat. The warm blood gushed down my hand. We lowered his body to the ground and I peered through the open door. Flat Nose was bent over Don Vicente and was searching him. In one motion I slipped open the door and strode across to the unsuspecting robber. Putting my bloody hand over his mouth I stabbed him up through his ribs. His body juddered and shook and then fell still. I dropped the body to the ground. We lifted Don Vicente on to a chair and made sure he was breathing. He looked to have been hit in the mouth with the butt of a musket. Poor Antonio lay bleeding on the marble floor.

I signalled for Rae and Cartwright to go to the kitchen while I led Sergeant Sharp towards the stairs. I put the stiletto in my left hand and drew my sword. I kept my shoulder to the wall as I climbed the stairs. I kept peering above me for a sight of the enemy. We should be evenly matched now but they had muskets. I assumed they would have bayonets fitted. In a fight, they would have the advantage over swords.

We had just reached the landing when there was a shout and a scream from the kitchen. A soldier leapt from a bedroom with a surprised expression on his face and a levelled musket. He saw me and shouted, "Jean!" At the same time, he lunged at me with his musket. I turned the bayonet with my stiletto and plunged my blade into his chest. Sharp pulled the body down the stairs and we leapt up to the landing.

The three men all erupted from the bedrooms at the same time. The sergeant raised his musket to fire. I rolled over as the gun cracked smoke and flame. The discharge singed my head. As I rose I stabbed with my sabre and felt it enter his groin and, as I stood, rip him open. He fell to the ground trying to push his entrails back into his body. I turned to face another attacker and found myself looking down the barrel of a musket. There would be no escaping this ball. There was a loud boom and then, miraculously, the musket and the dead soldier fell. Behind him, I saw Rae with a smoking pistol.

"Sorry, sir. It was my fault that the Frog screamed."

"Thank you, Rae, and don't worry. You just saved my life." All six were dead. "Sergeant Sharp, go down to the town, take Cartwright with you. See if there are any more French around. Rae, you get the bodies out of the villa we will need to dispose of them."

"We'll give you a hand." Sharp and Cartwright carried a body down the stairs. Trooper Rae took the second while I searched the sergeant. He was Sergeant Jean Moreau of the forty-second light infantry regiment. He had written orders to secure Maida and find accommodation for the rest of his company under the command of Captain Lapiste. He also had a large number of coins. Sergeant Moreau obviously believed in free enterprise. I pocketed the coins and dragged his body to the front of the villa. Rae had just completed the gory task of removing all the bodies.

"Keep watch and I will see to Don Vicente."

I grabbed a bowl of water and a cloth. I began to bathe his face. His nose looked to be broken and was out of shape. As he was still unconscious I decided to try to straighten it. I had seen it done before after soldier's fights. The repaired nose would never be perfect but it would not be so obviously damaged. As I twisted it into shape I felt his body move. I began to dab his face with cold water. The eyes flickered and then burst open.

"Antonio!"

"Dead, I am afraid, Don Vicente." I pointed to his body.

He tried to rise but I restrained him. "And the animals who did this?"

"They too are dead. Their bodies are outside. My men are checking the rest of the buildings but I think these six were working alone." He closed his eyes and sank back into his chair. "More French soldiers will be coming. We will need to hide the evidence of the fight."

"Why?"

"The French will not listen to our story. They will not believe that their men were rapists and robbers. Maida will be put to the sword."

"You are right and thank you for what you have done. Had you not been here then I would now be dead. Fortune sent you."

I smiled, "I will tell my cousin Cesar of his new name."

Don Vicente laughed and then stopped, "Oh that hurt."

"They broke your nose. I have tried to re-set it but I am no doctor."

Trooper Rae returned. "The Sarge is back sir. His face is as black as thunder."

Both soldiers looked angry when they entered. Sergeant Sharp snapped, "Those bastards died too quickly."

"Calm down Alan, "Tell us what you saw."

"We found half a dozen houses where they had been sir. The men had been butchered and the women and kids... well, sir, it's not right what they did."

"But there were only half a dozen houses which had been entered?"

"Yes, sir. It looks like they were working their way up here. All the rest have shut their doors. Even when we said we were friends they wouldn't open them. The women who survived are all hiding in the house of one of them. A big woman called Emilia. She was looking after them."

Don Vicente nodded, "She is a good woman. Emilia is the one who delivers the babies in the village. She knows how to care for people. Do not worry, they will all talk to us in the morning." He was now in control of things. "Well Scotsman, what shall we do?"

I pointed to the blood. "We need that clearing up and then the bodies burning."

"We have a place at the back where we burn rubbish." He looked at Antonio. "I think they qualify."

"Cartwright you clean up in here. Sharp, Rae, we'll burn the bodies. Put anything that won't burn in a pile and we'll find somewhere to get rid of it."

I went to the body of Antonio but Don Vicente restrained me, "He was my friend. I will see to him."

By the time morning came the house had been cleaned, Antonio buried and the bodies were a diminishing pile of burning ashes. Don Vicente said, "They will do good now that they are dead. They will fertilise the grapes and olives."

I pointed to the weapons and metal objects we had saved. "Now, sir. We will have to get rid of these. Have you horses?"

He nodded, "Three of them."

"Good. Alan, you stay here." I could see his objection written all over his face. "Your Italian is better than these two and Don Vicente will need you."

I would take the opportunity of adding to our knowledge of the area while disposing of the evidence. I had decided to draw a map now. We knew how long we had to scout this particular area and a piece of written evidence would be more use than a hazy memory. We rode back to the sea and found a cliff where the sea surged against the rocks. We hurled the guns, swords and unburned pieces of uniform as far as we could. They disappeared beneath the blue water

As we rode a long circuit back to the villa Trooper Rae asked. "Won't the French be suspicious when they arrive?"

"Probably but they get a lot of deserters and I think that the six we killed will have a reputation. However, you may be right and I would not like to be here when they arrive. We have two, perhaps three days at the most." I waved my arm around the bay. "This looks perfect for a landing and we know that Maida will welcome the General. What we need to do is to find out if there is anyone close to us."

I took us in a wide circle around Maida and we searched the area for a five-mile radius. We found no sign of the enemy and only a few isolated farms and houses. They all remained shuttered when we approached.

It was after noon when we reached Maida and I saw a large crowd in the square. Don Vicente was standing on a cart with Sergeant Sharp watching his back. As our hooves sounded on the cobbles everyone looked around in fear.

"These men are the ones who saved me." The crowd erupted in cheers. Don Vicente looked at me. "Well?"

"There is no one close."

"Good. I have explained that the French will be returning. They are all set on revenge but I have persuaded them that it would be better to pretend that the six never came here."

I felt guilty for I had deliberately not told Cesar's friend that the British were coming. I did not want a careless whisper jeopardising Sir John's invasion. "That is good." I addressed them all. "You will need to hide all valuables and food for the French will take whatever you have. You have some days to do this. It might well be that they move somewhere else if there is nothing to be had here." I saw the nods from many of the crowd. This was something positive they could do.

Don Vicente said, "Please, use my villa. I will be with my people. We have to bury the dead."

"I understand."

The four of us returned to the villa. After we had stabled and fed the horses we entered the cool building. "I don't know about you sir but I am starving."

"So am I. You two get some food on the go. Alan, come with me. We need to begin to make a map."

We spent the next hour drawing a map of the area and I put down all the features which I thought would be useful to Sir John. The villa had a good aspect and we were able to see for miles. The map was far better than most maps we had created before. It took us a couple of hours to finally complete it to my satisfaction but I knew that it would help Sir John Stuart to plan his campaign. By the time we had finished the smell of food had driven work from our minds and we sat in the garden of this beautiful villa in the shade of lemon trees drinking some good wine and eating a simple meal. It was hard to believe that less than a day ago there had been a bloodbath not far from where we ate. Such was life in 1806 in a war-torn Italy.

Chapter 17

When Don Vicente returned we were exhausted and ready for sleep but it was important that we talked. He poured us each a glass of his best wine. "Thank you for saving our people and now, Don Roberto of Sicily, would you like to tell me what brought you here. I do not believe you came just to save my life."

"I am a captain of cavalry and these are my men. We are here to find out the French dispositions."

"You are spies."

"Yes." There was little point in denying it.

"If you are found out of uniform you will be shot." Why did everyone have to keep harping on about that? I nodded and sipped my wine. "Good, you are honest as well as brave. How can I help?"

"You already have. We need a base for the next day or so. Do not worry we will leave before the French arrive but with the three horses of yours we can cover a lot of territory. I will leave one man here each day in case there are any more unwanted visitors."

He nodded, "The men in the village are preparing to defend themselves. Some of them fought in the militia and they are armed."

I shook my head. "They should not act hastily. The French can be ruthless believe me. Better to hit them in small groups when they are isolated but even that is risky for there will be reprisals."

"But the Neapolitan Army is finished and if those six are a measure of what we can expect then better to die fighting than see our women and children abused."

I had no argument to that. "We will leave in the morning and remember to hide your valuables. I will be leaving Trooper Cartwright tomorrow he will help you." I saw the disappointed look on his face. "And perhaps you can improve his Italian."

I let Sergeant Sharp take Trooper Rae to scout the south and east while I went alone to the north and east. They were less than happy about that but I brooked no argument. I rode hard towards the mountains in the north. It was as I remembered from the two other visits I had made. There was a wall of rock and narrow passes with few houses and farms. As I headed east in the afternoon, I reflected that Maida was the largest town in the region. If Sir John could hold that he would be able to stop troops from getting to the toe of Italy and Reggio.

I pushed both my horse and my luck. I could see the sea ahead of me. This was the narrowest part of Italy. I knew that there was a town ahead of me but I had no idea of its size. It was a shock when Cathanzario loomed up, almost from the sea. It was a larger town than Maida and had defences. Even more importantly the French tricolour flew from the walls. The French were there.

Even though it was late I knew that I needed to find out how many men there were there. Could this be where the Light Infantry we had killed were based? I rode as close to the walls as I could get without being seen and I sheltered in an olive grove close to the gate. I dismounted and pretended to be attending to the hooves of my horse. I kept glancing at the gate to see who was using it. There were no guards, which was a good thing. There were also people pushing carts and trudging out. It looked as though there had been a market for those leaving were laden with food. That in itself was interesting. It meant that there was not a large French garrison or else they would have confiscated it all.

I was just about to risk entry when I saw two monks come from the town and they were carrying two amphorae of what looked like olive oil. They were struggling. I watched them pass me and head west down the road I had used. I mounted and left the olive grove to follow them. When I caught up with them I halted, "Brothers that oil looks heavy." I dismounted, "If we are going the same way perhaps my horse could bear the load?"

They looked at each other and then nodded. The older one said, "Thank you, my son." They tied the amphorae on either side of the horse and I began to lead it. "Where are you headed for, my son?"

I waved vaguely towards the south-west, "To Reggio. I hope to get a boat to Sicily. And you father, where are you headed?"

"Our monastery is up the hill. We will leave you in a few miles but this is kind of a stranger and a foreigner to boot." He appraised me with a shrewd look. I became alert. He had recognised that I was not Italian. "Were you in the town?"

I decided on a version with some honesty in it. "No, father for I saw the French flag and I have no love for the French."

He saw my sword, "You were a soldier?"

"Something like that."

"We were told that the armies of Naples were destroyed."

I nodded, "They were beaten but many escaped."

He took that information in. "You could have gone into the town. There were but ten French horsemen in green uniforms there and they were busy drinking in the square. I think they were on holiday!"

So there were Chasseurs there and the French Light Infantry was elsewhere. "Even so it might have caused trouble."

"A thoughtful soldier; how refreshing." Again he gave me a look which made me think that he was not all that he seemed. "You are not Neapolitan, are you?"

"No, I am not." I ventured nothing more and he changed the subject.

We chatted about the monastery, the area and the climate until the brother said, "Here is where we leave you, my son. Thank you for your kindness." He made the sign of the cross over me, "I pray that you will stay safe."

Once they had disappeared from sight I mounted my horse and rode hard, taking the fork to the right. I had no reason to distrust the monks but I could afford to take no chances Besides some of the monk's questions had been too pointed for my liking and they had unnerved me slightly. As I rode home I began to imagine all sorts of plots and intrigues. I was becoming too much like Colonel Selkirk and concocted plots behind every bush. It was well past sunset when I reached the villa and Sergeant Sharp was watching anxiously for me.

"Sir, where have you been? We were worried."

I smiled, "And you are now my mother, sergeant? Don't worry. The nearest Frenchmen are twenty miles away and there are just ten of them."

Once inside, with the horses attended to I fell upon the food they had for me. While I ate they reported on what they had seen. "We saw no sign of Frenchmen for twenty miles around."

"And I had the same experience. Except when I headed for Cathanzario; I discovered that there are ten Chasseurs there. They are close enough to pay us a visit. We will leave here before dawn and hide near our rendezvous."

"The men of the town could deal with ten horsemen." Don Vicente ventured.

I shook my head, "No, there might be a chance that one could escape and that would bring the wrath of the French upon you. Better that we leave. The next rendezvous will be tomorrow night. If we delay our departure we might be here for another three days and risk capture. From what I have seen there are just two towns in the area which could be defended and my general needs to know that. And," I added, "the King and Queen will need to know of the atrocities committed by the French. It might spur them to action."

"Very well. What do you need from me?"

"Nothing, save some food and an oil lamp to signal."

That evening we spoke of the French and what they had done. Don Vicente had been something of a recluse and the horrors inflicted upon his neighbours had made him resolve to care for them more. "I will start the militia again." He patted his stomach. "Working with the young men might help me to lose this." His face hardened. "If the French come again then they will be given a hot welcome. They will learn to leave our women alone."

It struck me that six soldiers had done more for the British and allied cause than all of General De Damas' Neapolitan Army.

We left the next morning and were seen off by everyone from Maida. They all knew that, but for our presence, the French soldiers would have continued their orgy of destruction. Had we asked we would have gone back laden with food but I knew that they would need it more than we would. I said goodbye to Don Vicente at the edge of the town. "Thank you for your help and perhaps I can visit again in more peaceful times."

"I would like that." There was genuine affection in his smile and the firm grip told me that he meant his words.

As we were on foot we were able to hide more easily than had we been mounted. We kept low and stopped frequently. I had not seen another sign of the French but it would not do to be caught so close to safety. We had a mere five miles to go and we took our time; pausing frequently. We reached the beach just as the sun was dipping beneath the horizon. We gathered wood for a fire but, while the sun set we watched. Lying on the sand we were strangely at peace. It was a beautiful sunset and the red and yellow rays seemed to dance on the water at the edge of the sand. It was hard to believe that violence and destruction had ravaged Maida, just five miles up the road.

It soon became chilly and we lit the fire. I was not worried about the fire being seen. The nearest people were in Maida and they were on our side. Perhaps Lieutenant Hill might see the fire and close with the shore. We finished our food and Sergeant Sharp checked that the lamp functioned effectively. Then we sat to wait. Time seemed to drag. I kept looking at my watch and the hour hand had barely moved.

Rae had just asked, for the umpteenth time, "What time is it, sir?"

I had replied, somewhat irritably, "Ten o'clock. Two hours to go," when Cartwright's sharp ears picked out a noise.

"Horses sir and they are coming fast."

The only friendly horses belonged to Don Vicente and they were unlikely to be his. They had to be the Chasseurs. "Stand to!"

Moving away from the fire, which would have highlighted me, I stuck my sword in the sand and drew my two pistols. The other three had spread out and we all crouched to make smaller targets. It was the French and they hurtled at us screaming obscenities and leaning forward with their swords. We must have looked an easy target. Had I been leading them I would have used firearms first but, thank goodness, the Chasseurs were predictable.

We remained silent. We would be hard to see and any noise we made would draw them to us. If they were the same ones from the town then I knew that there were ten of them. If not then we were in even more trouble. We had to hurt them so much that they would pull back. Of course, that would mean we were still stranded on a beach without the means to escape. The leading rider made straight for Sergeant Sharp. I tracked him with my pistol but Sharp's own pistol cracked out and the rider tumbled from the back of his horse. The flash showed that they were all in one column but, following Sharp's kill, they spread out in a wider line; they were attempting to envelop us. I waited until the trooper who charged me was ten yards away and I could smell his horse. When I fired the trooper's head disappeared. I had to dive to the sand to avoid being trampled by his horse. The dive saved me for a second assailant swung his sabre at the spot my head had occupied a moment earlier. I rolled onto my back and fired at the figure. My ball struck him in the spine and he gave an animalistic scream as he fell to the sand, writhing in agony.

I stood and drew my sword from the sand. The odds were shrinking. It was now seven to four. However, the enemy had horses and my pistols were both empty. I had heard the cracks from the others but I had to focus on my own attackers.

Two horses made for me. The riders came from two sides. I dived to my right and did a roll. The front of the foremost horse brushed my shoulder. As I rose I slashed, more in hope than expectation and caught the horse on the rump. It reared and the unbalanced rider fell to the floor. I pounced upon him. He was quick and deflected my sabre. Out of the corner of my eye, I saw the other rider wheeling to come to his comrade's assistance. I reached down for my stiletto. As I caught the sabre on my sabre I stabbed upwards with the Italian blade and my knife penetrated his heart.

I was panting and out of breath. The sand was sapping my energy. I was aware of the rider hurtling towards me and I saw, in the same instant, Cartwright felled by a sabre. We had come close to safety but we were going to die. Suddenly there was a dull boom and then a sharper crack. I heard the whistling of a cannonball as it flew overhead. Then there was a ripple of muskets from the sea.

There were only a handful of riders left and the cannonballs suggested that we had friends. I heard someone order the Chasseurs to retreat. I ran to Trooper Cartwright. I could see that the wound was mortal. He was coughing up blood. "Sorry I messed up sir. It has been a…" And then he died. I did not even have the chance to tell him that I was proud of him and that he had not messed up.

Lieutenant Hill appeared next to me. "Let's get back to the boat, sir. They may come back."

I knew that they wouldn't but I wanted to be away from the beach anyway. Sergeant Sharp and I picked up our comrade's body and I saw Rae nursing an arm. He shook his head, "Can you believe it, sir. Last time it was my right leg. That gets healed and it is my right arm!"

As we edged away from the shore our rescuer explained. "We arrived early and we waited. We saw the fire lit but weren't sure if it was you or someone else. When we heard the firing and saw the horses I guessed that it had to be you and we rowed ashore. The shot from the cannon was just to let you know someone was coming. It is only a three-pounder." He grinned, "But it worked."

One of the sailors put a piece of tarpaulin over Cartwright's body. "Thank you, sailor."

Hill said, "Sorry about your man."

I shrugged, "He died doing his duty. What more can you ask of a soldier?"

It took two days to reach Sicily, the winds were against us. We decided to bury Trooper Cartwright at sea. He had no family and we would always remember our comrade when we sailed and looked at the water. It seemed fitting.

The other two spent a great deal of time with me on the voyage home. The brush with death had brought us closer. "How do you think the French knew we were here?"

I had wracked my brains for an answer, "The only thing I can think is the monk. He was suspicious of me. Or perhaps the six men we killed were missed and they came looking for them. Either way, we were unlucky and poor Cartwright paid the price."

I think that Lieutenant Hill was a little disappointed that his detached duty had ended so quickly. As we neared Messina he said. "Any time you need a ship, sir. Just ask for me. We have had more excitement in three days than in the last six months. You get fed up of delivering despatches day in day out. That was the first time we have fired our gun in these waters." He shook his head. "I feel more like a man delivering post than a sailor."

"Don't worry Lieutenant, your day will come and I shall inform the admiral what a fine job you did. We owe you our lives."

"I think you would have got out of it somehow sir."

Once we were back in our uniforms we felt more like soldiers and less like bandits. I left the sabres for Lieutenant Hill as a souvenir and he was delighted. The three of us made our way to the General's headquarters. He took in that there were just three of us.

"Trouble, Captain Matthews?"

"We were ambushed on the beach." He frowned, "Don't worry sir we had completed our mission."

He brightened, "It is a good spot then?"

"It is perfect. The country is only twenty or thirty miles wide at that point. There are only a handful of French soldiers. You could control the land as far south as Reggio from there."

He rubbed his hands together. "Excellent. I shall put forward a plan and send it to London."

My face fell, "They may move French troops in by then, sir."

"I know Robert but my hands are tied."

"A waste of a good man's life," I added bitterly.

"Look upon it as shortening the war."

I flung down the map we had drawn. "If we invaded now it would. Men will die because we delay." I stormed out knowing that I had breached etiquette not to mention King's Regulations. I didn't care. I was becoming sick of taking risks and then watching others wait. Perhaps I would be better off with the French and Napoleon. He had acted on my information at Ulm and defeated the Austrians and the Russians.

Sergeant Sharp came up behind me and said, quietly, "Let's get back to the farm sir. A hot bath, some sleep and some food and you'll feel much better." I glanced over my shoulder at the General's tent. "Oh don't worry about him, sir. We explained what went on and he understands." He lowered his voice, "I just wouldn't make a habit of it, sir."

Chapter 18

It felt like going home, returning to Giuseppe's farm. We received a hero's welcome muted by the death of Jeb Cartwright. I saw the looks which Lieutenant Jackson and Sergeant Grant gave me. They were the sort of look you give someone when you know you ought to say something but you don't know what. In a way, I was relieved that General Stuart had to delay the invasion for it gave me and my two companions the chance to recover.

We waited for almost six weeks before we knew that we were going into action. By Horse Guards' standards, this was almost instant but I fretted for I did not know what would have happened in our absence. Had the French-occupied Maida? What would happen to Don Vicente and the people of Maida? Had they fortified the beach? No one had been back so we could not know for certain. As soon as the decision was made I was at the headquarters almost every day. Colonels Kempt and Cole bombarded me with questions about the terrain and the French. Captain Sillery just collared me as I was leaving. "You realise that we are quite likely to be operating together?"

"It normally works that way."

He seemed relieved, "Good. I was worried that you might be like some of the other cavalry officers I have met who think it is a bloody fox hunt and charge after anything in blue shouting, 'View! Halloo'!"

I laughed. That was the stereotypical view of cavalry officers. "As I have never been on a fox hunt in my life I can assure you that I do not run my troop like that."

"I know. You are the oddest cavalryman I have ever met. I am intrigued how you finished up like this."

"Perhaps I am not the finished article and have some way to go eh?"

"Possibly but I shall keep my eye on you, my friend."

When we heard that we were leaving I went to see Cesar. I had told him of the privations of his friend and he thanked me for what I had done.

"By the way, your message was delivered." His impassive face gave nothing away but I knew that he would never betray me.

"We may not be coming back for a while and so I shall keep in touch by letter."

The farewell from Giuseppe was tearful. The farmer and his family had become genuinely fond of my troopers and it was reciprocated. The troopers had helped around the estate and they, in turn, had been treated like family. As we left the Sicilian pointed proudly to his lemons and olives. The fruit bulged. He said in halting English, "Thank you Captain your horse shit has done wonders!" The troopers laughed. They had obviously taught him the words.

We boarded the transports on the twenty-seventh of June and we sailed the next morning. I was delighted to see Lieutenant Hill and his sloop darting around like a collie dog rounding up sheep. It is silly, I know, but I felt safer with such a keen officer watching over us. We would not be surprised by any Frenchmen. It took until July the first to beat up to the bay. Mercifully it was undefended. Perhaps the Chasseurs had assumed they were chasing partisans. Whatever the reason the landing was unopposed. It took all day to land the horses, men, guns and supplies. Most of the horses were lowered over the side and they swam to shore. A couple had to be rowed. I was lucky; Badger swam happily to the beach and waited patiently for me.

As soon as we had landed and saddled up I sent out a skirmish line. This was just to ensure that we landed all the men without interruptions. We saw nothing save the people of Maida peering down at their red-coated allies. The General had decided that we would hold a line north of Maida so that we had mountains to our rear and we were halfway between Cathanzario and Maida. It was a good plan and I was pleased that the people of Maida would not have to suffer the bloodbath of a battle. We had an easy task for there were no French to be seen. The ridge to the north of Maida was perfect. We had a safe place to camp and a good field of fire. Captain Sillery was delighted. By July the second we were ready for the French, should they come, and General Stuart sent for me.

"Captain Matthews, I need you to find the French." We were standing on the ridge facing Maida. "I want to draw this Reynier chap here. And, if you could whittle down his cavalry then that would be useful too."

It seemed simple and yet it was anything but. In effect, we were goading a dangerous dog and attempting to keep out of the range of its savage teeth.

"Right sir." As I led the troop away east I saw that the position he had chosen to defend was a good one. The sea protected one flank and the mountains his rear. So long as he watched the mountains to the east then the solid red line should be able to hold off the French. All I had to do was to find the enemy.

The problem with this part of Italy was that there were no secret ways. You had to use the passes and valleys. They were easy to control. Had the French been more vigilant then they would have seen us. We were lucky. They were neither vigilant nor alert. The ease of their victory had made them complacent. When we neared Cathanzario I left Lieutenant Jackson in charge and rode with Sergeant Sharp to spy out the land. If the French were not here then we would have to head towards Reggio. I used the smaller road which did not go near to the monastery. I was still suspicious of the monks. We emerged behind a stand of trees and we were able to look down on the town while remaining unobserved.

There, below us, we could see a camp of Chasseurs. More importantly, on the other side of the town, I saw the unmistakeable smoke from campfires. There were elements of Reynier's army. It was hard to estimate numbers but logic told me this would be the main part of his army. I surmised that, if the cavalry were present then the bulk of his forces would be too. I had worked out my plan beforehand and, as I looked at the roads and trails, I refined it. "Right Sergeant let's get back to the men. I need to explain what we are going to do."

The troop waited on the hillside above Cathanzario. I moved them until we were at the top of the hill. We could see the camp of the two regiments of Chasseurs. It was where I expected it to be;

196

outside the town and close to water. We were a mile away and could neither be seen not heard. I gathered them around me.

"Men, today we are the only force of British cavalry on the Continent and we are going to take on two regiments of Chasseurs. Many troopers would be daunted by such a task but I know that you will relish the prospect." I grinned, "Taking on ridiculous odds appears to be the only way you know how to fight. We cannot hope to charge them and win. They outnumber us by at least six to one. I have decided that we are going to tire them out and stop them having an influence on the battle up the road today." I saw them nod their approval and grip their weapons a little tighter.

"We are not going to use familiar tactics today so listen carefully. We will ride in a column of twos. Trooper Rae and Bugler Jones will lead. Sergeant Sharp and I will be a third of the way from the rear. Lieutenant Jackson and Sergeant Grant will be at the back." I could see that I now had their interest and their attention.

"You will need to ensure that all of your guns are loaded. We will ride down a small trail over there." I pointed to the trail I had found when scouting the town. "We will ride to the camp and each man will discharge his carbine in turn. We will do this at the closest point to their camp. Rae and Jones will have to judge that. They have a great responsibility." I saw the other troopers looking at the two of them. "When you have fired then head up this road. The Spanish call this the caracole. You need to keep the gun level. Do not aim. Keep the barrel flat across your saddle and you will hit something. It matters not if it is man or beast. You will now see why Bugler Jones and Trooper Rae are leading the column. Bugler Jones must use the bugle and Trooper Rae seems determined to be one-armed." That brought a smile from everyone. "Each pair will do the same. I want the French to chase us. Therefore we will not gallop; we will keep a steady pace. There are fifty pairs of us and it is the ones at the back who will be in the greatest danger." They all looked at the Lieutenant and the Sergeant. Neither man seemed worried.

"I want them to catch us. When they are a hundred paces from us, the last pair will halt, turn and discharge a pair of pistols. They will then gallop up through the middle of the column and lead it. By the time it is One-Armed Rae and Bugler Jones at the back I hope to have discouraged the French enough for us to escape. But, if not, we all have another two pistols." I paused, "Except, of course, Rae and Jones." They smiled again. "We need discipline and trust in each other. Well lads, can you do it?"They all raised their carbines silently and we rode to war.

The plan I had concocted was unusual for me, I was not leading the men but I trusted both Jones and Rae. Trooper Rae carried the guidon. We wanted the enemy to know who we were. The Chasseurs might have been ambushed by us before and I wanted that hunger to get to grips with us. Sharp and I were following two troopers. It did feel strange. When they fired and wheeled, it would be our turn.

I heard the two cracks of two pistols and then the louder noise of the carbines as the men began to fire. The noise seemed to ripple as each pair fired. Then I heard the French drums and bugle; they were calls I remembered. They were calling the camp to arms. By the time we reached the firing point all that could be seen was a pall of smoke. The French were firing back. We fired and wheeled into the thick gunpowder smoke. We had no idea of the effect of our balls. I clipped the carbine to its sling. It would be some time before I needed to use my pistols. We trotted up the road and I heard the crack of carbines behind us. I risked a glance and saw that there were no empty saddles. I had been worried that the French might have organised something quickly. We had obviously taken them by surprise. We reached the rise where we had begun our advance. The horses naturally slowed at the steep part of the road.

"Keep a space between you!" Sharp moved further away from me so that three horses could gallop between us. I heard the thunder of hooves as Sergeant Grant and Lieutenant Jackson charged up between us. They were both grinning like children.

I heard Sergeant Grant. "We have stirred up a proper hornet's nest there sir!" Then they galloped up to the head of the column.

The pairs of troopers came up the road at regular intervals. I counted them. When fourteen had passed I knew that it would be our turn soon. I drew one pistol. I heard the four cracks from behind us and then Hargreaves and Wilson whooped through the middle. I joined Sergeant Sharp and we looked behind us. The French were eighty yards away. I saw one empty saddle indicating a hit by one of the last pair.

We halted and turned. Seeing the officer's uniform the leading riders leaned forward in the saddle to reach us. I had drawn my second pistol and I held them before me. When they were thirty yards away I fired both my pistols followed a heartbeat later by Sharp's two. I grabbed my reins and wheeled Badger around. Sergeant Sharp did the same and soon we caught the others and made our way up the middle of the column.

Four more pairs joined us and then there was a wait. I risked halting the column and I rode back to see where the French were. The last two men looked worried, "Sir, they just stopped and we didn't know what to do."

"Don't worry Corporal Ashcroft. You did what I ordered." I rode back with Sergeant Sharp. Half a mile down the road I saw the remnants of the French cavalry riding back towards Cathanzario. They had had enough. Because my men were halted when they fired they had more chance of hitting the enemy. If the Chasseurs tried that whilst riding them the balls would have been wasted. It had worked. Now we had to draw them on a little further.

"Well, Sergeant Sharp. We have completed the first part of our task. Now is the difficult bit. We have to wait for them to take the bait." We rode back to the column.

"Dismount, reload your weapons and see to your horses. Sergeant Seymour, take a man and watch for the French. Let us know when they resume the chase."

And they did resume the chase. There were at least two squadrons who thundered after Sergeant Seymour. Ten of my troopers fired a volley when they were eighty yards away and then we galloped towards Maida, some five miles hence. It was fortunate that we had rested the horses for they were really trying to catch us. They had fresh horses and would not allow us to halt and fire as we had before. They wanted to get to grips with us and destroy us. As we emerged above Maida and galloped towards our guns I felt some relief that we had done our duty and not lost a man. The Chasseurs reined in and watched as we regained our lines.

I ordered Lieutenant Jackson to see to the men while I reported to General Stuart. "You found them then, Captain?"

"Yes, sir. I could not ascertain numbers but I assume it is Reynier's force." I pointed behind me at the Chasseurs. "I dare say they will report to their general and he will come sometime."

"Excellent. Rest your men. Tomorrow I want a skirmish line the other side of Maida to give us warning of their approach."

The men appreciated the rest as did the horses. High summer in this part of the world was brutal. The horses were permanently sweating and our heavy uniforms, while fine for winter, were not suitable for summer wear. I took the troop along the road beyond Maida. That first day we saw no one. In the middle of the afternoon, I sent two riders towards Cathanzario. They came back with the worst possible news, the French were gone! The problem we now had was to find them. I sent riders back to warn the general and I took the rest of the troop west.

I rode at the front with Sharp and Jones. There were two riders a half a mile ahead of us. The twisting mountain roads were a nightmare for you found yourself coming around blind bends. We were approaching one such obstacle when I heard a pistol shot and the clash of steel. I drew my carbine as did Sergeant Sharp and the riders behind me. Before we had even reached the bend the two riderless horses came galloping towards us telling their own story. The men had been hit. The first three Chasseurs were met by a ragged volley which threw one from his saddle and forced the others to turn and flee, one clutching his arm.

I dropped my carbine and drew my sword. When we reached the bend we met a troop of Chasseurs. Before I could issue any orders we were fighting for our lives. I slashed at the face of the young lieutenant leading them who was eager to show his prowess. He concentrated on striking me which made my task easier. I flicked his sword and my blade ripped open his face like a ripe watermelon. Sergeant Grant shouted, "Open fire!" Ten carbines covered us in smoke. I heard the cries of some French troopers as they were plucked from their saddles. When the smoke cleared they had fled with their wounded. There was little point in pursuing for, beyond the bend, we could see the whole of Reynier's army marching towards Maida. The wily general had marched his men around to arrive at right angles to the British lines. Sir John had his men in the wrong place. We collected the troopers who had been wounded and the dead. "Back to Maida!" We galloped the three miles back to our comrades.

All of Sir John's plans were thrown into disarray. He was facing the wrong direction. I rode directly to him and pointed over my shoulder. "Reynier is less than three miles away. He must have gone to Reggio to collect more men. He is approaching from the south and not the east."

"Have your men form a skirmish line while I get the army moving."

I saw Captain Sillery already limbering up his guns. That was the advantage of Horse Artillery, it was quick! We rode to the far side of the Amato River. It was shallow enough for men to ford and was not an obstacle to anyone. The French appeared; their columns protected by a cloud of skirmishers. The Chasseurs were on their right flank. I glanced over my shoulder and saw that Sir John was busy marching the infantry to attack the French before they could deploy.

I turned to Lieutenant Jackson, "We need to buy the General some time. We will ride towards the Chasseurs and try to annoy them again."

"Sir, there are four squadrons there. We will be outnumbered eight to one."

"I know. I do not intend to stay and fight them toe to toe. We will make them chase us to Maida. The narrow streets will suit us and we can swing around and rejoin the army. Sergeant Grant, ready the men."

"Carbines at the ready."

We cantered obliquely across the front of the French skirmishers. The sight of cavalry made them halt, ready to go into square. It bought the general a precious few minutes. The French cavalry formed up to charge us. This time they had the advantage of an open plain. I saw that they only had two squadrons committed to this action. The rest stayed in column.

We halted in a line some hundred yards from the French. We both waited. I think they thought that we were going to charge. I raised my sword and shouted, "Fire!"

At that range, we were never going to hit many men but we struck enough horses and men to initiate a response. Some Chasseurs charged and then their leader gave the belated order to charge. Most of my men had drawn their pistols and they fired a volley. "Retreat!"

Jones' bugle was obeyed instantly and the line wheeled to form a column of twos and galloped towards Maida. As we led the two squadrons away from the battle I heard the crack of musket fire as the action and battle behind us, commenced. I hoped we had done enough. We were still outnumbered and our horses were tiring. We struck the narrow streets of the town and I shouted, "Head west down the hill. Split up and use all the streets." I hoped to confuse the enemy while giving my men the chance to escape their pursuers.

The French were gaining on us. These Chasseurs were not the ones who had pursued us the previous day and their horses were fresh. It would be a close call. I was not certain if we would make the safety of our own lines.

As we thundered through the narrow streets I caught a movement above me. There were men on the roofs. It was the men of the village. Suddenly the Chasseurs were falling from their horses as they were struck from above by muskets and rocks. The townspeople had the advantage that they could hide when the Chasseurs tried to fire up at them. I heard the French bugles sound the retreat. The Chasseurs began to drift back to their lines.

As we dropped down from the village and headed for our lines we saw the battle fiercely raging. The other Chasseurs had formed ready to charge and I saw Colonel Kempt's' men begin to form squares. The French guns were being deployed to fire into the squares. The infantry would be massacred. Our route had brought us to the flank of their cavalry.

"Jones, sound, form line."

The men quickly formed a straight line. I saw that some men had fallen but we still numbered over eighty. Our horses were tired but we would be charging downhill. The gunners were oblivious to the danger on their flank for the whole of Sir John's force was before them. The battle was at a crucial stage.

"Charge!"

We were just four hundred yards from the guns. The sound of battle, the screams and shouts of the dying and wounded all meant that the gunners did not hear us. It was only when one of the crew turned to load another ball that they saw us and, by then it was too late. Badger reached the guns first and, as he leapt over a limber I sliced down and struck a gunner across the neck. I carried on and leaned forward to slash a second gunner across the face. Those men manning the last two guns fled towards their own lines. Even Badger was tiring and I wheeled him around to finish off the rest of the gunners who remained. They stood with their arms in the air. They surrendered. They had nothing left to counter cavalry.

I looked over to the main battle. The 20th Foot had made a flanking moved and were pouring musket fire into the Swiss troops who, realising they were beaten, began to retreat from the field. The Chasseurs had not charged and they formed a protective screen to enable their comrades to march away. If we had not charged the guns then we could have pursued but there was no possibility that the 11th Light Dragoons could move from the plain of Maida. We had given our all but we had won.

We guarded the guns until some of Captain Sillery's men came to collect them. We had only lost two troopers. Four more were wounded but that was a tiny price to pay for such a huge victory. In all Sir John's force had only lost forty-five dead. With the captured guns and almost a thousand prisoners, this was the first defeat for Bonaparte's Imperial war machine.

We dismounted and walked our weary horses back to camp. We were applauded and cheered. Colonel Kempt rode over to me and shook my hand, "That was a damned fine effort, Captain Matthews. If those guns had blasted away at us then I think we would have lost. Well done sir!"

Sir John was equally effusive. He pointed to the bay. There were now four men of war anchored with open gun ports. "That is Sir Sidney Smith. We can now begin to drive the French back to their own lands. You and your men get all the rest you can. I believe that tomorrow we will be chasing the French."

He was wrong. After his conference with Sir Sidney, he sent for me, "Sorry about this Matthews. I am damned sorry to lose you."

"Sorry sir, lose me? I don't understand."

"Not just you but your whole troop. You have been ordered back to England."

"But sir, that will leave you without any cavalry. Now is the time when you will need them."

He shook his head, "I know that more than anyone. In my report, I have said how valuable your contribution has been. I dare say you will be gazetted but the fact remains that our lord and masters want you home. There is a transport waiting for you in the bay. I am afraid your Italian adventure is over."

And so we left Calabria. I hated to go because our task was unfinished but Sir John was correct. We had to obey orders and so we boarded the Indiaman and headed west for England.

Chapter 19

It took six weeks to get home to England. It seemed an anticlimax after what we had been through. There was also dissatisfaction amongst the men. We all felt that we had been pulled away when we had total victory in our grasp. The fact that we sailed from the blue Mediterranean and summer skies to the grey Channel and autumn also contributed. Our mood lightened when we saw the White Cliffs of Dover and knew that we were but a few miles from home. Spirits brightened. We would have tales to tell of our adventures.

We disembarked at Dover. I was pleased that we did not have to sail all the way up the Thames. For one thing it added a great deal to the journey and secondly, it meant that I would not be accosted by Colonel Selkirk with another task.

We rode up the road to our barracks. I took it slowly for the horses had had no exercise during the long voyage. Colonel Fenton must have been forewarned of our arrival for he, the Major and Sergeant Major Jones were waiting for us with a guard of honour at the barrack's gates. I halted the men and we dressed lines. The guard of honour saluted us and Colonel Fenton rode towards us. He stopped and took out a newspaper.

"Men, I have to tell you that you have done this regiment great honour. You have been mentioned in despatches for your courage under fire. In addition Captain Matthews and the troopers who rescued Queen Carolina of Naples and Sicily have been singled out for their incredible fortitude and bravery. Well done to all of you."

Sergeant-Major Jones roared out, "Number seven troop, dismiss!"

I turned to George Grant. "We will have a parade tomorrow afternoon. Until then they are off duty."

I dismounted, "I'll sort Badger out, sir."

"Thank you, Alan."

The two senior officers flanked me as we walked to the mess. "I hear you were knighted by King Ferdinand."

"Yes sir, but it is purely honorary I assure you."

As we walked towards the mess Colonel Fenton put his hand on my shoulder, "Honorary or not it is a mark of the work you have done and from the reports, we have read your charge at Maida saved the day. From what I can gather we would have lost but for that."

"I don't know about that sir. Sir John Stuart is a good general."

"You mean the Count of Maida. He has done well and Parliament has granted him a pension of a thousand pounds a year. That is slightly more than honorary."

I asked the question which had been on my mind since we had left Naples. "Sir, why were we pulled out? We had a job to do."

"It wasn't me Robbie. I think our lords and masters have plans. I daresay they will tell us eventually. Meantime we are damned pleased to have you back."

I was allowed a whole month before I was summoned to Horse Guards and Colonel Selkirk. I went alone. It seemed unfair to drag Sergeant Sharp there and have him cool his heels outside the Colonel's office.

He got straight down to business as soon as I sat down. "That was useful intelligence you sent back. I assume you sent the message to Bessières?" I nodded, "Good then he should think that there is discord between us and the King of Naples. Thanks to you and Sir John Stuart nothing could be further from the truth." He leaned back. "You did well young Robbie. You seem to have a flair for this sort of thing."

"What sort of thing sir?"

"Thinking on your feet. The rescue of the Queen was a masterstroke."

"It was not planned, sir, I just happened to be there. I couldn't leave her alone."

"I know. That is what I mean. You think on your feet. Now I have sent for you because I need to pick your brains about Copenhagen. You sailed from there did you not?"

"Yes sir, but I didn't see much."

"You are a soldier and you have a soldier's eye. That is important." He picked up his pen, "Now tell me all that you can. Leave nothing out."

I spent a gruelling two hours trying to remember as much as I could about Copenhagen and its defences. I hoped that they would not be sending me back there. Autumn was almost upon us and, much as I disliked the heat of Naples in summer, the thought of winter in Denmark was just as appalling.

"It is a pity we can't get you back to Bonaparte. We would like a little more intelligence about what his plans are but he is still knocking our Prussian allies about a bit." He chewed the end of his pen reflectively, "Still, so long as he is in Prussia he can't be over in Italy. We have managed to hold down a large force of French with Sir John's tiny force. If Boney went there I dread to think what would happen."

"That is what I couldn't understand sir. Why did you pull us out?"

He looked baffled, "I didn't." He seemed genuinely surprised that I didn't know the reason. "I thought you knew. It was the DeVeres' uncle, the one at the war office. I heard that when they read the report of the rescue of the Queen they had you sent back. It seems they were jealous of your glory."

"Damned politics! My troop was making a difference over there. Who is running this War Department?"

"I thought you knew Robbie, politicians. It is who you know that is important. The brothers might have been disgraced but that doesn't stop them having an influence. Forget them. They are unimportant."

I stood. "Listen to yourself, sir. They are patently not unimportant. They have the power to get a fine force of cavalry sent home for no good reason. To me, that sounds damned important." I stood. I was too angry to stay and it was not the Colonel's fault. "With your leave, I will get back to my regiment. The War Department leaves a bad taste in my mouth."

He laughed and held up a glass, "Why do you think I keep a bottle of whisky close to hand? It takes away the taste of politics."

I almost stormed from the building and I was so angry that I did not notice the pair of men I almost knocked over as I left. I was about to apologise when I saw that one of them was Captain DeVere. I almost drew my sword. He, for his part, was also angry and he snarled at me before he recognised me, "Watch where you are going you damned... It's the stable boy!"

There was little point in trading insults. I had always been bigger than he was and I used my size. I went very close to him and hissed, "Listen DeVere, you were an appalling officer and now I learn that you are a sad and twisted little man who feels he has to prove himself over and over again. A word of advice; keep out of my life and steer clear of me or you will suffer."

His piggy little eyes bulged so much I thought that they would pop. "Why you! You apology for an officer. I have a good mind to..."

My hand went to my sword hilt. I was almost willing him to draw his sword so that I could end this feud. "To what, DeVere?" There was real venom in my voice.

The captain with him stepped between us. "This is a public place, gentlemen."

I turned to him. "Then tell DeVere to mind his tongue or I shall teach him a lesson he will not forget. He might hide behind others who do his bidding but annoy me and it is I who will mete out retribution." I held DeVere's gaze until he looked down and stormed off towards Hyde Park.

The other officer said, "You must be Captain Matthews."

"I am and what of it?" I knew that I was being brusque but I was still seething with anger.

He smiled and held out his hands in apology, "Nothing, I was just going to say that was a damned good show in Naples. I wish I could have witnessed it."

I smiled, "Sorry if I am prickly but DeVere has a way of annoying me. You seem like a decent fellow; why associate with him? He is a rotten apple."

"We are brother officers we serve in the same regiment. I am Captain Roger de Lacey."

We shook hands.

I watched my former brother officer storm off in the distance, "I served with him but I would not walk down the same street as him. Be careful around him, Captain de Lacey. He is neither honourable nor honest. He is an untrustworthy snake."

He laughed at my vehemence and glanced at the sulking DeVere who had stopped and waited down the street. "I love a man who speaks his mind. Perhaps one day we can talk when he is not around. You sound like an interesting chap."

"I am just a captain who tries to do his duty. Good day to you, sir."

"And to you, Captain Matthews."

I hoped that would be the last encounter I had with any of the DeVeres but I was, of course, wrong.

Once back at the regiment I threw myself into the daily life of the regiment. I had told my brother officers about my adventures and we began to experiment with different ways of using our troopers. The troopers found it varied the diet of drills and training. For me, it just expunged DeVere from the recesses of my mind. Autumn and winter sped by.

In January I was again summoned to Horse Guards. Colonel Selkirk had need of me. Rather than use the mail coach and be reliant upon others for my transport I took Badger and stayed overnight in a coaching inn. It was cold and frosty on the road but the snow and rain held off. I was pleased that I had ridden Badger. I stabled him at an inn close to the Horse Guards.

I was ushered directly into the Colonel's office. He began without preamble. "Ah, Robbie. Do you still have the connections to the merchant ships?" I must have looked quizzical for he added, "The colliers and those wine ships…"

He was like a spider in a web and knew everything. "Yes, of course, why?"

"We would like you to go to Copenhagen, as a civilian of course, and gauge the mood of the place."

"Isn't that a job for a diplomat?"

"No. It is a job for a soldier. You have an eye for these sorts of things and you can handle yourself. I understand that Fouché has agents in Copenhagen too. It will only be a brief visit."

"It may be difficult to arrange. I do not know if any of the ships I could use are in port or plan to go to Copenhagen."

He gave me a cold look, "I thought that you were a joint owner." Before I could argue he continued, "Look we will make it worth the captain's while. We will give him a lucrative contract to bring back some Baltic timber. How is that? Whatever rate he chooses; he can command his own price."

"Let me go down to the river and see if they are in port."

"Fair enough."

I wandered down to the river. There appeared to be no ships that I knew in harbour. I did see a collier and I approached the gangplank. "Is Geordie due in any time?"

"Nay, bonny lad. He left this morning. He won't be back for a week or two."

Thanking the sailor I headed for the inn we usually used. I decided to have some beer and a meal and see what the afternoon tide brought. The landlord remembered me and we chatted. When I asked him about Matthew Dinsdale's ship he shook his head. "No, sir. He is not due in here for at least a week. Mr Fortnum was down asking about him too."

Finishing my beer I headed for Piccadilly. It would do no harm to speak with the owner of the emporium and part-time shipping agent. The store was closing up when I arrived. "Walk with me, Captain Matthews, my home is around the corner. I am sure my wife will have a pot of tea brewing."

I learned much in that twenty-minute stroll. Although Napoleon Bonaparte had imposed a blockade on Britain the merchant fleet and the Royal Navy meant that it was largely ineffective. It did have the effect of driving up prices and he told me that the profits from the family were rising month on month. "Captain Dinsdale is now a wealthy man. He has purchased a fine house here in London although he has yet to move in. I also understand that the two of you are seeking to buy a second ship. That is a wise move, sir."

His wife made me welcome and we drank China tea and ate warm scones. I was offered a bed for the night but I had decided to return to the barracks. Captain Dinsdale would be informed of my request when he returned. As I left I said to Mr Fortnum, "Tell him I may have a lucrative contract to the Baltic working for His Majesty's Government."

Mr Fortnum was an astute businessman and saw the potential in such a contract. "When you leave the army, Captain Matthews, I can see a great future for you. London will soon be the capital of business and your place is here."

"We will see. We have an Emperor to defeat first."

I picked up Badger and rode south. I would not make the barracks until the next day but there some fine inns on the Dover road and they would be quiet at this time of year.

When we crossed the river there was still a great deal of traffic and people to keep me company but within two miles I was riding along empty roads and making good time. This was not Calabria with twisting mountain passes and treacherous roads. This was England with well-maintained roads which went, largely, straight. I had decided to stay in Dartford. It was a pleasant little hamlet and the Coach and Horses was a good inn. I estimated that I would be there by ten o'clock. Just in time for a little late supper. With an early departure, I could be back at the barracks by ten.

Perhaps the beer and the tea had dulled my wits for I was not aware that I was being followed for some time. When I did realise that there were riders keeping the same pace as me they were less than half a mile behind me. The old Roman Road of Watling Street was mainly straight but there were some twists and turns when it negotiated hills and small valleys. It was after one such twist that I stopped to adjust Badger's girth. It was then that I saw the three men riding along the road and confirmed that they were, indeed, following me. Normally I would not have worried but when they saw me stop they also stopped. That was not normal. They were pursuing me. I cursed myself for my inattention. I should have heard their hooves had my mind not been distracted by the problem of Colonel Selkirk.

I quickly mounted Badger and set off slowly. As soon as the road turned again I kicked him on to increase the distance between me and those chasing me. I heard the thundering of the hooves of their horses. All pretence had now gone. They were after me. I leaned forward and urged Badger on. I kept looking around for some side road or some house but all was darkness and emptiness. I was alone.

I had my two-horse pistols and I had my sword but the men following me held the advantage for they could split up and come at me from different directions. I had to regain the initiative. Suddenly I saw a gap in the hedge which bordered the road and I jinked Badger's head to whip him into the track which, I assumed led to some farm. I stopped immediately and turned Badger to face the road. The three horsemen galloped by and I saw that they were armed. They hurtled down the Dover Road. It would not take them long to realise that I had hidden myself somewhere. Both Badger and I regained our breath. I drew, primed and cocked my pistols. The sound seemed loud but I knew that the hooves of my pursuer's horses would have disguised the sound. I edged Badger closer to the road. We were still hidden by the hedge and I waited.

The sound of the hooves receded and then stopped. After a few moments, I heard them as they returned down the road. They were going slowly now and searching for me. This was nerve-wracking. It would come down to which of us had the quicker wits and reactions. I heard them as they came closer and their conversation dispelled any doubts I might have harboured that they were innocent travellers.

"Where did the sneaky bastard get to?"

"He has to be somewhere close. Remember we were told he was a soldier. It stands to reason that he will be crafty. That's why the money is so good. He won't be easy to kill."

"Will you shut up, he might hear us."

"And he might run when he hears us! That way we will know where he is."

Their voices had told me where they were and they were getting closer. Suddenly one of their horses snorted and whinnied. "He's close."

The horse's head appeared and then the first man. He was holding a pistol before him. I did not move. There was a thin branch before me and it broke up my outline. He stared but did not appear to see me. When the second horse's head appeared Badger moved slightly and I saw the man's pistol swing around. I fired first and he was thrown from his saddle. I kicked Badger out and aimed my right pistol as I emerged. I fired at the same time as the first man. His ball struck the top of my Tarleton helmet; mine hit him in the face. I holstered my pistols and drew my sword. The third man had decided that enough was enough he galloped back up the London road.

I dismounted and walked up to the first man I had shot. I knew that the second man was dead for his face had disappeared but I saw movement from the other attacker. My ball had punched a hole in his middle. It was a mortal wound but he was still alive.

"Who sent you?"

The response was a mouthful of bloody phlegm spat in my direction. I began to search him. In his pockets, I found five guineas. Someone was willing to pay well. I left the dying man and searched the body of the man with the bloodied face. He too had five guineas. I slung the body across his saddle.

As I approached the dying man he tried to raise himself on to one elbow. "You'll get yours Captain bloody Matthews. You stable…" Then he fell back dead. Had he spoken the name it could not have been any clearer. DeVere was behind this. I found the other horse standing forlornly by the hedge. I retrieved it and put the second body across his saddle. I led the two horses towards the Coach and Horses. It was five miles distant. It gave me time to ponder the problem of the DeVeres. I would have to try to neutralise them in some way without ending up on the gallows myself.

The inn was still open. The innkeeper came out to inspect the bodies. "The nearest constable is in Canterbury, sir but I can tell you that this one, the one who still has a face, is Jem Harris. He is a notorious highwayman. I am guessing that the other is Dick Dawes. He looks to be the right build. There is a reward of ten guineas on each of them."

I shook my head. "You claim it. You might as well have the horses too."

He brightened. "That is very generous of you sir. Now the bodies won't hurt for lying in a stable until morning. We'll go and get some food and room sorted out for you sir. Hey Nob, come and see to these horses."

I called in to speak with the constable when I passed through Canterbury. I explained what had happened and where the bodies were. "I am stationed down the road with the 11th Light Dragoons should you need me."

"And the reward sir?"

"Give it to the landlord of the Coach and Horses. He helped me."

"Very generous of you sir. And you say there was a third?"

"Aye, he rode off to towards London."

"Well, you leave all of this with me, sir."

Back at the barracks, I explained to the colonel that Sergeant Sharp and I would need a week's leave. He smiled, "You have taken less leave than any officer in the regiment but you rarely get any time off. Don't you want to forget all this cloak and dagger stuff and just enjoy yourself in town with the other young officers?"

I thought of the DeVeres; if they were typical of young officers then I would prefer to work for Colonel Selkirk. "When I leave the army sir, then I will enjoy the life of a gentleman."

"You are thinking of leaving? I thought you were a career officer. You are one of the finest cavalry officers I have ever met. It would be a shame if you were to leave."

"No sir, I am not a career officer but I will not be leaving until Bonaparte is finished with."

"Looking at his successes in Europe, that will not be for some time yet. He thumped the Austrians and Russians at Austerlitz last year and the Prussians last month at Jena. Can no one beat him?"

It was a rhetorical question. Although I had no doubt that we had the soldiers to defeat him it was another matter when it came to the generals. I had seen little evidence of anyone with his ability to lead and to out-think his enemies. Our generals had let us down in the colonies and the Low Countries. If it had not been for Nelson and the navy the French would be in London already.

Chapter 20

Sergeant Sharp and I headed back to London just five days later. We rode along the London road. When we called in at the Coach and Horses for a drink I was treated like royalty. The landlord insisted on giving us food and ale on the house. The story of the dead highwaymen had increased his trade and I, of course, had put money in his pocket.

We stabled the horses close to Horse Guards and then went to Fortnum and Masons. Mr Fortnum was delighted to see me. "Captain Dinsdale is due in port tomorrow. I believe he has no cargo to take back to Sicily. I think the contract would be most welcome. I will draw up the papers."

"Good. I will speak with my contact and find the details."

Colonel Selkirk was more than happy that we were able to oblige him. For the first time since I had known him, he appeared worried. He espoused the same sentiments as Colonel Fenton. "I don't know who is going to stop this friend of yours, you know. I have been asking around and there are only a few men who might have the potential to beat him: Sir John Moore, Rowland Hill, Arthur Wellesley. The thing is none of them have fought the French yet. Still, that is my problem."

He handed me a sheet of paper. "Here is the order. Timber from Copenhagen. I have left the amount blank." He looked up at me. "Try not to make it too ridiculous a figure eh? You don't want to kill the golden goose."

We stayed at the inn near the river. I had told Sergeant Sharp about the attempt on my life and my suspicions about the DeVeres. "I'll keep my eyes open, sir. I'll watch your back." Sharp knew the brothers as well as I did and he would be able to identify them quickly.

We waited, the next day, by the river. We watched every ship coming to dock at the huge port. Captain Dinsdale would arrive, that much we knew, but we had no way of predicting the time. It was late afternoon when I recognised the ship making its way up the river to the quayside. We knew the berth for it was the only empty one that we could see.

His crew recognised me and they shouted to the captain. "Well, Mr Matthews, I am guessing this is urgent or you would not be here."

"It is, Captain Dinsdale."

As soon as the ship was tied up and the gangplank lowered we boarded the ship. I showed Captain Dinsdale, the contract and his eyes widened. "This is a licence to print money. They must want you in Denmark urgently."

"There will be no danger to you or your crew. In the time it takes to load your cargo I can do what I need to do and then we return here."

He laughed, "The danger does not worry me. For this sort of profit, I would sail up the Seine. Besides, Captain Matthews, you own half of this ship. I will throw the dice with you once again. We normally get double six!"

We changed aboard the ship while the cargo was offloaded. We had to wait until the midnight tide and so Captain Dinsdale let the two watches have a couple of hours ashore; watch on watch.

As he said to us, while we ate a meal delivered from the inn, "It is not enough time for them to become incapable and yet it will make them feel as though they have had a treat and," he tapped the side of his nose, "they will not realise that they have not had their pay until we are halfway to Denmark."

He opened a couple of bottles of Don Cesar's wine and he asked me of my mission. "This is not a dangerous one, captain. I merely need to gauge the mood of the Danish."

He laughed as he mopped up some of the gravy from the steak and ale pie with the freshly baked bread, "Then I can save you a journey. The Danish are more nervous than a cat in a room full of rocking chairs. They see the French gobbling up Europe like a chicken with a plate of corn and they wonder when their turn will come." He wiped his greasy hands on a piece of rope which hung above the table. "The only setback the French have had was when you lads gave him a bloody nose at Maida. Otherwise, he has had all his own way."

"What you cannot know though, Matthew, is will they join the French or fight them?"

"They have the biggest fleet now that the French and Spanish have been beaten. That fleet could hurt Britain if it fell into Bonaparte's clutches. Oh, do not get me wrong. I am more than happy to sail to Copenhagen and make a tidy profit at the Government's expense but I just worry that you will be tempting fate once again."

"We will barely have to leave the ship."

Matthew looked at Alan and they both shook their heads. Neither believed for a moment that it would be as simple as I made out.

I had forgotten how cold the North Sea could be, especially in February. We were chilled to the bone. We had dressed from the ship's slop chest so that we appeared as the other crew. We even helped out on the voyage. I had learned that there was no such thing as a passenger on a merchant ship. You all pulled together for the good of everyone. The winds were not in our favour and it took more than ten days to reach the Skagerrak. We had to pass many Royal Navy ships as well as those of the Danish navy. All appeared suspicious and nervous in equal measure.

I remember Copenhagen harbour from my previous visits. The houses were right on the harbour wall. They were all old houses and the port looked homely. It was a pretty little town and I liked it. If I had known what was in store for it I might have changed my report.

I went with Matthew to the warehouse and handed over the order for the timber. It was good timber and vital for the spars and masts of our ships. Although we had not lost many ships at Trafalgar our fleet had suffered much damage and this would go some way to remedying the situation.

"We'll take a turn around the town, Captain, while you load the ship."

"We'll say on the late tide." He winked at me, "There is no point in hanging around any longer than we have to."

The sergeant and I looked like two sailors. There was nothing to distinguish us from any of the others who frequented the port. We walked around the harbour noting, casually, which ships were in port and their nationality. As I had expected there were many British ships as well as Swedish and Russian. It meant that there was a cacophony of languages being spoken and we did not stand out.

We had plenty of time and so I headed for a bar in a side street just off the harbour to have a drink and listen to the conversation. This might confirm what Captain Dinsdale had said. It was in the area frequented by whores who shouted to us lewdly as we walked by them. Sergeant Sharp seemed happy to be away from their attentions. As I had expected the owner could speak most languages; it was in his interest to do so. After he had brought our drinks I waved around the bar. "Business appears to be good."

He waggled his hand back and forth, "It seems that way doesn't it but," he lowered his voice, "the French are not far away and there appears to be no one who can stop them. We are a small country with a weak army. Who would stop this Bonaparte?"

I leaned in to him. "Why do you speak quietly? There are no French here."

He laughed, "Do not believe it, my friend. You are English I can see that but there are others who pretend to be a nationality they are not. They are French spies."

I feigned shock and looked around the crowded bar, "What in here?"

He nodded. "Any of them could be a French spy so be careful what you say."

"Two more beers please."

We had not finished our first but I wanted to keep him on our side. When we had the beers I led Sharp away to the side of the bar where we could watch others. Sergeant Sharp and I had done this too many times to be careless and so we talked of the ship and what we would do with our bonus when we returned to London.

A Danish Captain of the Navy entered with another Captain of the Merchant service. They managed to get the table next to us. The captain was not Danish and so they spoke in French. I listened attentively while Sharp rambled on about some fictitious girl he intended to wed at home.

The Danish captain was speaking. "I am telling you my friend that you Russians are lucky. Even though Napoleon defeated your army your country is too big for him to conquer. All he has to do here is to defeat our militia and he can walk across the whole country in half a day."

"Yes but you have a powerful navy. I have seen it. You will be protected."

"There are many in the navy who sympathise with the republican ideals of the French."

The Russian laughed, "Bonaparte is an Emperor; how is that Republican?"

"Even so he has shown that he has democratic tendencies. Look at the Ligurian Republic and the Batavian Republic; those nations govern themselves under France's protection."

"It sounds like you have those tendencies too."

"No my friend, but I am pragmatic. I will go with whoever rules but tell me can you take my little chest with you?"

"Of course, my friend, I will secure it in St Petersburg. No matter who invades your nest egg will be safe with me."

The Captain seemed relieved, "Good. Let me get it for you."

They stood and left. I had heard enough and I would be able to write a comprehensive report for Colonel Selkirk on the voyage home. It had been one of the easiest missions I had ever had to do and I left the bar feeling happy. I had forgotten the long nights this far north and when we emerged it was dark. The whores were busy inside with customers and the street appeared deserted.

"Come on Alan let's get back to the ship. We don't want to be late."

Before we reached the water two men stepped out in front of us. It was then I realised how deserted and how badly lit was the street. One of the men held a cudgel in his hand which he tapped against his palm. The other was better dressed with a short sword in his scabbard. We stopped and I glanced behind us. There were two more men there. They both held wicked-looking cudgels. I held up my hands, "We want no trouble and we have only a little money."

The man in front of me took out his sword. He looked like less of a thug than the one with the cudgel. He spoke to me in French. "Why not speak French. You appeared to understand it in the bar."

I went cold. This man was French. He was one of the French spies. This was no common assault. He wanted to question us. I lowered my hands. "I understand French, what of it? You speak French and you understand English, what does that make you."

I slipped my right hand behind my back and under my jacket as I spoke. My fingers found the handle of the stiletto. Sergeant Sharp also had a long lethal knife. We would not be taken without a fight. I pointedly reached into my pocket. "Look we have a little money." As I reached inside my pocket I stepped forward to get me closer to the pair of them. Sharp took a step back. He would deal with the two behind. The one with the sword, the dangerous one, and cudgel man were mine.

He laughed, "I do not want your money. I want what is in your head."

I had a handful of coins and I opened my palm to show them. The man with the cudgel stared at them. Taking another step forward I threw them in his face and, when he put his hands up for protection I slashed his throat with my knife. The man with the sword was taken by surprise but he slashed with his sabre. It was a wicked-looking weapon and I had to pull back to avoid being eviscerated. I grabbed his hand with my left hand and kneed him hard in the thigh as I brought the stiletto over and round. He half crumpled allowing me to stab him in the ribs. I twisted the sharp blade as it went in, sliding between his ribs. When I withdrew it I saw the red bubbles already coming from his mouth. I had punctured his lungs.

I whipped around picking up his sword in my left hand. One of the two men Sharp had been fighting lay in a pool of blood but, as

I turned the second thug swung his cudgel and caught Sergeant Sharp on the side of the head. I threw the sabre and it spun in the air and then stuck in his chest. He had a surprised expression on his face as he fell to the ground, dead.

The noise had attracted attention and the windows opened. Light flooded the death filled alley. I picked Sharp up and threw him over my shoulder. I raced for the harbour. The path was slippery with hoard frost and dirt. I almost slipped and fell into the harbour. I managed to keep my feet and I turned to run to the ship. We were berthed four ships down. I dared not shout for fear of attracting attention and I did not know how many other confederates our attackers had.

Fortunately for me, the deck watch saw me and four sailors ran to my side. I saw that three of them were armed and they stood around us as we carried the inert body of Sergeant Sharp aboard Captain Dinsdale's ship.

The captain assessed the situation quickly and shouted. "Prepare to set sail!" The crew raced up the lines to lower the sails whilst the ropes holding us to the shore were unceremoniously thrown to the land. I saw a crowd appear from the street. There looked to be a couple of uniforms amongst them.

"Robbie, get below deck. Leave this to me."

Alan had been carried to the captain's cabin where the sailor who administered first aid was seeing to my friend.

"How is he?"

"He will live but his skull suffered a nasty crack. Keep an eye on him and make sure he doesn't turn on to his back. I have seen unconscious men choke before now. I am needed on deck." He grinned as he turned at the door. "It is always interesting when you are around, captain!"

I could hear voices from the harbour but I could not make out the words. I washed Sharp's head with water and was pleased when the bleeding stopped. The voices stopped and I could feel the motion of the ship. We were moving. I knew as soon as we had left the harbour for the ship began to move up and down far more. Captain Dinsdale joined me, "How is the lad?"

"Your man says he will live but he will have a lump the size of an egg on his head. Did you have trouble getting out?"

"Nah. Some of the militia asked had I seen three men leaving the harbour. I said they had run down to the next ship. They seemed happy with that. What happened?"

I told him and his face became serious, "Sounds like they were French spies. You were lucky. I should have sent a couple of my lads with you for protection."

"We would have stood out like a sore thumb. No, it turned out for the best. We found what we had to. I am just sorry that Alan got hurt."

"Robbie you could have both got dead, never mind hurt!" Just then Alan started to come to. "Right let's get this young man seen to."

He opened his eyes and stared around fearfully. Then he saw where we were. "Sorry about that sir."

"Don't be silly Alan. You had two men with cudgels. You did well."

He laughed and then held his head, "So did you, sir. I still have a lot to learn."

I spent the next few days putting the information I had gleaned to paper. The fact that it took nine days to sail back helped me to refine my thoughts. The Danes would hand their fleet to Napoleon; that much was glaringly obvious. They had a militia army. Their only asset and their only strength was their fleet. Napoleon would not come by water. He would come by land! The Danes would capitulate. I suppose I could have learned al lof this by just talking to Matthew but I felt better having the hard evidence.

Alan was completely healed when we docked. Matthew was more than happy with his profit. "If you have enough money for a third ship, Robbie, I think we can use her."

I shook his hand, "Money isn't a problem. My needs are small. See Mr Fortnum; let's do this."

Colonel Selkirk was delighted with our intelligence. He took my report and shook my hand. "A little bird told me that you had an altercation with a certain officer when you left here recently and then two highwaymen were killed." I shrugged. "If you want the DeVeres out of your hair I can arrange it."

"No!" I felt cold at the suggestion. "I will deal with Mr DeVere in my own way. He is my problem and not yours."

He nodded, "Tell your colonel that some of his men may be needed sooner rather than later."

I looked at the report I had just given him. "Copenhagen?"

"You always were a bright lad Robbie!"

Chapter 21

Colonel Selkirk was delighted with the results of our mission. It confirmed what others had said. I was not sure that it was worth the risk we had taken. "Damn good job, Robbie! I may need you again in a month or so."

As Sergeant Sharp and I rode down Watling Street, I began to question my work for Colonel Selkirk. Was it worth it? It seemed to me that I was being used by the colonel because I was cheap. Poor Sergeant Sharp could have lost his life and I am not sure that the Colonel would have been bothered. For his part, Sergeant Sharp was quite philosophical about the whole adventure.

"The way I look at it, sir, I get paid as a sergeant. There are risks involved in that no matter what I do. I could end up like Jeb Cartwright, couldn't I? At least this way I get to see a bit of the world and I know that you won't order us to do something stupid. You are not Captain DeVere."

That, once again, put that treacherous officer and his cronies into my mind. I had thought that when the two brothers had been cashiered and joined another regiment that would have been the end of things. Instead, my notoriety and success had made him hate me even more. Had duels not been banned I would have called him out and that would have been an end to it. That could not happen and I would need to devise some other means of ending the feud.

Back at the barracks, there were new recruits to train and horses to school. It was a relief to be back in an ordered routine although my troop did miss the sun of Sicily and the easy life on Giuseppe's farm. Their tanned faces and hands marked them as the troop who had fought the French. The other troopers were envious. It was a shame that we could not be sent to Italy. We had heard that Sir John and the British forces controlled Calabria and Sicily but King Joseph, Napoleon's brother, controlled the rest. With a few more troops I was convinced that we could have defeated the French and recovered Naples for the King and Queen.

In May I was summoned, along with Colonel Fenton and Lieutenant Jackson to Horse Guards. None of us had any idea of the reason but I took Sergeant Sharp as a precaution. This time it was not Colonel Selkirk alone who greeted us but there was a General, Sir David Dundas. I had heard of him but knew nothing about the man.

"Ah, gentlemen sit down." The three of us sat stiffly on the chairs. None of us were used to speaking with generals and it felt awkward. He smiled but there was no warmth in the smile. "Now you two young officers have been drawn to my attention because of your success in Calabria. Sir John Stuart was fulsome in his praise. We are going to use your skills in a campaign we are planning." He sat back as though he had finished.

Colonel Fenton looked confused, "Sir, why did you need me here."

"Protocol sir, protocol. We have to do things by the book. These two fellows will be detached from your command for a few months. You will need to make arrangements while they are away."

I saw the tic of anger in the corner of the colonel's eye but he was too much of a gentleman and too experienced an officer to allow it to be seen by the general. Sir David stood, "Well, I shall take my leave and the colonel here will continue with the briefing."

We stood to attention as the General left. When the door closed we sat and Colonel Selkirk poured us all a glass of whisky. "Sorry about that, Colonel Fenton. He likes to do things properly. He is a stickler for regulations."

"I know it is not your fault but it is a damned waste of my time." He swallowed some of the whisky. "I might as well hear what you have to say and then I shall get back to the regiment."

"You two will be sent as aides with General Arthur Wellesley to Denmark. I know that you will keep this to yourselves but the Danes have been given an ultimatum by Bonaparte to close their ports to us and, at the same time, we have demanded that they hand over their fleet. I feel sorry for them. They are between a rock and a hard place. They either face the might of Bonaparte and his army or our Navy."

The colonel nodded. "It will be good experience for you two." He smiled at me, "And it might keep you out of trouble Captain Matthews."

"If you would get yourself some accommodation you will be needed by General Wellesley to plan the campaign and give him advice. This is where your last little jaunt will come in handy Robbie." He stood, "Report here tomorrow morning at ten o'clock. Be punctual."

We walked back to the horses with Colonel Fenton. "Well, I shall stay at my club, gentlemen." He shook his head, "I thought old Dundas had been put out to pasture. The man is a menace."

We made sure that we were prompt for our meeting with Sir Arthur. We had left Sharp with the horses and we were in Colonel Selkirk's rooms by nine. "Well done. It will impress the general."

"Tell me, sir, I have never been an aide, what do we do?"

"Fetch, carry, advise. That is about it. You are expected to think on your feet and move quickly. I hear that Sir Arthur is very demanding which is why there are two of you."

"Who is he sir, the general I mean?"

"He has been in India for a few years. He was very successful there. He asked for the chance to go to Copenhagen and so I think he is keen to get back into the saddle as it were."

When he came into the office, at precisely five to ten, he strode in as though he owned the building. He was an imposing figure but his face was dominated by a huge nose. The soldiers used this as his nickname but that was in the Peninsula and was some years away. His nose meant that he had a tendency to look down his nose at you; both literally and metaphorically. I never liked him. In all the years I served him he was one of the most unpleasant men I had ever met. He was a brilliant general but you would not want him as a friend. To be fair to him he reciprocated in kind keeping everyone, including, apparently, his wife, Kitty, at arm's length.

The meeting began badly. We stood to attention and he imperiously swept to the other side of the desk where Colonel Selkirk had provided a chair. He sat down, removed his hat and then stared at us. He picked up a piece of paper and read, "Captain

Matthews and Lieutenant Jackson. You are to be my aides." It was not a question, it was a statement of fact. "Tell me a little about yourself. Where are your people from?"

I saw Colonel Selkirk give a slight shake of his head. I began. "My mother was a Macgregor from Scotland."

"Yes, but who is your father? Where is his land? What is your title?"

"My father is dead and I own a little land in Sicily."

He looked appalled. "And you, Lieutenant, tell me your family has land."

Poor James was totally intimidated. He stuttered, "Er no sir, my, er father is a parson."

Sir Arthur turned to the Colonel. "This won't do Selkirk, it simply won't do. I am not one of these damned republicans who believe you put anyone in a uniform and they can become an officer. You need breeding. I need blue bloods, not some parson son and a Scottish mongrel. Won't do sir!" I felt myself colouring at his insults.

"General, these two young men are highly qualified. Captain Matthews is the one who was sent to Copenhagen. He is the one who wrote the report you liked."

"A damned spy to boot! This gets worse and worse."

The colonel sighed, "And Captain Matthews also rescued Queen Carolina from the French. He was knighted by the King of Naples himself."

"Another damned foreigner. Well if this is the best there is I will have to put up with it. But let me tell you, gentlemen, I want none of your lower class nonsense. You are both officers and I expect you to behave as such. Now, Captain, tell me what we can expect."

I went through the defences of Copenhagen and what I knew of the army. James just sat next to me like a frightened rabbit. I was just angry with the way we had been spoken to and treated. If this was the way the British Army conducted itself then I found myself wishing for a French victory. We had both proved ourselves on the field of battle and that was where it counted. It struck me that he would have preferred the DeVeres rather than us.

At the end of the briefing, he seemed satisfied. "Well, you appear to know your stuff. We leave on the morning tide. Get yourself a couple of horses. We are sailing on the 'Rose of Calcutta'. Dismissed."

We left and I did not say a word all the way to the inn. James kept looking at me. "Why do we have to go, sir? He doesn't like us."

"I think we are there because Colonel Selkirk asked for us." I smiled, "Don't worry, James. He is like one of those big dogs that bark a lot. If we upset him he will just send us back to the regiment and I, for one, am happy about that."

"Shall we take our horses, sir?"

I shook my head. I would not inflict another voyage on Badger. "No, we'll get a couple of nags. There is no point in hurting our horses for him."

Sergeant Sharp was less than happy. "But sir, you will need a servant."

"We will get a couple of soldiers for that. We need you to take the horses back to the barracks." I softened my tone. "Believe me Sergeant Sharp, you would not enjoy the company of the General."

James nodded vigorously. "He is right there Sergeant Sharp, you are well out of it."

In the end, we bought a couple of decent hunters courtesy of Mr Fortnum who had contacts all over London. I knew that James had been worried about the cost of a horse. "I will pay James. We can sell them back when we return. We might even make a profit eh?"

We arrived before dawn at the Indiaman we were to take. The captain was like all the captains of Indiamen; he liked order and a tidy ship. He appreciated our early arrival for it meant he could get our horses loaded while it was quiet.

Gradually, as we lounged on the deck, the others arrived. It seems that we were to travel with the senior officers, the artillery and the 43rd Foot. The officers seemed pleasant but that was in contrast to Sir Arthur. None had served with him and they were all keen to find out about this unknown Indian general. James and I were discreet, pointing out that we had only met him ourselves the previous day. When they heard my name they were all interested in hearing the story of the Neapolitan campaign. It filled the time until Sir Arthur arrived. He had timed it so that he was just fifteen minutes ahead of the time of sailing. I discovered that he liked to be punctual but not early.

We left the wharf and slowly headed downstream to join the rest of the convoy and the fleet which would be attacking the Danes. I felt sorry for them. They had no idea of the destruction which was to be unleashed upon them.

His lordship wasted no time. He commandeered the officer's mess and began to tell the officers what he wanted. James and I were relegated to becoming servants. We hovered behind him and he would snap an order out and we would be expected to fetch and carry. I had not been treated in this way since my father had been alive. I was little better than a serf.

"None of your officers know me. You do not need to know me. You just need to obey my orders, to the letter. The troops you command are little better than the scum of the gutter. If they were not in the army then they would be in gaol."

One or two of the officers bridled at this, "I say, General Wellesley, that is a little strong. My men are all good chaps."

"Then you have seen something which I have not in fifteen years of soldiering. I will accept no breach of discipline. I know that the British infantry can stand and fight but I need them to obey every order instantly. The cavalry at our disposal will be the King's German Legion. I have yet to meet their officers but I would expect the highest standards from our allies. I hope to God they speak English! Now, let us get on with the campaign and my plan of action."

He went through every detail until every officer knew his standing orders and what he intended once we arrived at the Danish capital. Those last weeks of July and the first week of

August were intolerable. I was desperate for us to reach Denmark and get the experience over with.

We were approaching the Danish coast when we were told that the Danish had refused the ultimatum; they would not hand over their fleet. As their fleet was still in the harbour we were forced to land some way away from the port. It took many days to unload all the men, horses and cannon we would need. James and I were kept busy delivering messages to various officers and regiments. Finally, his lordship was ready to begin the bombardment of the city. We had twelve guns and some rockets. The six pounders and five-inch howitzers were not really suitable for a bombardment and we could see that it would take a long time to reduce the walls sufficiently to allow an assault.

Sir Arthur seemed happy for it to take as long as it took. He summoned James and myself one morning as the cannons began to fire again. It was like rolling thunder and the air was thick with the smell and taste of gunpowder.

"Ah, Matthews. Colonel Selkirk told me that you are something of an expert at going behind enemy lines."

I nodded, "I have been of service to the Colonel before now."

"And you, Lieutenant Jackson, have you such experience?"

"A little."

"Good. We have seen little of the enemy save those tucked up in Copenhagen. I wish to know where they are. I need to know if they have an army! Find them!"

With a perfunctory wave, we were dismissed. Although a daunting task I was delighted for it took us away from the odious general. I made sure that we took supplies both for ourselves and our horses. This was all enemy country.

We headed north first. I was anxious to cover as much ground as I could and yet avoid being ambushed. Riding along the coast enabled us to do that. I had made sure that we carried four loaded pistols each. We were going to be too far from friendly forces to be able to summon aid. We would have to rely on our own wits. The two hunters were fine horses. Mine, called Jack, was not Badger but he was a fine horse. When we had ridden for a couple of hours the track we were follow began to head south. I held up my hand to halt James.

"What's up, sir?"

"The land around here is flat. If you look ahead you can see smoke. Is that a village? We need to approach carefully."

We rode down lanes lined with hedges to deflect the icy wind which would have blown across this island in the winter. We rode down the track for a mile or so and then I heard the sound of Danish voices. We slipped behind the hedge and dismounted. I slipped a pistol from my holster and gently cocked it. We crouched behind our horses to disguise our uniforms. Thankfully the twenty men who marched down the road with their ancient muskets over their shoulders had their heads down as they tramped along the track. I recognised them as militia.

Waited until they had passed and then we mounted and rode along the field side of the hedge. It was some sort of grain crop which was unfortunate as it marked our passage as clearly as footsteps in the snow. It could not be helped. I did not want to risk being surprised by another band of militia. We could not return to Sir Arthur yet. He would not be best pleased with information about a mere twenty militia.

I then had an idea. "James, stop here." I took off my Helmet and attached it by its chin strap to my cloak which was secured behind my saddle. "Take off your tunic." I began to unbutton my tunic. Once done I slung it across the front of my saddle. With no helmet and just our shirts and breeches, we, too, looked like militia. We would not bear close scrutiny but, at a distance, we might be taken for Danes.

We rode for another mile or so and drew closer to the fires. I could now see that it was a camp. There were not many tents but this was August and the nights were warm. I spied a barn and a farm building. We dismounted and led our horses to hide behind the huge building. Leaving James holding the reins of both horses I walked to the end of the building. The farm was to my left and before me was the camp. It was clearly the militia camp. I spied the artillery park. It was close to the front of the barn. In the distance, I could see the horses of their cavalry and between the two were the infantry. There was some semblance of a uniform. They mainly wore hats rather than shakos but they all had a musket and many had a sword.

Suddenly two artillerymen approached. If I ran they would be suspicious. I pretended to examine the bottom of my boot as though I had stepped in something. I guessed that the Danish for 'shit' was similar to the German. I used the word as they neared and they both laughed. I had managed to use an approximation of the word. They walked along the front of the building and disappeared into the farmhouse.

I turned and walked back to James. "We can go back to Sir Arthur now. We have seen their army."

As we mounted he asked, "How many men?"

"It looks to be about the same size as ours but it is hard to tell because it is spread out in an untidy fashion. And they are militia."

We turned the horses and headed back the way we had come, "Does that make a difference?"

"Remember the Neapolitan militia?"

He nodded, "I see what you mean…"

He got no further as a dozen Danish cavalry suddenly appeared twenty paces from us. They looked to be regulars. They had come from our left and were obviously heading into camp. We were so close that they recognised us as cavalrymen and that we were not Danish. Their officer drew his sword and shouted at us. I drew my pistol and fired. Their horses were not gun trained and, when the officer fell, the other horses began rearing and jumping. I dug my spurs into my horse and we leapt down the lane. There was no question of riding across the fields. We would have to take our chances on the track.

Someone had organised the Danish cavalry and I saw them hurtling after us. We had a lead of some hundred yards. I decided we would head directly for our camp and not risk the circuitous route we had taken to reach the Danes. I heard bugles in the distance. The camp was being alerted. We could expect more pursuit but, so long as it was just these ten or eleven men and so long as we maintained our lead, I was confident we would escape.

Suddenly, as we turned a bend, I saw the militia who had walked by us an hour earlier. They were returning to camp. There was only one thing for it. "Draw your sword and charge!"

We had been cantering but, when I applied the spurs Jack leapt forwards. If we had been galloping towards regular infantry then we would have died. The officer shouted to his men to kneel and aim. In the time it took them to complete the action we had covered twenty yards and were almost upon them. I saw the fear on their faces as the two massive horses galloped towards them. I leaned forward and pointed my sword at the men. Even as the officer shouted, "Fire!" they all took to the hedgerows to avoid being trampled.

I slashed my sword at the officer but he jumped out of the way. I allowed James to get ahead of me and I looked under my arm. The militia were belatedly firing at us but, more importantly, they were blocking the lane and preventing pursuit by the cavalry. They followed us for another few miles but, as we were gradually increasing our lead they gave up and we were able to slow down and rest our horses.

James grinned at me. "That was jolly good fun, sir!"

I began to dress again. I did not want a trigger happy sentry mistaking me for a Dane. "If they had fired first then we might not have got by them. Thank God they were militia."

"What will Sir Arthur do now sir?"

"He has to deal with them. If they attack us while we are bombarding Copenhagen they have a chance of winning. It will merely delay the inevitable."

It was late when we reached Sir Arthur's headquarters. The man never seemed to need rest and he was busy writing a report. He seemed to write reports about everything.

He glanced up and took in our dishevelled appearance. He frowned, "I hope you have an explanation for your appearance gentlemen."

I bit back the retort and said, instead, "Sir we have found the Danish camp and we were attacked as we escaped. I deemed it more important to bring you the news rather than changing sir."

He nodded, seemingly satisfied with my explanation. "Well, where are they and how many are there?"

"They are about eighteen or twenty miles west of here sir. They are mainly militia but we saw at least one regular cavalry regiment. They have about thirteen or fourteen artillery pieces and there are between five and seven thousand of them, sir." I paused, "We did not have time to count."

He allowed the rare hint of a smile to form on his lips. "You have both done well. I shall overlook the uniforms. "Find the senior officers. I want them here at six o'clock in the morning and warn the pickets that there is a Danish army close by. When you return, I shall have a message for Admiral Gambier."

It was midnight when we were done with our duties. Jack was exhausted and we had not eaten all day. However, the general seemed pleased with us. As we reported to him for one last time he nodded. "Well done for today. You have both surprised me."

We saluted, "Just doing our duty, sir."

He seemed to look at us for the first time. "Isn't that an Austrian sword?"

"Yes sir, I acquired it in the Low Countries."

He frowned, "Weren't the Austrians on our side then?"

"Yes sir but the sword wasn't it was wielded by a Chasseur."

"Ah, the spoils of war. Why did you not acquire a better one?"

"Lieutenant Jackson and I were awarded fine swords for our rescue of the civilians from the Pas de Calais but this is a good sword sir. I prefer it."

"Ah, so you were the chaps who helped to rescue the civilians. That was a fine show but I don't approve of all this cloak and dagger shenanigans."

"Sometimes sir shenanigans are the only way to get results."

"Hmm, I suppose you are right. Better get off to bed. I will need you two tomorrow. Do not be late and make sure you have a smart uniform!"

Both Wellesley and Bonaparte shared the ability to do without sleep. Physically they could not have been more different and in their attitudes too but there were so many similarities that it was frightening.

The Battle of Køge, as it became known, was a messy little battle. Sir Arthur left the guns bombarding the town while he took the rest to deal with the militia. The cavalry did the job we had done in Calabria. They found the enemy. The camp had moved for another force had joined it and they were just twenty miles away at Køge.

The Hanoverian who returned to tell his lordship where the enemy had been found did not speak English. I wondered if it was a mistake or a ploy by the Colonel. Sir Arthur looked angry and then I translated. After the lieutenant had gone he said, "A man of many surprises captain. Thank you. I would suggest you stay close to me in case that fool of a colonel sends another messenger who does not speak English."

The army moved south. Now that we knew where they were it was now important to move quickly. The cavalry would be able to pin them in place while the ponderous infantry manoeuvred into position. We found the enemy close to the coastal town of Køge. The Danes had dug in. The sea protected one flank while the cavalry guarded the other. The infantry was drawn up in between them. Their artillery was spread out across their front. It was obvious that they outnumbered us but Sir Arthur appeared to be quite confident.

He turned to James and me. "I would like to see all the commanders now. I will give them their instructions for the battle tomorrow."

Everyone who attended spoke English and I was not needed to translate. The plan was quite simple. The cavalry would threaten their horse and, hopefully, make them either flee or charge. When the cavalry were out of the way then the cavalry would threaten the infantry. Sir Arthur hoped that the Danes would move their artillery to counter the threat and, when they did so, and then the infantry would close with them and give them five rapid volleys. I had seen the effect of British volleys at Maida. The Danish militia would stand no chance.

We breakfasted before dawn and we waited with Sir Arthur as the regiments and battalions took up their positions. The Danish waited and, if it is possible for an army to be nervous then the Danes appeared to be nervous. There was much movement. Riders rode from one flank to the other and from the back to the front. Regiments changed positions while the British and Hanoverians waited.

The Danish artillery opened fire. Their balls did little damage as they had been fired one by one. There appeared to be little coordination. Sir Arthur gave the signal and the King's German Legion moved towards the Danish left flank. Their cavalry made as though they were going to charge but when the Hanoverians formed into line they fled. Even before the King's German Legion had begun to move towards the Danes the Danish commander had begun to shift half of his cannon from the centre to the left flank. One had to admire Sir Arthur. His plan was working perfectly. It was as though the Danes were doing what Sir Arthur wanted. The regiments on the left of the Danish line echeloned back and their centre became proportionately weaker. I saw the ghost of a smile play upon the peer's lips. He could launch the infantry soon and punch a hole in the middle of the Danish line.

The Hanoverian cavalry moved forwards towards the Danes. The Danish guns opened up and this time they fired together. I saw some riders and horses struck. To my horror, I heard the bugle sound charge and the first four squadrons began to charge the cannon. They were half a mile away from the Danes and would take many casualties during their approach.

"Damned fool! Captain Matthews, ride to those Germans and tell them to get back into position. I cannot afford to lose a single horseman!"

I kicked Jack and we sped across the front of the British lines. I heard a cheer as we galloped towards the Hanoverians who were now enduring the musket fire of the Danes as well as their cannons. I rode obliquely across the front of the infantry to try to cut off the Hanoverians. Some of the Danes tried to hit me but as they did it individually I was never in any danger.

I watched as the first squadrons began to retreat having been badly handled by the Danes. There were mercifully few bodies on the field. I veered to my right and headed for their colonel who was busy preparing his next charge. I reined in next to him and said, in English, "The General orders you back into position."

The colonel feigned ignorance of English even though I knew he spoke it perfectly well. He grinned as he shrugged. I repeated the order in German and his face turned to a snarl. "Colonel, you will be court-martialled if you refuse. I beg of you to withdraw your men back to their allotted position. The infantry are about to begin their attack."

There was a pause and then he nodded and ordered his men back. They all turned around. I had just started to wheel Jack around when I heard the crack of the Danish cannon. Suddenly Jack was struck and it felt as though someone had smashed my leg with a sledgehammer. The air was filled with dust and I seemed to fly through the air. I saw the blue sky and then all went black.

Chapter 21

When I opened my eyes I was in a tent and there were strange faces peering at me. I found hearing difficult. I could see the man above was speaking to me for his lips were moving but I could not make out any of the words he was saying. I tried to rise but the effort was too much and all went black again.

When I finally came to I heard noises before I opened my eyes. I was not deaf. I could hear voices. "He is lucky to be alive, Sir Arthur. If the horse had not taken the cannonballs and the muskets then he would be dead. As it is his right leg has been damaged and his hearing seems damaged. This officer's career may well be over."

"Dammit Doctor, he is a dammed brave fellow you have to do something."

I opened my eyes and tried to speak. All that came out was a cough. I saw Sir Arthur and the doctor above me. I tried again. "I can hear sir."

They both smiled. The doctor knelt over me and held a lamp before my eyes, "Remarkable. An hour ago I was getting ready to bury you."

I looked up at Sir Arthur, "The battle sir, how did…"

"Oh, we won, of course. We barely lost a man. The Danes just ran. I sent those damned fool Germans after them. It looks like this little war is over and we can all get back to England. Well done, my boy." He patted my hand and turned around. It seemed a little perfunctory to me but I learned that it was his way.

After he had gone I asked, "My leg, what is the problem. I won't lose it will I?"

He smiled, "Oh no, well at least I don't think so. The cannonball went through your horse and it cracked your knee. I don't think anything is broken and, even if it was, there's nothing I can do but you won't lose the leg. Whether you can use it is another matter. You rest now and we'll get you aboard the transport in the morning."

I lay back and closed my eyes. Was my career over? I was thirty years old and I thought I had a future in the army ahead of me. I thought of all the battles I had fought in. This one was nothing. It was an army of farmers with ancient weapons and it looked like I was one of the few casualties. I felt angry because there was nothing that I could do about any of this.

I felt a presence in the room. It was James. He looked relieved when I opened my eyes. "Oh, sir! I was really worried. When they brought you from the field you were covered in blood. It wasn't till later I found out it was Jack's blood."

It was only then I realised that the fine hunter had been killed. I had had two horses die under me. I was gladder than ever that I had not brought Badger. If it had been him who had died I do not think I could have borne it.

"What happened to him?"

He looked appalled. "I am sorry sir. I was so worried about you that I ..."

He looked almost ready to cry. "Don't worry James. It was a silly question."

"We are going home tomorrow sir. The General says we have done our job."

"Copenhagen?"

"They used those Congreve rockets, sir and the city just burned and burned; they surrendered. The war is over."

I was carried on a stretcher and then by wagon to the beach where there were rowing boats waiting to take us to the ship. I was carried, like a baby to the boat and then rowed, along with James to the Indiaman. When we reached the side they had a bosun's chair waiting to lift me up the side.

I shook my head, "I am not a piece of cargo! You can take the damned horses that way but not me. I shall enter by the tumblehome."

James grabbed my arm as I tried to rise, "But sir! Your leg!"

"I have one good leg. If necessary I will hop up the bloody ladder."

I put all the weight on my right leg and held the rungs of the ladder. As the blood rushed down to my left foot I felt an excruciating pain shoot to my knee. I felt like sitting down again but I had said I would do this and I had to. I pulled on the ladder and hopped my right leg on to the first rung. I hopped up six of the rungs and then I slipped on one which had some weed on it. I just reacted and put my left leg down to save myself. I heard a gasp from James and then felt such pain as I had never felt before. I closed my eyes and held on for dear life. Miraculously the leg held. I began to climb up but I put as little weight on my left leg as possible.

When I reached the tumblehome I fell forward on to the deck. Two sailors grabbed me. One said, "You are a game 'un captain and no mistake. Now stop acting the hero and let us carry you to your cabin eh sir?"

I nodded and gave a weak smile, "I think you are right."

As I was carried to the cabin I would use for the voyage home I found myself smiling. I could use my right leg. It might hurt but I could walk and I would ride again. I was still a Captain of Light Dragoons and my war had not ended just yet.

The End

Glossary

Fictional characters are in italics

Trooper (later Sergeant) Alan Sharp- Robbie's servant

*Captain Robbie (Macgregor) Matthews-*illegitimate son of the *Count of Breteuil*

Colonel James Selkirk- War department

Colpack-fur hat worn by the guards and elite companies

Crack- from the Irish 'craich', good fun, enjoyable

Horse Guards- the British War Department in Whitehall

Joe Seymour- Corporal and then Sergeant 11th Light Dragoons

Joseph Fouché- Napoleon's Chief of Police and Spy catcher

Lieutenant Jonathan Teer- Commander of the Black Prince

musketoon- Cavalry musket

parky- slang for cold

pichet- a small jug for wine in France

*Pierre Boucher-*Trooper/Brigadier 17th Chasseurs

Pompey- naval slang for Portsmouth

Paget Carbine- Light Cavalry weapon

Rooking- cheating a customer

Slop chest- the chest kept aboard ship with spare clothes[1]

Snotty- naval slang for a raw lieutenant

Tarleton Helmet- Headgear worn by Light cavalry until 1812

Windage- the gap between the ball and the wall of the cannon which means the ball does not fire true.

---

[1] Normally from dead men

Historical note

The 11th Light Dragoons were a real regiment. However, I have used them in a fictitious manner. They act and fight as real Light Dragoons. The battles in which they fight were real battles with real Light Dragoons present- just not the 11th.

The books I used for reference were:

- Napoleon's Line Chasseurs- Bukhari/Macbride
- The Napoleonic Source Book- Philip Haythornthwaite,
- The History of the Napoleonic Wars-Richard Holmes,
- The Greenhill Napoleonic Wars Data book- Digby Smith,
- The Napoleonic Wars Vol 1 & 2- Liliane and Fred Funcken
- The Napoleonic Wars- Michael Glover
- Wellington's Regiments- Ian Fletcher.
- Wellington's Light Cavalry- Bryan Fosten
- Wellington's Heavy Cavalry- Bryan Fosten
- Wellington's Guns-Nick Lipscombe
- Wellington's Army- Colonel Rogers

The buying and selling of commissions was, unless there was a war, the only way to gain promotion. It explains the quotation that 'the Battle of Waterloo was won on the playing fields of Eton'. The officers all came from a moneyed background. The expression cashiered meant that an officer had had to sell his commission. The promoted sergeants were rare and had to have done something which in modern times would have resulted in a Victoria Cross or a grave!

The character of Colonel Selkirk is based upon a number of characters who existed in World War 1 and 2. I have no reason to believe that such characters did not exist a century or more earlier.

Subterfuge and duplicity are two weapons which can be used by the military when needed. The colonel symbolises such cunning.

The Naples invasion was written largely as described. The King and Queen of Naples reneged on a treaty with Napoleon who ordered Masséna to invade Italy. The King left Naples on the 23rd of January 1896 but the Queen waited until the 11th of February to leave; 2 days after the French crossed the border. She eventually arrived in Sicily. I have made up her rescue by the 11th although it is similar to the rescue of Queen Cartimandua by Roman cavalry in 69 A.D.[2]

Roger de Damas was a young émigré who was given command of one wing of the Neapolitan Army. However, I have made up his characteristics. It struck me that anyone who had fought on the émigré side, bearing in mind they lost to half-trained revolutionary armies, would not be good enough to face the well trained French Army of 1806. The fact is he should have been able to hold the French at the site he chose. His flanks were secured by high ground and he had the height advantage over the French. However, he omitted to leave men on the mountainside and French Light Infantry climbed the mountains and descended on their flanks and rear. His men were bottled up in the valley and, out of the two armies of almost 17000 men, only 3000-4000 escaped back to Sicily.

---

[2] Sword of Cartimandua- by Griff Hosker

Roger de Damas

The French did behave badly in Calabria. Following the battle, they rampaged through the farms and villages taking food and women as they saw fit. The French observer Paul Louis Courier reported that they robbed, raped and murdered. There appeared to be no order. The result was that the Neapolitans reacted in kind and it was a precursor to the guerrilla war waged in Spain a few years later.

Wellington, as Arthur Wellesley, did serve in Copenhagen. I have tried to portray him as the real man and not the larger than life general who helped to defeat Napoleon. He was a snob in every sense of the word and a true elitist. From contemporary accounts, he was not a very pleasant man and could be quite vindictive. His attitude towards ordinary soldiers can best be described as feudal and yet the soldiers who served him would follow him anywhere.

Most ships both merchant and Royal Navy used a rope suspended above the mess table to use as a kind of napkin. It would be an old piece of rope and would be unravelled to help it function as a napkin. If the ship ran out of food or became becalmed then the rope could be cooked to make a gruel which would have bits of grease and food to give sustenance.

The Battles of Maida and Køge happened largely as described however there were no British cavalry at Maida and the KGL did not have to be ordered back. That was just an homage to Captain Nolan at Balaclava.

Captain Matthews will continue to fight Napoleon and to serve Colonel Selkirk. The Napoleonic Wars have barely begun and will only end on a ridge in Belgium in 1815. Robbie will be back to the same place he fought his first battles as a young trooper.

Griff Hosker June 2014

Other books by Griff Hosker

If you enjoyed reading this book, then why not read another one by the author?

Ancient History

The Sword of Cartimandua Series
(Germania and Britannia 50 A.D. – 128 A.D.)
Ulpius Felix- Roman Warrior (prequel)
The Sword of Cartimandua
The Horse Warriors
Invasion Caledonia
Roman Retreat
Revolt of the Red Witch
Druid's Gold
Trajan's Hunters
The Last Frontier
Hero of Rome
Roman Hawk
Roman Treachery
Roman Wall
Roman Courage

The Wolf Warrior series
(Britain in the late 6th Century)
Saxon Dawn
Saxon Revenge
Saxon England
Saxon Blood
Saxon Slayer
Saxon Slaughter
Saxon Bane
Saxon Fall: Rise of the Warlord

Saxon Throne
Saxon Sword

Medieval History

The Dragon Heart Series
Viking Slave
Viking Warrior
Viking Jarl
Viking Kingdom
Viking Wolf
Viking War
Viking Sword
Viking Wrath
Viking Raid
Viking Legend
Viking Vengeance
Viking Dragon
Viking Treasure
Viking Enemy
Viking Witch
Viking Blood
Viking Weregeld
Viking Storm
Viking Warband
Viking Shadow
Viking Legacy
Viking Clan
Viking Bravery

The Norman Genesis Series
Hrolf the Viking
Horseman
The Battle for a Home
Revenge of the Franks
The Land of the Northmen

Ragnvald Hrolfsson
Brothers in Blood
Lord of Rouen
Drekar in the Seine
Duke of Normandy
The Duke and the King

New World Series
Blood on the Blade
Across the Seas
The Savage Wilderness
The Bear and the Wolf

The Reconquista Chronicles
Castilian Knight
El Campeador
Lord of Valencia

The Aelfraed Series
(Britain and Byzantium 1050 A.D. - 1085 A.D.)
Housecarl
Outlaw
Varangian

**The Anarchy Series England
1120-1180**
English Knight
Knight of the Empress
Northern Knight
Baron of the North
Earl
King Henry's Champion
The King is Dead
Warlord of the North
Enemy at the Gate
The Fallen Crown

Warlord's War
Kingmaker
Henry II
Crusader
The Welsh Marches
Irish War
Poisonous Plots
The Princes' Revolt
Earl Marshal

Border Knight
1182-1300
Sword for Hire
Return of the Knight
Baron's War
Magna Carta
Welsh Wars
Henry III
The Bloody Border
Baron's Crusade
Sentinel of the North
War in the West

Sir John Hawkwood Series
France and Italy 1339- 1387
Crécy: The Age of the Archer

Lord Edward's Archer
Lord Edward's Archer
King in Waiting

Struggle for a Crown
1360- 1485
Blood on the Crown
To Murder A King
The Throne

King Henry IV
The Road to Agincourt
St Crispin's Day

Tales of the Sword

Modern History

The Napoleonic Horseman Series
Chasseur à Cheval
Napoleon's Guard
British Light Dragoon
Soldier Spy
1808: The Road to Coruña
Talavera
The Lines of Torres Vedras
Bloody Badajoz

The Lucky Jack American Civil War series
Rebel Raiders
Confederate Rangers
The Road to Gettysburg

The British Ace Series
1914
1915 Fokker Scourge
1916 Angels over the Somme
1917 Eagles Fall
1918 We will remember them
From Arctic Snow to Desert Sand
Wings over Persia

Combined Operations series
1940-1945
Commando
Raider

Behind Enemy Lines
Dieppe
Toehold in Europe
Sword Beach
Breakout
The Battle for Antwerp
King Tiger
Beyond the Rhine
Korea
Korean Winter

Other Books
Great Granny's Ghost (Aimed at 9-14-year-old young people)

For more information on all of the books then please visit the author's web site at www.griffhosker.com where there is a link to contact him or visit his Facebook page: GriffHosker at Sword Books

Printed in Great Britain
by Amazon